Forever

Family

Friends

By
Dorothy Ketterer

ISBN: 978-1-913275-84-6

This book was published in cooperation with Choice Publishing, Drogheda, Co. Louth, Republic of Ireland.
www.choicepublishing.ie

For Pat, Susan, Paul and Mary.

Chapter 1

George and Ethel Boles were happily married for sixteen years and had three sons. Joseph was a quiet spoken boy, thirteen years old, tall and thin, with black hair and brown eyes and very good looking. He loved school, enjoyed homework and liked being left alone in his room to study for long periods of time. Philip was ten, small for his age with chestnut brown hair and deep blue eyes. He had no interest in studying and he was always up to mischief. He was the joker of the family, which at times annoyed Joseph so they did not get on well with each other.

Trevor was seven with red hair and blue eyes, not the best looking of the three boys, but he was so kind and pleasant everybody loved him. He was the one in the family who worried about everything. Always ready to help his mother and father without having to be asked.

Their Dad George was an only child. The minister of the local Protestant Church. A tall handsome man with black hair and blue eyes, very pleasant and well liked in the village. Their mother Ethel was the eldest of three girls, and Beatrice, who was the middle child, were both fantastic dressmakers and designers.

Beatrice had been married to her childhood sweetheart, who died suddenly after only four months of marriage. She was broken-hearted and said she would never marry again. She came to live with Ethel and her family. That was the best thing to do at that time. They all got on well and she never left, and never did marry again.

They made clothes for all the gentry in the surrounding area for every event. They loved making wedding dresses and outfits for the wedding party. They always covered a real horseshoe in the same material as the bridemaids' dresses just as a little keepsake of their wedding day. They liked adding these little touches and the clients were very pleased at the trouble they went to over and above their expectations.

Holy Communion dresses were the next things they enjoyed working on. They always dressed a small doll in the same material as the child's dress and gave it to her on her big day. That was a nice thing to do. The children loved getting a doll to keep as a reminder of their Holy Communion. They did not charge for the doll.

Ethel enjoyed this, as they did not have a daughter of their own, they did not have any dolls in the house. Ethel always longed to have a little girl but never mentioned this to anybody because she knew her husband felt the same way as she did, but it was never spoken about. Until Trevor was born he just said,

'More toys for boys, we'll have to try again.'

When he saw the look on Ethel's face he realised he said the wrong thing. He said, 'Sorry, I was only joking,' he then gave her a big smile.

Looking at the baby he said, 'He is a beautiful baby'.

She was hurt but let it go. She would always remember his remark. If George wanted a girl as much as she did they would have to adopt a girl.

Chapter 2

People came from far and near to have outfits made by the two sisters. Every design was completely different so if there was a big occasion in the county none of the guests would arrive dressed in the same style. They made a good income from their work. They were not rich, but they had a lot more than most of the village people.

Their house was on a hill just outside the village, built on an acre of ground.

Mr. Boles took great care of the gardens, back and front. In summertime, when the front garden was in full bloom, it was so beautiful it was the talk of the whole county. He had a yellow climbing rose tree round the front door and red roses around the window frames. Along the garden path, he had sweet William, night-scented stock, jasmine and a variety of flowers with a strong perfume so there was always a beautiful aroma from the garden. Around the sidewalk, he had a section where he planted flowers for birds and bees. Just outside the back door he planted wallflowers. Not because he liked the look of them, but the perfume from them that filled the air was stunning. He was very proud of all his hard work in the gardens, but he never realised how much pleasure the local people got from the front garden flowers and the wonderful perfumes. At the back of the house he had fruit trees, apples and pears. Soft fruit bushes and all types of herbs growing. When the berries were ripe he made jam from them with the help of the boys. If he had a good crop of fruit he would give a selection of the jam to be sold at the Christmas fair. The locals liked the jam and were delighted to buy it, at very low cost. They knew how much work he had put into making it. They liked to show how much they appreciated it. They would never expect a pot of jam for nothing and they never got one.

The Christmas fair was a big event in the village. Everybody did their best and helped out to make it a success. All the prizes for the raffle were donated by those that could afford to do so, and the rest of the prizes were made by the most talented people in the village. There were many beautiful knitters, and hand knitting was a great seller. Every year that was the stall that made the most money. The children also played their part doing whatever they could. It was a good, fun day and everybody enjoyed it. The proceeds from the fair went to both the Catholic and Protestant church funds, as the amount of members of both churches were almost equal. It was a good way for both religions to work together and support just one big event. Nothing was ever left over, at the end of the day if there was, they would give the youngest in the hall free goes spinning the wheel until everything was gone. The little ones loved that part of the day. It got the Christmas spirit feeling going in the village.

Because there were so few people with money, it put the poor on a level playing field. The poor had big families. So there were always plenty of children to play with. None of them had expensive toys so there was no competition among the children. The boys would play hoops, marbles, and if they were lucky, and somebody had a rubber ball called a *bouncer*, they played football. The girls played with little dolls and a cardboard shoe box for a pram. The lid was cut to make a cover. The sides of the box cut down and little holes punched into the side, string put throughout the holes tied into a bow to make a hood. A long string in front to pull it along the ground. The only competition here was if a father with big feet got new boots, that child's pram would be bigger than anybody else's. This didn't happen very often. The only time most children got new shoes that came in a box was for Holy Communion or Confirmation. Then every little girl had a pram. Sometimes the shoe box would be made into a doll's house. The doll's house furniture was made out of matchboxes and cigarette boxes; covered with pieces of material they made a lovely sitting room suite. Bits of lace left over from a wedding veil made nice curtains. Simple things but the children got hours of play from them.

Some women in the village were talented but had no money to buy the things they needed to make use of their talents. Which was very sad. Money was like a sixth sense: you could not make use of your senses without it. Ethel was very good to some women who could make beautiful things out of very little material. When the sisters made anything for their own family and friends they always gave the leftover pieces to the women who could sew. It was amazing what some women could do. Making so much out of so little and nothing was wasted. In large families everything was passed down. Clothes, shoes and toys if they had any. Boys made a cart from two planks of wood and four little wheels called a gig. Twine tied around the front wheels provided the steering and when pushed from behind it was like owning a car. If you had a gig every kid on the street was your friend. Sometimes the boys might give the girls a go; just to frighten them. They would push the gig so hard and then let go. If your feet were not right on the steering the gig went all over the place and sometimes would end in a nasty fall. If a girl had a few brothers they would teach her how to steer properly and she would be as good as the boys and never fall off. Girls that could drive a gig were tomboyish and disliked by the other girls.

Having little money makes people very creative. Those childhood memories were very special, and boasted about when they became adults and had plenty of money.

The Boles family were the only family in the village that had a pony and trap. They were very happy to help out the neighbours, transporting them to and from the railway station. There was no public transport to the station at that time in Ireland. Things were very hard for a lot of people. It was normal to have a big family and some had as many as fourteen children. The old people had funny sayings, when another child arrived in a family that already had a lot of children, they might say,

'God never sent a child to let it go hungry.'

The answer they got was,

'None of mine came with a loaf of bread under its arm.'

When there was only a year between babies in a family they referred to this as being *Irish twins* and there were many families in the village that had *Irish twins*.

To make matters worse, there was very little work for men except a few weeks here and there doing some farm labouring or handyman jobs for those who had a big farm. Some of the employers were very good to these men and at the end of a working day would give them milk, bread or meat, if they killed their own cows, or lamb. This was greatly appreciated by the workers. A lot of men went to England to work and send money home. Some of the younger ones joined the British Army or Navy.

If a poor family had any relations in America they might be able to send the price of a sea journey ticket to the oldest of the family. If the oldest was not working and in good health they would be the one who got the opportunity to go to America. When the time came for a member of a family to go away to work in America there would be a collection made in the village and a big party thrown to give them a good farewell. This party was called an *Irish wake*. Everybody took part in saying goodbye and tears would flow from broken-hearted mothers, fathers, all the family and girlfriend or boyfriend. Despite all the sadness, these parties could be great fun and go on all night long. When anybody left Ireland at that time, there was very little chance of them ever coming back. When the party was over and the traveller left, there would be terrible sadness in the village for some time.

When the first person that left for America made enough money he would send for another family member to join him. As well as trying to send money home. He would have to work very hard, sometimes three different types of work, if he could do it. Life was hard for the first member of a big family who went away. But that was expected of them, and they did it as their duty.

Apart from all the sorrow, the village was a lovely place to live. Everybody knew everybody and a lot of bartering was used when neighbours were in need. They would borrow or exchange goods of all kinds. That worked very well in a place where there was so little money. Everyone was doing their best with what they had. There was great community spirit. Being poor did not matter, being nice was more important.

The village was small, with a few shops, a couple of houses owned by the shopkeepers or the local council, which they rented out, to those who could afford to pay the rent. There were two small rows of county council cottages in the main street, for very low rent, but none of them ever became vacant except when a whole family left, or a person who had been living alone passed away. So when Mrs. Fogarty, the best loved old lady in the village passed away and all her family were long gone, there was great consternation, long discussions and meetings about who would get the cottage. It had been so long since one had become vacant nobody could remember who was next on the list. Like most things on lists in Ireland, the list had gone missing and some on the list had already died. There was a lot of talk and so many meetings and disagreements over who would get the cottage, it was locked up and left there idle. It was the first time in the village that anything like this had happened. If Mrs. Fogarty had known this would happen, she would just have passed it to a friend or relation with no questions asked. This is what people did in Ireland at that time.

One day when Trevor, the youngest of the Boles family, was coming home from school with his friends they knocked on the door of the empty cottage as usual, sat on the window ledge and were laughing at the state of the cottage when the door opened and a tall, fat man with long grey hair and a big beard made a run at them. Trevor got such a fright he ran without stopping until he reached home. When his mother saw the state of him she asked what happened. When he told her, she asked why he had knocked on the door. He said they did that every day since nobody lived there.

'Well,' she said, 'you will not be doing that again, that man lives there now. You will have to go back down there now and say sorry. I will come with you and explain to him. I'm sure he will understand.'

'No Mum, I will get the boys who were with me and we will all go together,' Trevor answered.

'Well, then go now and hurry back,' said his mother.

Off he went, but none of the friends would go back with him so he thought long and hard about it and then he went and knocked on the door himself. After a while the door opened and the man stood there looking at him, he said in a very strange accent,

'Vat do u vant?'

'We didn't know you lived here, I'm sorry for knocking on your door,' Trevor said.

He patted Trevor on the head, said some words Trevor did not understand and then he closed the door. When Trevor told his mother he didn't understand what the man said, she smiled and said, 'How could you understand? He is from Russia and he does not speak English very well.'

Trevor asked what a Russian man was going to do living in the village. His mother said she did not know but it won't be long before the whole village will be asking the same question about him. When Mr. Boles came home and heard Trevor's story, he was surprised to hear that the man opened the door. He had been living there for a few days and this was the first time he had spoken to anybody. The local gossip, Mrs. Moore, who knew everything about

9

everybody, had missed out on this huge news and she would be very annoyed to think that a child like Trevor had been speaking to him without her hearing about it.

Ethel and George had a great laugh then Ethel said, 'Wait until she hears how much we know about him, she will be really mad. She won't sleep a wink until she finds out all about him and what he is doing in this village.'

Ethel's parents John and Mary Cramp owned the biggest shop in the village that sold everything from groceries to hardware, vegetables, drapery and some stationery. In a small section divided off from the shop was the local post office. Their youngest daughter, Lydia, worked in the post office. This work suited her very well as the post office was a great place for getting all the information about what was going on in the village. As nobody had a phone in their home and the only public phone was in the post office, Lydia as post assistant answered all the calls. She had to go and get the person the call was for. That person had to take the call there at the counter where anybody in the shop could hear all their business. If she could not leave the shop to get the person she would ask them to tell her when would be a good time for the person to ring them back. When she had time she could relay the messages to the person the call was for. Then they came to the shop at that time, and rang the person from the shop. This didn't happen very often as most phone calls were from family members who would have already written home and said they would ring on a certain day at a certain time and the person expecting the call would be there ready to take the call. If there was an important telegram it had to be brought to the person by the postman, telegrams usually brought bad news, of death or an accident, when anybody in the village got one it was not long before the news travelled around the village like wildfire, until everybody found out what the news was. It usually was not good news. The local nosy parker Mrs. Moore was not shy of asking questions in the shop about what was going on in the village. Especially, if there was nobody else in the shop, she would spend ages asking questions. Then she would tell the latest news she had heard. Mrs. Cramp did not want to hear about the other people who came into the shop, but she did not like to be rude to her. If Mrs. Cramp was quick enough and saw Mrs. Moore coming into the shop, she would run into the back room and Mr. Cramp took on the task of serving his least favourite customer. She never asked him questions. He never knew anything or pretended not to know. She would leave the shop in a bad mood if she got no information. She was a widow with no family, nothing in her life to occupy her mind but other people's business. There was no real harm in her but she was a terrible news monger. She was desperate to know who the strange man was that got the cottage that a local could not get from the council. She would not be happy until she found out who, what, where, when and how this strange man had found his way into this village, one of the smallest places in County Wicklow. How could she have missed not seeing Trevor and his friends running away from him, nobody could understand? It will be hard for her to understand how a Jewish Russian man got the derelict cottage. So she will be on full alert sitting at her front door or behind the curtains making sure she will get a good look at him when he comes out.

The next time he came out of the cottage was early on Monday morning, he went right through the town, with

11

a little sack on his back. Where he was going nobody knew, but he was not seen for the rest of the day. This happened for the next four days. Now everybody in the village had nose disease. Then he started using a little hand cart when he left the town early in the morning and did not get back until late at night. One day he came home early and a few of the older lads standing near his cottage shouted after him.

'Hey Louie, is it true the Jews killed our lord?'

Thinking he had no English and would not understand they all laughed. He walked back to them and said,

'Me did not know the man.'

They nearly died, but he roared laughing and started talking to them. His English was bad but he made himself quite clear with the few words he had and some gestures. He told them he had a *vife* and two children in Russia. They were leaving Russia next week and coming to Ireland. They did not believe him. He looked very old to have a wife and young children.

All his life he pronounced a word starting with *w* as *v*, although his English was very good after a very short time. He became very friendly with these lads and they all loved him. He had great stories to tell. Sometimes they thought he might be colouring the truth but that did not matter to them. He had a really funny laugh, the guys got a great kick out of him.

They told him stories sometimes that were far from the truth but he seemed to enjoy their company and they were delighted with him. He was a real novelty in the village. Everyone was still wondering where he went every day with his little cart and what he had in it, but nobody had the courage to ask him and he never told them.

One day when Trevor was playing near the cottage, Mr. Solomons came along pushing the cart and Trevor asked him what he had in it. He opened the sack and showed him what looked like a heap of rubbish and he asked Trevor,

'Vat think you this is?'

Trevor said, 'It looks like rubbish to me.'

'Well,' he said, 'there is money in this rubbish.'

Trevor laughed and said,

'My Dad has a load of stuff like that and he just told my Mum yesterday that he would get rid of that rubbish this week.'

Mr. Solomons got so excited he frightened Trevor.

'He still got it, yes? Do you know?'

'Yes, he has. Come home with me, see for yourself,' answered Trevor.

When they arrived at the house he told his Mum that Mr. Solomons had come to see the rubbish that they had to get rid of, he wanted to buy it. His Mother said he could take it for nothing whenever he wanted, it was no use to them. Mr. Solomons thanked her and almost broke her fingers he crushed her hand so hard when he shook it. Then he left smiling and muttering to himself. He could not believe his luck, he knew the real value of what they were calling rubbish.

That night he came back with a small scale and started to put the small pieces of the rubbish on the scales. He told Mr. Boles he would pay him for it. Mr Boles said not at all they were going to dump it anyway. It was no use to them. He could take all of it for nothing. Mr. Solomons asked if any of his friends had any rubbish like this he would buy it from them.

Mr. Boles thought for a moment and then said,

'I will tell them not to get rid of rubbish, you are willing to buy it. That will be great news for the locals.'

Mr. Boles knew that nobody in this village would have this kind of rubbish. It was pieces of lead, brass, and other bits left from the new workroom they had built at the back of the house for Ethel and Beatrice. They had put the best of materials into the building. They had waited a long time for it. It was really comfortable and had a fitting room, separated from the sewing room, which they always wanted. Ethel had always worked with her sister Beatrice over her parents' shop which was nice enough at that time, but her business had become so big now she had to have more space. Now she could take a local girl into learning the trade. The extra pair of hands would be a great help to them.

Chapter 3

Some weeks passed and then one day a beautiful young woman, two children, a boy and a girl were there in the cottage. It was a mystery how they had been brought into the village so secretly, but everything about these people was a mystery. The woman was a bit shorter than her husband, stunning looking, with long black hair, ebony eyes, and when she smiled she had the most beautiful teeth, her skin was glowing and she looked like a film star. She started to clean the cottage windows, washing the paint work. Sweeping out the whole cottage. In doing all this work, at times she took a little break and smiled at anybody that passed by. As a result the village people warmed to her immediately. They accepted and agreed that it was nice to see the cottage looking good again, and nobody ever asked how they came to get it.

The Solomons' children were small for their ages. The boy David was nearly nine and the girl Sybil was six. They both started school in the village and made friends quickly. They were a great novelty because they could not speak English, all the children wanted to help them. Seven weeks in school and it was David's Birthday. His parent's invited all the school boys and girls to a party in the cottage. There was so much excitement in the village no child had ever been to a birthday party. Some children in the village never knew they had a birthday. This caused a strain on the parents, finding money to buy a present. It would be a pity if children could not go because their parents could not afford to buy a present. So Ethel decided rather than the poor should not be allowed to go to the party because they could not afford a present she would take it on herself to sort something out. She suggested to George that they should take this opportunity to talk to the Solomons and to offer the church hall for the party. They could buy one big present for David and say it was from all the class and make it a great day for the children. The adults could come along later and keep the party going for Mr. and Mrs. Solomons to welcome them into the village and get to know their neighbours. It had been a long time since there were any kind of celebrations for all the parish to get together and this would be a great opportunity to show the newcomers what we are most famous for; our Céad Míle Fáilte or Hundred Thousand Welcomes.

Ethel and George would buy the present for David, and the women who were good at baking could all do something. Ethel knew that her mother would sell the ingredients to them cheaply and everyone would have a great time. It was about time there was something cheerful going to happen in the village. The parish hall belonged to the Protestant church, but every event that happened in the area run by the Catholic church was held there. Now if the Solomons agreed to have the party in the hall, and they were Orthodox Jews, there was another religion going to join them. That would be really great. Three different faiths all getting along together.

There was no bigotry in the south of Ireland and everybody respected each other. When children fell out they would call each other names. The Prods would call the Catholic Cats and meow, meow at them, imitating cat calling. The Cats would sing a song they made up.

Proddy waddie on the wall, half a loaf would feed you all. Look at your mother, you will soon discover she fed you on hay so you could eat all day.

These fallings out did not last very long and they would all be friends again. Sometimes a Catholic child might be best friends with a Protestant child and she would take her to mass with her. Then in the afternoon the Catholic child would go to Sunday school with the Protestant child. The parents never minded this. The one thing that made the Protestant children very envious of the Catholic children was when they made their Holy Communion and collected money.

The first year the Solomons were in the village, in the month of May when the procession was in the village for four Sundays, Sybil cried to go with them. At first her Mother said no. All her little friends begged her to let her go. Sybil cried so much her mother promised her she would make her a dress and get a veil for the following three remaining Sundays. But Sybil ran away from her mother and joined the procession with her friends. Nobody objected, the locals thought it was great that she wanted to be part of the goings on, so her mother kept her promise to Sybil and she went dressed in white with a beautiful veil borrowed from her friends for the next three Sundays. After this, Ethel and George had no hesitation in going to see if the Solomons would like to use the parish hall.

The next evening, Ethel and George called to the cottage and were invited in. The place was sparkling clean and really cosy. When they told Mr. and Mrs. Solomons why they were there, they could not believe it. They were so pleased, delighted, and in shock, with the offer. Mrs. Solomons said she would do all the baking and make some special treats that were popular with Jewish children at parties in her country. That was agreed. No need for the local women to do any baking. Nothing to be done now except the decoration of the hall and look forward to the big day.

In school on his birthday, the teacher brought in a cake for David with the candles lighting on it. The class sang Happy Birthday. David was thrilled, he ran to the top of the class and thanked everybody. He got very emotional and almost cried. The local children were delighted with all the fuss being made of David, all of them wanted to be his friend. It was so exciting to have a foreign family living in the village.

The following Sunday was the day of the party. From early morning the children were waiting dressed in their best, ready to go, although the party was not starting until three in the afternoon. Beatrice and Ethel had stayed up late on Saturday night to make the hall beautiful. All that had to happen tomorrow was for Mrs. Solomons to bring the food.

When the Solomons arrived, they had with them the cart filled with the most wonderful variety of food. Ethel did not know where to start to help so she left it to Mrs Solomons to do it her way. She was a fantastic worker and the speed she worked at was great to watch. The tables were fit for a wedding, not a party for children. The children were very shy when they came in and saw how beautiful the hall was arranged. They were so excited they were at a loss to know what to do. But in a short time, Mr. Solomons had all of them out on the floor doing everything he showed them to do. The games were simple but new to all these children, in no time they were doing exactly what they were told. With hand signals, sign language and the little English he could speak. It was so funny for the parents to watch. The adults were enjoying it as much as the children. When the children had played for a long time they were dying to eat. The food was so unusual even the adults were not sure what some of the things were. But then Mr. Solomons took a break from playing the games and sat everybody down at the table. David and Sybil started eating and then the rest followed. Plates were cleared in no time and although a lot of the things they were eating were not known to them, they were loving the food. Even the drinks were different from anything they had ever had before, they loved every bit of it. Time for the birthday cake. Mr. Solomons, after lighting the candle stood David on a chair, said a few words in Russian to him and sang Happy Birthday with Sybil and Mrs. Solomons in their own language. Then the children from school sang Happy Birthday in Gaelic, and then all the guests sang it in English. The Solomons were overwhelmed. Mrs Solomons started to cry, she could not believe how kind and welcoming the Irish people were, making such a fuss of her child. They had only lived in Ireland for such a short time. She felt now that they were going to be very happy living here. Then the best surprise of all, Mr Solomons took a balalaika out of its case and started to play. It was the most beautiful music they had ever heard. Everybody was taken by surprise and just sat there listening, without saying a word. The children were dumbfounded, they had never heard anything like it. After about an hour he put the balalaika away and got everybody into a circle and made them skip around while he sang a Russian song. He then took Mrs Solomons and his two children out into the middle of the circle and they did a Russian dance. It was fantastic to watch. When he finished he put his hands in the air, thanked everybody for coming and the lovely welcome and said this would be a party to remember forever. The guests realised that was the end of the festivities.

As each child was leaving they were given a small gift and the surprise on their faces was a sight to behold. They had never had anything like this before, they were so happy going home. They were delighted that this family had decided to come to Ireland and live in their village. None of the local people could ever give a party like this one. They would remember it for a long, long time.

On Monday morning, the talk in school was still about the party and some of the children were wondering if there would be another party like that when it was Sybil's birthday.

Trevor decided he was going to have a party for his next birthday. It was a few months away so he had plenty of time to get up the courage to ask his parents' permission. He and his brothers always had a birthday cake and blew out the candles but they never had a proper party. He hoped this might start a trend in the village. Deep down he really did not think it would, but he was going to give it his best shot. He would have a word with his aunt Lydia. Like him she was the youngest of their family and he adored her. Lydia was full of fun and he always had a great time when he was with her. If anybody could talk his mother into doing anything for him it would be Lydia. He loved her, and some of her boyfriends were very nice to him. He didn't like the one she was going with now. He never wanted Trevor hanging around with them. When she was going with James Taylor Trevor had a great time with them.

Chapter 4

Weeks went by and nothing exciting happened in the village. Then one evening when Ethel and Beatrice were working late to finish an outfit for an important client, Lydia called into the workshop, which was most unusual. She asked them to stop working for a second. She had something to tell them. They both lifted their heads at the same time and knew this was serious. They thought something was after happening to their parents. No, this was a bigger shock than that.

She just said, 'I'm pregnant.'

They both looked at each other and asked,

'Who is the father?'

When she told them, they could not believe it. But they knew she was serious. The father of her baby was the most awful person she had ever gone out with. He was not from this village. She was not long going out with him. They both knew their parents could not stand the sight of him. Especially her Dad, he could hardly be civil to him. They never said so to Lydia. They thought it was just a fling and she would drop him after a while as she did with most of the guys she went out with.

Although she had been going out with James Taylor for a good while and everybody loved him, she seemed to pick up with this guy very soon after James went back to college in Dublin.

Ethel and Beatrice were in such shock they did not know where to start.

Then Beatrice said, 'Look we will sleep on it and come up with some solution in the morning but don't say a word to anybody, especially Mum or Dad, this will kill them.'

Their youngest child, the beautiful daughter they adored, especially her Mum who had spoiled her so much she would never get over it. Having a baby outside marriage was such an awful thing to happen to any family in those days. A baby for this awful guy whom nobody liked. Lydia would have to leave the village. There was no way she was going to bring this trouble on the family. Ethel was awake all night. What were they going to do? In the morning she told George and he could not believe it. He suggested that she go to England and have the baby and give it up for adoption.

'That is not going to go down well with Lydia. But she is not going to have any say in it. Our problem now is how we are going to tell Mum and Dad that she is going away. They will go mad because she is so good in the shop and how will they manage without her.'

Such news and so sudden out of the blue. It could have a terrible effect on their health and Dad not so well at the moment, and not getting any younger.

Then Ethel thought,

'We won't tell our parents. I have to go to Dublin next week and I will bring her with me. I will tell them when I come home without her. Lydia and I will go and visit Aunt Phyllis.'

Phyllis was their Mother's sister who was not married, but had a big house and owned the house next door.

Phyllis kept lodgers but Ethel added,

'She will take Lydia in even if she has to give her a room in the attic, when she hears this dreadful news. They get on great with each other. So I don't think there will be a problem there. We will ask her if she would agree to have her live with her until the baby is born. Then she can give it up for adoption and go and live in England.'

Ethel was not looking forward to this journey. She was so annoyed with Lydia. It would be hard to spend so much time with her under these circumstances, but it had to be done. We will just have to lie and tell them she is going to England for a while to experience a bit of life outside the village.

'How am I going to come home from Dublin without her and try to tell all these lies to Mum and Dad? They are not stupid and I am not good at making up stories, especially on a scale of this magnitude. If I tell the truth and say she is in Dublin they will want to go and see her sometime, and we can't let that happen. I feel like killing her. How are we going to cope trying to keep this from them? I know what would happen if the real story got around the village. A lot of the fellows who were in love with Lydia and she broke their hearts, would be delighted this happened to her. Especially for the awful guy she said was the father. The whole thing is such a mess.'

Beatrice suggested she would call into the shop when they were gone and stay there until Ethel got back and see how the parents took the news. She would act surprised and offer to help in the Post office and say Lydia won't last long away.

'She will soon be back, tomorrow on the next train if I know Lydia.'

Beatrice was good at making light of situations that Ethel found more difficult to handle. Beatrice knew that Ethel would be worn out, when she got back. It was going to be a difficult task for both of them. When Ethel arrived on her own and broke the news Beatrice thought the mother was not very surprised.

She said, 'Lydia mentioned she might stay in Dublin for a few days, but I didn't think she was talking about now.'

'She did not take anything with her to stay.'

'Well, no," Ethel told them, "it was a last minute decision. We went to see Aunt Phyllis and Phyllis encouraged her to take a little break. She thought she looked very tired. Personally, I thought Phyllis was the one needing company. It will be good for both of them. They get along so well together. Lydia being in Dublin will be a great way to get her away from that creep she insisted on going out with.'

'I suppose,' the Father agreed and said, 'every cloud has a silver lining.'

The two sisters could not believe how well this was going. They both thought the parents knew there was more to this story than they were being told. Especially the Mum deep down they felt she was not so easy to fool.

Mrs. Cramp told them to go home, they were all very tired. Both girls hugged their parents and left. As they walked home together they decided it might be better to tell the mother the real truth. There was no way they were going to be able to keep lying to both of them. It would be good to have their mother on board. The mother could always know when they were lying so why did they think they could fool her this time. She would not be very happy with the situation but she would understand what they were trying to do. They walked in silence. They were so tired they just went to bed hoping tomorrow might be a better day.

The next day Ethel decided she was going to get on with her own life and not mention Lydia's name. Lots of girls in this position in Ireland had to leave their home and go to England. They would not have the support that Lydia was going to have. Their hope now was that she would agree to give up the baby when it was born without making a big fuss.

Ethel decided to leave it until evening time to call into the shop to see how the parents were. They were fine and Mrs. Cramp was in the post office tidying papers and seemed to be enjoying herself working away. Ethel was taken aback, surprised, and relieved. She realised then her mother knew the real truth. Ethel felt the strain vanish from her body. Her mother put her arms around her and gave her a big hug. Nothing needed to be said; they both understood the magnitude of the problem. The mother and the two girls would work things out to the best of their abilities, but the Dad could never be told. So for now they could relax a bit and allow Lydia to stay in Dublin. Ethel had warned Lydia to write letters to her Mother, saying things that her Mother could read out to the Father.

Like, 'Tell Dad I'm sorry for not coming home with Ethel. I love you both so much. I will write soon etc.'

Then the mother told Ethel,

"Lydia can write to us here because I'm the one that gets the post first and your Dad need never see the envelope with the Irish stamp on it. He will think it came from England. Having letters from her will keep him happy and that is the most important thing at the moment.'

Ethel left the shop a much happier person than she

had been when she came. When she got back home Beatrice was busy at work. She was surprised at how happy Ethel looked. Ethel told her the story and how well things went.

'That will take a bit of pressure off for the time being, so we can get back to business.'

George called into the parents' shop every day before any of this trouble, so now he would still do the same, but stay a bit longer and see how the parents were managing. Ethel and Beatrice were very busy so George staying a bit longer in the shop was a great help. If he thought the parents needed help one of the girls, whichever one was available, would go to them and sort things out. They were very independent people and did not like to bother anybody. The two girls were always very good at helping out, but now they were so busy in the workroom it was going to be a bit harder for them. They could manage that, easier than keeping Lydia's secret. That was going to be the toughest thing they had to do. How were they going to face the next few months?

Chapter 5

One day when Beatrice was in the shop Mrs Solomons came in and was overjoyed with her news she was going to have a baby. She had wanted another baby because she was so lonely since the other two were at school. Most of the day she spent making clothes, knitting or cooking. She loved the company of other people. What did Beatrice think of the idea she had of setting up a knitting, cooking or sewing, club? Beatrice congratulated her on the good news of the baby and told her a club was a great idea.

When Beatrice told Ethel the news about Mrs. Solomons' baby, Ethel was delighted for them and then it just struck her that it was just a while before Lydia's baby was due.

'Oh my God, if Lydia comes home after giving her baby away she will be very upset to see the Solomons with a new baby.'

Then Beatrice told her that Mrs. Solomons was thinking of starting a club. Ethel could not believe it.

'She told you she can sew, are you serious? I wonder if she would be interested in coming to work for us.'

'Well, we will ask her. That would be great. If her sewing is anything as good as her cooking she would be a terrific help. We are so busy.'

Beatrice decided she would be the one to ask her, as she was the one she told of her idea.

Ethel said, 'Ask her tomorrow, we need her now.'

'Consider it done,' Beatrice said, and got on with her work.

Ethel was excited at the idea of Mrs. Solomons coming to

work for them, she couldn't sleep.

'What if she is not interested?' she thought. 'Stop,' she told herself. 'We will make her an offer she can't refuse. That would be the answer to all our troubles. Oh please, please God,' Ethel prayed, 'please let Mrs. Solomons come and work for us.'

It was 4am before Ethel fell asleep, and she was awake again at 6am. She could not wait to hear what the answer would be from Mrs Solomons. When Beatrice came into the workshop she was so excited Ethel knew the answer was yes. The sisters hugged each other, then Beatrice said,

'God works in mysterious ways. Did we ever think, this time last year we would be in any of these situations?

'Lydia is living in Dublin. A new workroom. Thelma, the young girl training to be a designer. A Russian woman who needs no training at all working with us. It's not easy to take it all in. We will have to pinch each other to realise it is true.'

That day got off to a great start, Mrs. Solomons arrived an hour earlier than expected. She said it was better for her if she came to work just after leaving the children to school, if that suited them. That was better for all of them so everybody was happy. It was so pleasant now with four people in the room. It was just what the sisters needed to take their minds off the family problems. As time went on in the workroom, Mrs. Solomons was so good the girls gave her more freedom to suggest some changes as to the way they worked. She suggested to Ethel, the next time she was in Dublin she should buy a roll of material. When they had time between orders they could make up dresses, blouses, and things like that to sell in their parents' shop. She had a friend in Dublin who would sell her a roll of material wholesale, and they could train Thelma in this work and make her day more interesting. Instead of having to stop what they were doing now and then to explain things to her. Making designer pieces was very nice, but if Thelma was doing the same thing for a certain amount of time, she would get better and better. Thelma was delighted with this idea and said she would love to make a dress for herself. Ethel thanked Mrs. Solomons for her suggestion and decided the next time she was going to Dublin she would bring Mrs. Solomons with her and she could introduce her to her friend. If this worked out well then they would buy material on a regular basis and supply these small items to other shops around the county. They would be at low cost so the locals could afford to buy them. At the same time, Thelma would be getting trained in working on a production line although it would only be when she was waiting for outfits to be finished.

Thelma loved working with the girls. She did not mind what she had to do. But working on a production line really appealed to her. Able to make a dress for herself that these girls had designed would be wonderful. She could never be able to afford to have one of these dresses but if she could make her own she would be over the moon and the envy of all her friends. This might never happen, but when Mrs. Solomons made a suggestion it usually happened and happened quite quickly. Thelma found it hard to wait for this and she was so excited she thought she would burst. She was so lucky to be working with these three beautiful women.

Two weeks later when the last client's garments were

almost finished, it seemed the Dublin trip could go ahead. Mrs. Solomons wrote to her friend and asked him if he could meet them at the station. He replied at once. It was decided that on Monday morning Ethel and Mrs. Solomons would go to Dublin. They were met at Harcourt Street station by Mrs. Solomon's friend, in a pony and trap. It was a beautiful day and Ethel was delighted because she loved travelling in the open air when the sun was shining like today. Well, her pleasure was short-lived. Mr. Goldberg drove like a bat out of Hell. Ethel thought she was going to be sick. If he kept going like this Mrs. Solomons would surely lose her baby. They were jerked back and forth. Then he stopped so suddenly she was nearly thrown out.

'Here we are,' he said.

Ethel said, 'Thank God, I thought we were going to lose our lives.'

'Ah no,' he said, 'sure, that's the only way to travel in the city when it's very busy.'

He brought them into what looked like a shack. When he opened the inner door Ethel could not believe the sight in front of her eyes. Materials of all types. The most beautiful colours. Shades of spring and autumn. How was she going to be able to pick one roll from this huge collection? She did not have to. Mr. Goldberg had a few rolls on a table that he thought might be suitable for her. Since it was her first time buying from a wholesaler, he said these were the best sellers to get started with. He would sell her any of these rolls very cheaply to get her new venture started. They were all very good quality. He only bought the best as he thought it silly to put hours of work into cheap material.

'You put the same time into making a garment that's cheap as you do making a good quality one. So why not put the

31

time into making something that will last?'

Ethel could not argue with that and she thought he was very fair. Pointing out these things to her was a great help. She was used to people bringing their own material to her. She never bought a whole roll herself, it was such a new experience. She hoped she was making a good decision. Mr Goldberg told her she could not go wrong.

'You have to speculate to accumulate in any business and this is really a winner. Material does not go bad. It doesn't have a shelf life. If stored properly it will not fade. So if you make a few samples and sell them quickly you will have a good idea of what works well for you then go for it. He who never made a mistake never made anything. I can tell you right now, if you make a good garment and it wears well you will never be out of business. Word of mouth is the best advertising, you know yourself if a brand gets a good name, it's on the market forever.'

Ethel was delighted with all this advice. She thought Mr. Goldberg was a great business man and she liked him a lot on the business side at least, although she would never get him to pick her up at the station again!

He had made it very easy for her to make a decision on the material after all. Mrs. Solomons and herself both picked the same one. They laughed and Mr. Goldberg thought they had great taste. That was the dearest one. He sold it to them at a good price and everybody was happy. He said he would bring it to the station in the evening and they could bring it home with them in the guards' van on the train. They thanked him so much, Ethel was delighted he was not taking them back to the station.

They had a lot to do in town when they left him. The one thing Ethel was most worried about was that she might bump into Aunt Phyllis and Lydia, so her best bet was to stay on the south side of the city, which they did. After they did their shopping Ethel decided to take Mrs. Solomons up to Grafton street and then to the Shelbourne Hotel for dinner. It would be a treat for herself also as she had never had dinner there before. After dinner they could rest in St.Stephen's Green and then make their way to the railway station for the evening train. They just arrived at the station and there was Mr. Goldberg bringing the material into the station. He was used to putting material on this train for his customers and all the staff on the train knew him very well. He really was very nice but if she was ever going to buy more material from him she would never get into his mode of transport again. If there was a next time. She would walk when she got off the train. It would be a pleasure to go to his store on her own two feet and enjoy seeing parts of Dublin she never had time to see.

The train journey home seemed to take a long time. Mrs. Solomons had been lovely to travel with. She was great company and so interesting. She did talk a lot but she was a good listener also. They were both very tired now but they had really enjoyed the day. George would be there at Rathdrum station to meet them. Ethel was happy to see he was at the station when they arrived.

Chapter 6

Things had gone very well in the workroom with Beatrice and Thelma while they were on their own. They had finished the suit they were working on in record time for a very important client. All they had to do now was wait for it to be collected and then they could get on with the new venture. They were looking forward to Ethel coming home with the material and getting started. Beatrice had decided to stay a bit longer in the workroom. She was excited about the dresses. She always wanted to work on children's clothes. Although they were only going to make three sizes, 5 to 6 years, 7 to 8 years and 9 years, it would be nice to do something different. Beatrice stayed working on the patterns so they could start cutting out first thing the next morning. She picked three designs that could be altered with very little changes to them. They would still look beautiful but different from the Holy Communion ones, much less trimmings on them. She left the workroom very pleased with herself. Tomorrow will be very interesting. Rolling out their own material for the first time and making dresses for the local children would be very special. It was a risk, but it could work well. If it failed at least they would have enjoyed the excitement of trying and the loss would not break the bank.

The next morning when Ethel came into the workroom and saw the designs Beatrice had chosen, she could not believe it, they were the very ones she would have chosen herself. She quickly cut out three in the Holy

Communion size and started to work on them. It was so easy to work on such beautiful material. Making these dresses without all the trimmings of the Holy Communion ones, she flew through them. When the other three came in they were so surprised. Ethel had three dresses hanging on the wall, just waiting to be hemmed, pressed and delivered to their parents' shop. Beatrice thought Ethel had been up all night making them. When Ethel told her how quick she made them she smiled, 'Great that's it then, we are in the rag trade now.'

Mrs. Solomons machine stitched the hems and Thelma pressed them, she could not wait to bring them to the shop. Ethel started cutting out the next two dress designs that Beatrice had chosen. As decided she cut three of each size, now there was work for all of them to start together. There was a lovely feeling in the workroom. Everybody was enjoying being busy. Except Thelma who thought she would never get down to the shop with the dresses and show them to Mrs. Cramp. Ethel told her she could go with these three that were finished. She could feel how excited Thelma was. She was off like a shot, she could not go quickly enough. When she arrived at the shop Mrs. Cramp thought something was wrong with one of the girls. It was the first time Thelma had come into the shop during working hours.

Thelma said, 'Wait till you see what I have here.'

When she opened the parcel. Mrs. Cramp was really surprised.

'My God Thelma,' she said, 'this can't be the material Ethel just brought home yesterday?'

'Yes, it is.' Thelma said, 'and she made them in such a short time and they are so beautiful.'

35

'My God,' said Mrs. Cramp, 'they really look fantastic.'

She put one in the window straight away and Thelma left. The dress was only in the window for about an hour when Mrs. Moore the local gossip came in and wanted to know, if the the dress in the window was for sale. Mrs. Cramp said, 'Yes and at a very reasonable price for such beautiful material.'

She showed her one of the other dresses and said, 'I have three of them. My girls are making them in their spare time.'

'Oh they are lovely, I would buy one if I had a little girl to wear it. When I go to heaven I'm going to ask God, Why did he never give me any children? I love little girls and to have just one I would have been so happy. We have to accept what we are given.'

Mrs. Cramp said, 'Look at me, three girls and I would have loved a little boy. That's something we have no control over.'

'No, I suppose not. By the way,' Mrs Moore said, 'How is your youngest one, Lydia, I haven't seen her in quite a long time, has she gone away?'

Mrs. Cramp was so taken aback, it was the first time anybody had mentioned Lydia since she left.

'Oh, she is in England,' Mrs. Cramp said.

She could feel the blood rushing to her face, telling a lie did not go down well with her. She was not good at it and hoped she would be believed.

Then Mrs. Moore left the shop muttering to herself. Mrs. Cramp knew she had not been believed, she looked up to heaven, rolled her eyes, and thought to herself,

'How are we going to keep this secret? God forgive Lydia for bringing this cross on all of us.'

Lydia's letters were happy. Her pregnancy was going well. Herself and Aunt Phyllis were getting on very well. She was delighted with the money her mother sent her on a regular basis and she loved living in Dublin.

'So she might enjoy herself, while those left behind have to cover for her, by making up stories.'

Mrs. Cramp felt disgusted with Mrs. Moore asking about Lydia. She felt sick to her stomach, she had taken the whole good out of her day.

Ethel and Beatrice called to see their mother that night to talk about the dresses. She was delighted to see them. She thought they weren't charging enough. The price was very reasonable for the beautiful material that they are made from. They could charge more if she could take a deposit and allow the customer to pay by the week.

'God! Mother!' Ethel said, 'Will you stop? They are a great price, we know.'

Beatrice said, 'Mum, they are not going to be expensive. We are just going to cover our costs and make a little profit. We will be happy with that. It's only an in-between thing to give Thelma experience and give us a bit of variety from our real work. We want to give something to the locals, they are so loyal to you and Dad. These dresses will last and can be passed on to other children. That's what we really want.'

Their Mother was so proud of them.

'What a great idea!' she said, 'how did you think of doing that?'

'We didn't. It was Mrs. Solomon's who thought of it.'

'Well, that's really fantastic. She is such a lovely woman, with such great ideas. No wonder she is so popular in the village,' answered their mother.

'We are delighted with her working with us. Thelma loves her and they get on so well. We are so lucky that things are going so well.' Ethel said. 'You both deserve all the luck in the world, you are two wonderful daughters. Your Dad and I really appreciate all you do for us,' said their mother.

'Enough of that now,' Beatrice said, 'I'm putting the kettle on and we'll have a cup of tea. Then we will be going on our way, it's been an excellent day.'

After the tea they talked about other business, they never suspected how upset their mother was. Their Mother herself could not believe how well she held it together. She still had to get through hiding her hurt from her husband, he must never find out what had really been going on. Sometimes she suspected he was aware that things were not right, but he never said anything. She thought in the last week or so he did not look very well. But he did not complain, he never did if anything was wrong. She felt she had so much on her plate to worry about, if anything serious happened to him, she would never be able to cope.

With all the things that were happening, Ethel felt she had been missing out on her own family's life. Joseph had been interested in becoming a minister. Both she and George were pleased about that. Now his latest talk was about joining the British Army. What had brought this on? They were both in shock.

George asked, 'Are you serious?'

'Of course I am. I have filled in the forms and I want you to look at them before I post them. If I'm accepted please don't try to stop me,' Joseph answered.

'We would never stop you doing whatever you want to do with your life,' his mother said. 'But if you go away we will miss you so much.'

Joseph said, 'I will miss you all, especially Trevor. He is such a good kid. But this is something I really want to do.'

'Well, that's it then. I'll read the forms and then you can post them if that is what you really want.'

Joseph could not tell his parents the real reason he had to go away, he was gay and he knew his mother would never cope with that. It was treated as a serious crime at that time in Ireland. He could never bring that kind of trouble on his parents. He would leave Ireland before anybody suspected. Deep down he did not want to go away but he knew he had no other option. His parents looked at him and sadness came over all of them. His mother turned her head so that Joseph could not see how upset she really was. Both she and George left the room without saying another word. 'Broken-hearted,' she thought to herself.

'That's our first born leaving the nest. 'Please God,' she prayed in silence, 'please grant that he is not accepted into the army. Trevor would be so upset, Philip would be happy to see him go. The grandparents would be very sad. This will have such an effect on so many people.'

Ethel wondered when they were going to get a break from big problems. One thing after another, she couldn't take much more. She was going to bed, but sleep was the last thing on her mind.

Ethel slept for a couple of hours but woke with a heavy heart. She decided not to tell anybody about Joseph. Then if he was not accepted nobody would know. She would leave it at that for the moment. She had two other children to look after. She would do what mothers do best. Put on a happy face and hope she could get through the day, hour by hour without breaking down. It was not going to be easy, she would tell Beatrice she was not feeling well and stay out of the workroom for most of the day. She would call in later and see how things were going.

It was late in the evening when Ethel popped into the workroom, looking bright-eyed and bushy-tailed. She just had a visit from a wealthy farmer's daughter in the next village. She wanted her wedding dress, three bridesmaid's dresses and her mother's outfit all made by them. There was nothing unusual about an order like this, but she pretended it was great because the wedding was not until next year, so that would give them some time to work on the dresses. Beatrice had made the 5 to 6 year old and the 7 to 8 year old design and was working on the 9 to 10 year old size. Ethel thought that was a great amount of work done in one day so she told them to leave what they were doing and go home early, they had done enough for one day. When they left Ethel sat in the workroom with her head in her hands and cried as she had never cried in her life. She felt as if her life was going out of control. If anything else goes wrong, she will not be able to deal with it. When she stopped crying she went back into the house. To her surprise George was there and had started to look after the boys. He realised how upset Ethel was. He nodded to her and made a sign to her to go out for a walk. A walk was what always cured George's problems. She walked out, turned left away from the village. This was a lonely road, so there was no chance of her meeting anybody. She walked for one hour and she had to admit to herself that George might be right, she felt a good bit better when she turned to walk home. She went straight to bed. When George came up to her with a cup of tea, she was fast asleep, he was so pleased, she really needed sleep.

Chapter 7

Ethel had a great sleep and woke up feeling a bit better. When Mrs. Solomons arrived for work, looking so happy and in great form, Ethel asked her what she was so happy about? Mrs. Solomons told Ethel that she had just had a letter from her brother and he, his wife and their son, six-year-old Nicholas had left Russia safely and were on their way to England. She was so excited. Ethel was so delighted for her. They hugged like sisters and when Beatrice and Thelma heard the news, they were also delighted for her. That was going to be a very happy day in the workroom.

It was a great day and they got so much done. When Ethel went into the house George also had good news. The three dresses in the shop were sold to a strange woman. Her mother was surprised and wondered where she came from. She was not sure about selling the three of them, but when she asked if she had any more of the dresses in the window she just said,

'Yes, I have two more.'

The woman said, 'I'll take the three of them.'

Mrs. Cramp could not believe it.

'They must be way under-priced,' she thought to herself again. How come that woman, a stranger happened to be in the village today? She bought nothing else. She knew a bargain when she saw one!'

Mrs. Cramp was taken by surprise when the woman asked if she had any more and she did not expect her to buy three the same size .She never expected this to happen. She will

42

have to have a word with the girls about the price. In one way it was great to see them sell so quickly, but three the same size looks a bit suspicious, where did this woman come from? Well, it was a good start to the day for Mrs. Cramp also. It was the little lift they all needed and which everyone was very thankful for.

With three dresses selling so quickly, Mrs. Solomons suggested they should cut out six of the 5 to 6 year old size and charge the same price as the 7 to 8 year old size. Beatrice thought this was good thinking, maybe they were under-priced.

'Then we can charge extra for the 9 to 10 year old size.'

Ethel said, 'Now girls let's not get greedy, we said we were going to charge a reasonable price, so let's stay with that. Same price for the three sizes no messing about. It will make it easier for the paperwork at the end of the day. We had better get working on more dresses. If they are selling that fast we must be doing something right.'

The next few dresses sold to the locals and it looked like they were going to be a big part of their business from now on. It looked like a trip to Dublin for more material was on the cards. Next time Ethel would go alone. The girls were so busy she could not take anyone with her. It would be great to pay a visit to Aunt Phyllis and check up on Lydia while she was in the city.

Another good thing had happened the same day. This time to Mr. Solomons. He had great luck with his business. By chance he met Mr. Marks, a man he had bought some scrap from a while ago. He said he had a few more bits of scrap back at his house. If he wanted it, he could have it for nothing. He thanked him and made hand signals and said, 'I'll take it now, if that's ok?'

Then Mr. Marks told him, Jonny Wall, a friend of his, had a big amount of scrap he would sell for next to nothing as he wanted to get rid of.

'He just lives up the road from here.'

Mr. Marks told him to leave the cart in his yard and take his bike and go and see if the scrap is worth buying.

'If it's no use to you then no harm done.'

When Mr Solomons reached the house he could not believe the amount of scrap the man had. He told him Mr. Marks sent him to see if he was willing to sell the scrap he had to him. He did not hesitate for one second and told him,

'You can have it for a good price if you take the lot. I don't want you to mess about, it's all or nothing.'

He made the deal and paid him cash straight away.

'I'll have it out of your way as soon as I can get transport organised.'

Jonny told him, 'there is a neighbour who delivers turf, a Mr. Paddy Murphy, he has a big lorry. I'm sure if he had time and if his lorry was empty before he went to the bog, he would be delighted to make a few extra pounds.'

'I will pay him whatever he asks if he collects and delivers it all on the same day.'

'If you are going through the village now you will pass his cottage on the way. The name on the gate is River View, you cannot miss it and the lorry might be outside anyway. He is a nice old guy and he will do it for you if he can, if he can't do it he will know someone who will do it. That's what we are like in this country.'

Mr. Solomons thanked him and made his way back to Mr. Marks and told him he bought the lot.

'That's great,' he said, 'I hope you got a good deal.'

'Oh I did,' Mr. Solomons said, 'I am so happy. I know the person I have in mind who will buy it all.'

He told Mr. Marks he was going to try and see if a Mr. Murphy who had a big lorry might be able to help him. Jonny, the guy he bought the scrap from, told him he would do it if he could.

'Oh that's right,' Mr. Marks said, 'I never thought about old Paddy, sure he's your man, sound is old Paddy. Always ready to help out. I know he will do it for sure.'

'I had better get down there now,' Mr. Solomons said, 'while the getting is going good.'

Mr. Marks smiled and agreed with him. He knew he got the wording the wrong way round, but he seemed so pleased with himself he did not correct him. Mr. Solomons could not get over how helpful the Irish were to him always. They went out of their way many times to tell him to find the way to places he would never have found. He had been offered so many cups of tea, so many times from people he bought scrap from. If he accepted them he would never have made a go of the business at all.

Mr. Solomons left and went as quickly as he could to find Paddy's house. He could see the lorry in the distance and hurried in case the man came out and left before he got to him. When he got to the lorry he could see it was empty. He could not believe his luck. He checked the name on the gate, *River View*, and he walked to the front door. It was open as always is the case. Doors are left open all day in

45

this country village. Not like where he came from in Russia. He coughed and ahemmed a few times but nobody came. He could hear voices inside, but he did not know what to do. Then he began to sing out loud, a voice inside said, 'Come in Mick, we would know your voice anywhere, come on in.'

He asked himself what to do now.

So he shouted, 'I am not Mick,' and then a big man came to the door. He had a really friendly face and asked,

'Then who are you?'

He told him who he was and what he wanted.

'Come in, come in! You could not have come at a better time if it's an empty lorry you are looking for. I would be happy to drive you there and back if the price is right.'

'Name your price and I'm sure we can agree.'

Price fixed and after having to take a cup of tea, they were off. The trip to collect the scrap took only five minutes. Filling the lorry took half an hour. The drive to the buyer was a little over half an hour. The quickest part of the whole thing was it emptied in less than five minutes. The whole trip was a lot less time than Paddy had expected. Now he was in no doubt he might have overcharged him. He was thinking of telling him and then decided not to say anything. After all when the price was arranged he had agreed and he would leave it at that. He did not deliberately try to rip him off. He could make it up to him if there was a second request for the lorry and driver.

Paddy never stopped talking through the whole thing, and although Mr. Solomons didn't understand a lot of what he was saying, he really liked him a lot. It was only

46

a couple of hours of work, but it was good to get it all done quickly. It meant so much to him and he had made a lot of money. He was a very happy man. That was a great day of work. He was going to find it hard to keep the good news to himself until his wife came home. Life had been really good for them since coming to Ireland, he had made lots of money. He had not met one nasty person. He sometimes had difficulty trying to make himself understood, but most times he was able to laugh at himself about the way he spoke and the hand signals he made. It never stopped him getting what he wanted. He really loved doing business with the Irish. He could never understand why people always wanted to give you things for nothing. A lot of the time he got so embarrassed, he felt they were sorry for him. But he was well off and did not need sympathy. After a while he realised it was just the Irish way. They were such nice people, it took time to get used to their ways.

Chapter 8

Ethel was just about to arrange her travel to Dublin when a big order came from the local fox hunting club, to make the hunting jackets for all the members. It would be a lot of heavy work and time consuming, as each member would have to be measured, fitted and there would be a lot of coming and going. Now that they had got used to making the dresses and nobody was bothering them, she would have to think about it. Ethel decided to put the idea to the girls in the workroom at the tea break. Whatever they decided, that would be her decision. She had never been asked to do such a big order before. The amount she could charge for each jacket would be a lot more than the money they got for each dress but the enjoyment would be a lot less. Sometimes life is not all about the amount of money you make, you need to have a bit of quality in your life also. Beatrice thought they should do the order. Thelma thought they should stay with the dresses. Mrs. Solomons thought they should do both. Ethel asked how they could do both?

'Well,' she said, 'never turn down business. What you have to do is tell the club that you will supply the material for the whole club. That makes it easy for them and you. As a result all the jackets will be exactly the same. Each member will just have to be measured. Then as you make the patterns, you will just cut as many as you can in one go. That will save hours, rather than trying to have a member come in one by one with their own cloth.'

'That sounds great but then I am going to have to get the material, which takes time,' answered Ethel.

'Not if you send a sample of the cloth to Mr. Goldberg. Tell him how much you think you will need and he will put it on the train, you can collect it at the station, problem solved. When the other clubs see how beautiful our club's jackets are they will all want a designer hunting jacket. You could set a standard in all the clubs around the country,' explained Mrs. Solomons.

Ethel, Beatrice and Thelma were speechless.
'That's it then, we will do both. I will tell the club we will do it, if they agree that I supply the material.'

Tea breaks over, all back to work with big smiles and a promise of a rise in wages if the club were willing to allow Ethel buy the material. Ethel decided to wait for the reply from the club before taking a trip to Dublin.

Chapter 9

Joseph received the word from the army. He had to go for an interview, then a medical. If he was accepted then he would have to go to Belfast first. Where he would be posted did not bother him as long as it was as far away from this village as possible. He was thinking England would be great, but he really did not mind as long as it was further than Dublin, so he would not have visitors from home. He knew he would be upset when the time came to leave but this was what he wanted. Ethel was very upset and tried not to show it. His Father was disgusted and walked out of the room to try and compose himself before he could wish him luck. His parents told him not to say anything to the boys until he had passed the medical and he was really ready to go. No point in upsetting them if he was not going. Joseph was praying the whole thing would go well and he could get out of this village as soon as possible. He hated the way everybody knew everything about everybody. He couldn't care less about anybody in the village .He loved his grandparents and his aunties, they were family. Other than that, he was happy on his own. If he didn't make it into the army he did not know what he was going to do. He would worry about that another time, for now he had to wait.

It was a pity Joseph had got this news from the army today. It had been a great day for so many, and this had taken all the good out of what could have been a perfect day, if there was such a thing.

Not in her life, there was always some hitch at the end of a great day to take the good out of it. Ethel went to bed with a heavy heart and thought to herself, being the eldest of the family was the worst place to be born. Only Beatrice had such a lovely way of bringing her back to some kind of sensibility she would never cope with life. How often had she gone to bed hoping tomorrow might be a better day?

Well, this time tomorrow was a much better day. She was only in the workroom a few minutes when George came home from the shop with good news. The hunting club was under the impression that she would buy the material. They were delighted to give her a sample and then she could name the day when she wanted to come round to the club and measure all the members on the same day or night whatever suited her best.

'Why did I not think of doing that? That is a much better idea than having them come round to the workroom one by one. That's great news. I'll get that sample posted right away and as soon as I get word that Mr. Goldberg has the material I will go to Dublin and bring it back with me.' Ethel thought.

When Thelma came to work she had good news, her Dad who was a great voluntary worker in the church, had been offered a properly paid job by the parish priest. The old clerk who had been sick a lot had suddenly retired and he was the one most worthy of the job. He had done it for nothing so many times when the clerk was sick. Her Dad was delighted, he had been out of work for a long time. It would be great to be earning money again. Now with Thelma getting a rise in her wages, things were getting better in one household at least. Thelma was getting so good at making the dresses she asked Ethel if she could use the base of one of their patterns to make a dress for herself. She would

51

make a few changes to the style to keep it unique and different. Ethel said of course she could, and she could use the machine and any of the trimmings she wished. If that turns out well you should make a pattern yourself for the next dress.

'You are well able to do that now, you have plenty of experience. I will give you a hand with it. When things get a bit slower. Don't attempt to do anything apart from what you have to do at the moment.'

Thelma thanked her so much and said she would work as hard as was necessary, she would do whatever it took to get all the orders out. When Beatrice came in to work she felt the atmosphere was pleasant. Ethel looked a bit better and she was actually smiling. It was going to be a better day than yesterday. When the working day was over they were all in agreement it had been one of the most exciting days. Things had gone very well, after work Beatrice and Ethel had arranged to go to the shop that evening and stay a while with Mum and Dad. They also had great news to tell Ethel and Beatrice.

About a mile from the village the Taylor family, owners of the biggest farm in the whole county, had just bought the flour mill. Mr. Taylor had been into the shop and told Mr. Cramp the good news. He was going to make big improvements in the mill. He was planning on opening a bakery shop. There would be plenty of work for the local people from the village. Some people from the village already worked for him on the farm. He was very pleased with all of them. He was a great employer in every way. If you worked for the Taylors you had a job for life. He treated those who worked for him very well. He paid great wages. Had proper

52

working hours that very few other employers practised. He gave all his staff a week-long holiday every year with full pay. If a farmhand was ill he still got paid while he was out of work. There would be great excitement in the village when this news went round. To get working for this family was the best thing that could happen to you.

The Taylors had eight children, five boys and three girls. They had three boys in four years. Michael, James and Patrick. All very good looking like their dad, with beautiful black hair and big brown eyes. Then they had a girl named Mary. She had blond hair and blue eyes. Next twin boys, Mark and John. They also had the black hair and big brown eyes. The next four years there were no babies and Mrs. Taylor was very happy with five boys and one girl. The Dad adored Mary and used to joke about her needing sisters and him needing more daughters. The next year they had twin girls, Margaret and Anne-Marie. Mr. Taylor asked where they came from. These girls had flame red hair and blue eyes. They were not like anybody on either side of the families. They were born in Dublin and he always said they could not be his children. If there had been another set of twins born the same night he would have believed the hospital gave his wife the wrong babies. They are so alike he could not tell one from the other. He could not take his eyes off them. He was like a first time father. He was over the moon with them and was dying to hold them. They were tiny and had to be treated with great care. Nobody was going to be allowed to handle them for a few weeks, and then only for a very short time. Martha, the nanny and Aggie the housekeeper who lived with the family, and worked for them for years, were on high alert. If anybody went near the nursery door they were in big trouble. Mr. Taylor was the worst offender. Martha caught him on a few occasions sneaking into the nursery. She would shake her finger at him and say only look, do not dare to lift them. She knew he would never go against anything she said.

He always said back to her, 'whatever you say Martha you're the boss.'

He said this to her so many times, she really did think she was the boss! He got a great kick out of cod acting with her, the banter between them was fantastic at times. He would not dare to upset her. He depended on her for lots of things. She had rescued him many times from his wife and his children. When he was under doctor's orders on a special diet, many times she caught him eating things he was not allowed. She warned him she would tell, but she never did. At times like this he felt like a child caught raiding the food cupboard. He was very fond of her and they got on really great, although she treated him as one of the children. If Mrs. Taylor found him standing over the cribs looking at the babies, she would have to smile. He would stare at them as if he never had a child before. He wondered about the red hair!

If she asked him, 'Does Martha know you are here?'

He always told a lie and said, 'No, no, not at all, sure she would kill me if she knew I was in here without her permission.'

Martha was very funny, she was small and fat, with snow white hair, big red cheeks, and a big loud laugh. She loved all the children and they loved her. They did play tricks on her sometimes. She never minded that, she could take a joke. She was strict at times but very fair. When Martha was serious everyone knew then her orders were adhered to. The atmosphere in the house was not nice if Martha was having a bad day. That did not happen very often, she got her own way most of the time. She was such a good worker she was forgiven all the time. Mrs. Taylor was as nice to work for as her husband. Mr. Taylor was happy to bring employment to the village. Any employment was good news, but this news was the greatest ever. It had been a long time since The Taylors had taken on any staff. There would be no shortage of people trying for any of these jobs. A bakery would be a great asset in the village. Mr. and Mrs. Cramp sold cakes, but they were no different from cakes you could buy from any village shop. All the shopkeepers bought their cakes from the same suppliers. They were OK but a choice would be very welcome. If the cakes from the bakery were nice, people would come from far and near to buy them. Ethel and Beatrice thought the bakery was a success already before it even opened. There were plenty of people in the area who could afford to buy good cakes. A nice cake for a treat every now and then would be lovely.

The first to get started was the improvements on the flour mill. Already six men had been employed. Mr. and Mrs Cramp were very busy in the shop. The difference it made when the locals were working. On a Friday when the men were paid, the sales of chocolate, sweets and lemonade were up. The Dads bought these as treats for the children who might not have as much as a sweet for a while. But if they gave a few pence to the children to buy their own, Fiz Bags were a big seller, because they had a lollipop in them, and Lucky Bags, always a sweet or two in them, so this seemed better value. If a child bought a Lucky Bag and only got one sweet Mrs. Cramp would give them another sweet to cheer them up. She loved children and could not bear to see a child miserable with what they got, an extra sweet always did the trick. Sales in the groceries department were up also. It was great to see the pure joy of the women that could now afford to spend money more freely and buy without the strain of counting every penny. If this was anything to go by, it would only get better when the bakery opened. The talk in the village was that the bakery would take a much longer time, as a big extension was going to be added before they opened the shop. The big question was how many were going to get work on the extension. It looked like there would not be a man left in the village without a job. At last this little village would have something to bring in people from outside, which was just what they needed.

Chapter 10

The letter arrived from Mr. Goldberg telling Ethel the material for the jackets had arrived. She decided to go to Dublin the following Monday. This time on her own as she wanted to see Lydia and Aunt Phyllis. She would go there first and check on Lydia. They were not expecting her, so this was going to be a big surprise to them. Well, it was Ethel who got the surprise of her life. Lydia was huge, it must be nearer to her time than she said. She was not happy to see Ethel and let her know it. Ethel had a few serious questions to ask her but she knew by her attitude she was wasting her time. She passed no comment on her size, but knew she had lied about the date. She was so disgusted she did not ask her any questions.

She just said, 'Let us know when the baby arrives if you need anything.'

Then, just as she was leaving, Lydia dropped a bombshell.

'I have decided to keep this baby.'

Ethel said, 'You what?' She repeated herself. 'How do you propose to do that? You cannot come home with a baby.'

'No,' she said, 'I am not coming home with a baby; you are.'

'What do you mean?' asked Ethel.

Lydia said, 'What I say, I am not giving this baby away, so you have to take it.'

'I am not taking the baby, are you mad?' said Ethel.

'Then I am coming home with it. That's the choice you have.

57

Take it or leave it,' answered Lydia.

Ethel did not know what to say.

'You cannot do this to Mum and Dad, that's not fair. What made you change your mind about giving the baby away?'

Lydia answered, 'I just did that's all.'

'When were you going to tell us about this?' questioned Ethel.

'I wasn't going to tell you at all. I was going to come home with the baby. Phyllis said not to do that, if I did not write she would.'

'Thank you Phyllis,' Ethel said, 'after all the trouble you caused, you are so selfish.'

Ethel left in such a state, she had to go to a cafe and sit and think about what had just happened. If the baby was a girl then she would love to take it. That could be easy to explain to the village people, but if it was a boy, nobody would believe she wanted another boy. She could not think clearly. She was in shock that nothing was ever easy with Lydia. She did exactly as she wanted and she always got her own way.

Ethel made her way to Mr. Goldberg, saw the material was perfect, paid him for it and said she would see him at the station. She sat in St. Stephen's Green thinking, 'What are we going to do about this?'

She couldn't come up with any answers. All she could do was wait until she got home, talk to her mother and Beatrice and hear what they thought of Lydia's plans. When she got to the station the material was already in the guards' van and there was no sign of Mr. Goldberg. She was delighted she did not have to see him that evening, she was so confused. She spent the whole journey thinking of what had happened. The train seemed to take forever to reach Rathdrum station. When the train stopped, she saw George on the platform. She ran to him, fell into his arms, and burst into tears. George got such a fright he held her until the sobbing stopped before he could ask what on earth happened in Dublin to have her in such a state. When she stopped crying she said,

'It's Lydia she wants to keep the baby.'

'Well, Ethel, what's so bad about that?' asked George.

'I am so tired now I can't talk about it, I'll explain everything in the morning, I just want to go to bed,' answered Ethel. She did not say a word the whole way home.

George said, 'I'll tell the boys you are not well and will speak to them tomorrow.'

She went straight to bed and fell asleep immediately. When George came to see if she wanted anything and found her fast asleep so quickly he was pleased. He closed the bedroom door and slept in the spare room so as not to disturb her.

Ethel could not believe it when she woke up at midday. The boys had gone to school and George was in his office. When he heard Ethel coming downstairs he came out from his work and gave her a big hug. They went into the kitchen and he put the kettle on for the third time that morning, thinking he had heard her twice before. Each time he was wrong. This time he made sure his hearing was right and he was delighted to see her looking a lot better than when he collected her last evening.

'Well now then, how are you today? Ready to talk yet?' asked George.

'Oh yes,' she said, 'I will start with the good news. Everything about the business went fine. It was when I saw the size of Lydia I got such a fright. She either told us lies about the delivery date or made a mistake. Looking at her now she should have gone into labour yesterday. She is adamant about keeping the baby and she wants us to rear it. So she will see it and enjoy taking part in its life. If we refuse to do that she is bringing the baby home and does not care what the village people think. That would kill Mum and Dad and she knows that. She also knows that I would never let that happen to them. Especially now Dad is not very well.'

'Well then, that's it, we will take the baby,' said George.

'But what if the baby is a boy? Everybody would wonder why we adopted a boy already having three boys of our own.'

'We will love it whatever it is and it will be great company for the Solomons' baby. I would like a little girl if I'm honest Ethel, but under the circumstances I really don't mind,' explained George.

'Oh! Thank you so much.' Ethel kissed him. 'I'm so sorry for thinking you would object, but I got such a shock I could not think straight. After Mum being so good to her, sending money, making sure Dad never found her letters, and having to make up stories about how well she was getting on in England. That was such a strain on Mum it might have killed her. Lydia cares about nobody but herself. How am I going to tell Mum we are taking the baby?'

'Stop worrying about it. Wait until the baby is born then tell her we want the baby, after all, it is her grandchild and when she sees it she will love it. You more than anybody understands how soft she is when it comes to babies. Have faith in the Lord, leave it in God's hands and all will be fine. Just pray that things will go well for Lydia at her time of delivery, and that the baby will be perfect.'

Taking Ethel by the two hands, with a big grin on his face he said, 'Pray for a girl.'

This time she knew he was trying to make her smile and she did. George made a lovely brunch, while Ethel told him about the rest of her day in Dublin.

After they finished eating, Ethel felt she would go to the workroom and put on a brave face. Tell the girls about the good part of her day out and show them the material she had bought and see how they liked it. Things had gone great in the workroom and the girls were so happy with all they had done in one day. Ethel was delighted, and told them to take it a bit slower today. The afternoon went quickly and when the girls left Ethel said nothing to Beatrice about Lydia. That would have to wait for another day. When she came into the house the boys were so pleased to see her. They had set the table with candles, flowers from the garden, and a beautiful meal ready.

She was so surprised she asked,

'Who's coming for dinner?'

George looked at the boys and in unison they said, 'You Mum! Dad told us you were not feeling well when you came home, but you were feeling better today. So, we decided to make a fuss of you. Now sit down and enjoy your meal.'

Ethel found it hard to hold back the tears, she was so impressed with their kindness. George told her it was all their own idea. He was as surprised as she was. He had been out all afternoon and when he came back they had everything ready. The kitchen was in a mess but he cleared that up for them, and helped to set the table. Ethel knew George would not have been best pleased with them cutting flowers from the garden, but under these circumstances he said nothing. The meal was very good and they all enjoyed it. After the boys cleared everything away. George told them to leave the washing up and he would do it. Joking, he said he would do it in half the time, and use half the water.

'Oh Dad,' they said, 'we are not that bad.'

While he was in the kitchen Ethel told the boys she had not brought them anything from Dublin. She was so busy and not feeling good, she would make it up to them another time. They didn't mind as when Ethel told you she would do something she always did it. They were sure of that. When George finished the dishes the four of them played board games. Something they had not done for ages and they had great fun. When they were in bed, Ethel thanked George for being such a good husband and father and said how lucky they were with the beautiful kind children they have. They were so relaxed when they went to bed, they made love and just as they were about to settle down for the night there was a loud knock on the front door. They got such a fright they jumped out of bed. George looked out the window and saw Mr. Solomons at the door.

'Oh Ethel! It's Mr. Solomons you had better get up.'

He went down and when he opened the door he knew exactly what it was. Mrs Solomons had gone into labour and he was in a terrible state. Ethel got dressed and was so relieved that there was nothing wrong with her parents. She put her coat on and asked him how long she is in labour. Babies don't usually come that quickly.

Mr Solomons said, 'All day, and she would not let me call the doctor. She kept insisting it was you she wanted.'

'Well,' Ethel said, 'I have helped deliver a few babies in my time. I hope she will last a few hours longer and then we can call the doctor.'

But when they got to the house and Ethel saw the state she was in she knew there was no time to waste. The baby's head was already on its way and Ethel knew that this baby was in a hurry and was not going to wait for any doctor. Within an hour the baby arrived safe and sound. It was a beautiful little girl with a head of black hair. Ethel was overjoyed for them but found it hard to hold back the tears. Then she made sure everything was as it should be. She wrapped the baby in a big white towel, handed her to Mrs. Solomons and called Mr. Solomons to come and see the baby. When Mr. Solomons looked at the baby the tears began to flow and then all three of them were crying. They were tears of joy, Ethel congratulated them with a big smile on her face, while in silence she wished and hoped with all her heart that Lydia would have a baby girl.

When everything had settled down and mother and baby were comfortable, Ethel said she would go home. Mr. Solomons said he would go with her.

She said, 'Not at all, you are needed here and it is almost daylight now. I have walked this way for years, I'll be home in no time.'

She wanted to walk alone to collect herself before she got home. All the years of longing for a little girl came flooding back and she did not want George to see her in that state. By the time she got home she was fine. George was waiting for her. He had the kettle on and she said she would love a cup of tea. Ethel dropped down in the chair exhausted. When she told George the baby was born he could not believe that Ethel had done all this work on her own. He was so proud of her and happy for them it was a girl. It had been the easiest birth she had ever helped with, in fact it was the first time she delivered a baby on her own. Everything had gone well, but she told Mr. Solomons to get the doctor today to make sure mother and baby were doing OK. She was not a midwife and she did not want anything to go wrong. They both had a cup of tea and went to bed. A couple of hours later, they were up again ready for whatever the new day would bring.

When Ethel told the girls about the baby, they could not believe it. They wanted to see the baby immediately.

Ethel said, 'No, give the mother a chance to rest and we will go when we are invited. These people are not Irish. They might do things differently. So we will wait and see what they do. I can tell you the baby is beautiful.'

They were disappointed but agreed and wanted to know if she knew the baby's name.

'I never thought of asking, I was so happy that everything went so well that never entered my head.'

Beatrice said, 'Why don't we buy a big present from the workroom and then a few small things from each of us.'

They all agreed that was a great idea.

'I'm sure they will get plenty. They are so popular and well liked in the village. It is the first baby born of Russian parents here and that might never happen again. This will be a very spoiled baby for everybody. I'm so proud I did such a good job bringing her into the world,' Ethel exclaimed.

'Oh stop boasting!' Beatrice gave her a playful thump. 'You must have been scared out of your mind. I have to admit though, you were very brave.'

'Thanks a million for your kindness,' laughed Ethel.

It was all good banter between the sisters.

'Now we must get back to work. With Mrs. Solomons out for a while, we are short of a great pair of hands.'

They worked very hard all day, the atmosphere was so pleasant. Nobody thought the birth of a baby could bring such joy to so many people, who were not related in any way to the child.

Ethel had still to break the news of Lydia wanting to keep her baby when it was born, to her Mother and Beatrice. She just could not bring herself to drop such a bombshell at the moment. It was going to be a big shock to them, and she was not prepared for their reaction at the moment. So she was not going to say anything, until everything was arranged. They were not going to make any excuses to anyone in the village. If the baby was a girl it would make things a lot easier, but if it is a boy we will deal with that when the time comes. The next couple of days she was going to enjoy sharing in the excitement of the Solomons' baby. Just then she saw Mr. Solomons coming up the garden path. He looked really happy so she hoped it was going to be good news. When she opened the door and was about to greet him, he took her in his arms and held her so long, she could hardly breathe. He thanked her so many times for all she had done. He did get the doctor the next day and the doctor said she had done a great job. He and Mrs. Solomons would never forget her kindness. How could they ever repay her? He told her the baby's name was going to be Sofia after his mother and Ethel after her. She started to cry and said, 'That's so kind, I am honoured, but you don't have to do that. What about the baby's other grandmother? She might be hurt.'

'No,' he said 'Sybil is named after her so we want to do this, if you don't mind.'

Ethel was charmed and thanked him so much. He then took a beautiful bottle of perfume from his pocket and said,

'We hope you like this. It is very popular in Russia.'

'Oh no,' she said, 'you cannot do this, please I would rather Mrs. Solomons used the perfume and I would love the bottle to keep forever.'

He thought she was mad, 'You must take please.'

She was mortified but knew she had to take it. He then asked if the girls would like to come on Saturday at three o'clock to see the baby, and Mum, of course.

'Yes, they would be delighted to come. We would love that. We won't stay long and you are not to go to any trouble for us. Mrs. Solomons must have plenty of rest.'

'Of course,' he said, 'she is longing to see all of you.'

'We are all longing to see her and the baby. We miss her so much, we will come on Saturday thank you.'

He left very pleased with himself and Ethel was in shock. She always knew how grateful they were, but to call the baby's second name after her made her cry again. When George came home and saw her crying he asked, 'What is it now?'

When she told him he said,

'Thank God. It's getting to the stage where I'm afraid sometimes to come home. I'm not sure what I'm going to find. That was a nice surprise, enjoy it and be grateful. At least somebody appreciates your kindness.'

He held out his arms and they embraced.

'What a woman you are. Always ready to drop everything and go help others. Bringing babies into the world, helping to lay out the dead. You really are Mrs. Parish. Is there no end to your talents?'

'Stop that,' she said. 'I could not do any of it, if I did not have such an understanding husband.'

In silence she thanked God for her blessings and how lucky she was to be loved so much.

Ethel was looking forward to telling the girls about Saturday. She knew they would be thrilled. She said nothing about the names of the baby. They would hear all that news when visiting on Saturday.

When the boys came home from school she told them all the good news. They all sat down to dinner and the boys told their news. It was lovely having time with them, after all the trouble with her family. She decided that whatever happened in future with her family, she was going to go back to making proper meals and sitting down with the boys for the main meal every day as it used to be. She could not believe how much time she had been putting into looking after everyone, and neglecting those that should come before anybody or anything else. The family is going to come first from now on, she could not remember when all this rushing round started, but not any more. She enjoyed helping people, but lately she had taken on more than she was able to handle. She was feeling very tired and knew she was overdoing it. If they were going to take on Lydia's baby she would need all the energy she used to have. To enjoy being a Mum again to a newborn. She wanted to have plenty of time to enjoy and love this baby as she did with her own boys.

Chapter 11

The following Sunday morning Ethel's parents were at church. She was delighted to see her Dad there. That was a good sign he was feeling better. After the service her Mum asked them to come home with them for a chat. It seemed like a long time since her Dad was feeling good. He missed going to church and meeting them after the service. The girls went along with them, they talked all the way home. After they had a coffee, their Dad thanked them for coming, and told them not to leave it so long before coming again. He went off to the sitting room with his newspapers and Beatrice asked her Mum if there was anything wrong?

'No,' she said, 'but it has been a while since you have been here. I know how busy you are, but Trevor told me Ethel, you came home from Dublin not feeling well.'

Ethel decided this was the time to tell them about Lydia.

Beatrice looked at Ethel and said, 'I did not know you were not well.'

'No,' Ethel said, 'I was suffering from shock, and I could not tell you. I had to wait until I was ready. So now is as good a time as any, because you will not believe what I am going to say.'

She put her finger to her mouth, tilted her head towards their Dad, and lowered her voice so they understood whatever she was going to say was not for his ears.

'You will get a shock when I tell you what happened when I met Lydia. You will get upset, but everything is sorted and I will tell you now. She wants to keep the baby. I told her she could not do that. Then she told me I will have to take it. I agreed to, because I knew there was no way she was giving it away. She would have come home with it, and I was not going to let that happen, we are going to adopt it. If the baby is a girl that will be fine, if not we are still going to take it and deal with that if it happens.'

Beatrice's mouth fell open, but she could not speak.

Mum said, 'Please tell me that's not happening.'

'It is Mum, I'll tell Dad when the time comes, that we are doing a favour for a friend by taking the baby. He need never be told the truth. I know it will be hard for you Mum to keep the truth from him. That is the best thing for the moment. He is so well we don't want to upset him. Have you any better ideas?' Ethel asked Beatrice.

'Well, I don't know how you have kept all this to yourself. You have always said you would love a little girl. You had better start praying that Lydia's baby is a girl.'

'George said we are taking the baby. The boys will be delighted with it, especially Trevor. I am going to Dublin early in the New Year and Beatrice, you are coming with me, I cannot face Lydia on my own again.'

Beatrice agreed to go but she felt sick at the thought of having to see Lydia.

'She is so full of herself. How dare she say what she wants! She needs to be told what we want.'

'Well, there is no point in going over all that now. What's done is done, we just have to get on with it.'

70

Their Mum was so upset, Beatrice told her not to cry. If Dad saw her upset, he would want to know what was going on.

'We have to get through Christmas and make the most of it for the boys' sake. Joseph and Lydia will not be with us,' Ethel said.

'So Mum if that's ok with you, I will have Christmas dinner in my house. I am going to invite the Solomons. That will make the day enjoyable and we won't have time to think about the ones that are not here. If you or Dad don't want to do that then we will come here as usual, and we will invite the Solomons family here.'

Mum said, 'I don't mind, I just want it to be over. This was the most awful year of our lives. I hope next year will be a better one, please God.'

'It is going to be a great year every year from now on. With all the changes going on in the village. The way the Taylor family is getting on with the work, things will be quite different. People will be so busy they won't have time to notice who is doing what. Mum, when people come into the shop with plenty of money to spend, they won't be asking about Lydia. They will have much more interest in their own lives. Anyway, there will be no time for small talk. You will be so busy you will need extra help. Start thinking of taking on somebody mature and smart. You could also think of taking on that nice little Sheila Kelch on a Saturday. When she helped you out last time the customers loved her and she liked working here, she is a little flyer. You and Dad were delighted with her as she livened up the shop. It was a pleasure to come in to buy. Philip, Trevor and both of us will also do our best to make things easier for both of you, and of course, you can depend on George to check in every day as usual.'

'I hope you are right,' their Mum said.

'Mr Taylor told me last week, he has a huge amount of men ready to start work in January. He wants to get things moving fast now. The work that has been done so far has made a great difference in the village. When everything is finished it will be like a big town. Things will never be the same again, and that's good. I hope people won't lose the run of themselves and get greedy.'

'So what if they do? It will be lovely to see the place busy and happy smiling faces for a change. It's just what the village needed. Thank God for the Taylor family, having the money and the energy to take on a big project like this.'

Ethel was happy the conversation had taken on a lighter note before it was time to go.

'Now Mum, think of all the good things the new year will bring. Don't worry about the things we cannot change. Once we are healthy we can face anything.'

Her Mum thought she was right, but it was not going to be easy for her. She hated keeping things from her husband. Ethel said,

'George is here now. Mum, would you and Dad like to come to our house for dinner this evening? You will be better able to keep the secret from Dad, after having a break from the house. Staying here on your own will be a lot harder for you.'

'I would love that,' said Mum, 'I'll ask your Dad. If he agrees that's what we will do, thank you love, for asking.'

Dad was off his chair like a shot, he was fed up having

dinner with just the two of them. Sunday after Sunday not being able to go to church, dinner in Ethel's was always lovely. He liked having a bit of fun with the boys. It had been a long time since they were invited for Sunday dinner. He often thought it strange that Ethel had stopped inviting them. Ethel told him while he was not going to church, she did not want to take him out in the cold. Little did he know she was trying to see as little of him as possible in case he started asking questions about Lydia that she could not answer. He was out the door before they had their coats on. The three of them had to smile. It was great to see Dad feeling so well again. He was sitting in the carriage ready to go, telling them to hurry up like a bold child. It was fantastic that things had gone so well. Ethel knew when the parents had gone home, Beatrice would want to know what exactly happened in Dublin. She was determined not to talk about it again. She was trying to concentrate on getting ready for Christmas.

Chapter 12

On Saturday, the baby visit went very well. Mr. Solomons had gone to so much trouble, the girls were very annoyed but they enjoyed it. When they were leaving Ethel invited them to Christmas dinner at her house. They were really pleased and accepted immediately. The girls left feeling really happy.

Thelma said, 'What a difference that family made by coming here to live. None of this would be happening if a local had been given the cottage.'

They all agreed she was so right. Thanks to Mrs. Fogarty. They finished in the workroom four days before Christmas. It was going to be busy this year.

Beatrice was great at preparing for Christmas, and Ethel gave her all the freedom she wanted to do as she liked. She was expert at wrapping presents, decorating the house, dressing the tree and setting the table. Ethel would do all the cooking with help from the boys and George. It was going to be frantic in the kitchen. With so many coming. Mrs. Cramp said she would cook the turkey and ham as Ethel had never done that before. Ethel was thrilled with that offer. She would never have asked her mother to do it. But when she offered Ethel thanked her so much, she gave her a big hug and whispered in her ear, 'You know, we all love your stuffing.'

They had a good laugh. Ethel told her with all that cooking being done for her, she and Beatrice would be able to help out for a lot more hours in the shop. That freed her mother to work in the post office, which she loved, so everybody was doing their bit.

On Christmas morning the sun was shining. It was cold, nobody minded that as long as it did not rain. They went to church and after George brought them home, he collected the parents and all the food. When he arrived home, things got very busy. All the vegetables were ready to cook, but dinner was not going to be for a while. They wanted to wait for the Solomons family, before opening any presents. There was a lot to open as they had bought presents for the Solomons although it was nothing to do with their religion. They were being included in all the festivities. When they came they had presents for everybody. The joy and excitement was super. It took a long time to clear up all the wrappings and leave the sitting room tidy to come back to after the dinner. The meal was a great success. When they returned to the sitting room Mr. Solomons played the balakia and everybody relaxed and enjoyed the music. Then the Solomons decided it was time to leave as the adults were falling asleep. They had really enjoyed the day. Ethel was happy the day had gone so well. They did not have time to miss Joseph or Lydia. The parents stayed the night. They were all in bed by ten o'clock. Thankfully the day had gone so well.

Chapter 13

Ethel and Beatrice decided to go to Dublin on the 2nd of January. Having just had Christmas cards from Lydia and nothing since, they hoped everything was OK with her. They were not looking forward to going. It was getting too near her time to leave it any longer. They had lots of presents for Lydia, Aunt Phyllis and the baby. The 2nd of January was a beautiful day. The train journey was very nice. But they did not know what would be facing them when they got to Dublin. When they arrived at the house, there was nobody in. They waited and waited and then Aunt Phyllis came along. They knew by the expression on her face it was trouble. When she saw them she was so pleased.

'My God, I am so happy to see you two,' she said.

'Where is Lydia?' they asked.

'Come in first, you will have to sit down before I tell you. Lydia gave birth yesterday on New Year's Day to a baby girl and a baby boy. Yes, twins!'

'Oh my God!' they both said.

'She is in the Rotunda Hospital. The babies are beautiful, she is doing fine, and getting the best of attention.'

'Leave it to Lydia, she never did do things by half.'

'How are you going to get her to give up the little boy? I could not take on twins,' said Ethel.

'She is not giving him up. She said you will have to take both babies or you are not getting the little girl. She will under no circumstances separate twins.'

The girls looked at each other in disbelief.

'What time is visiting hour?' Beatrice asked.

'Oh, you can go in any time. She is in a private room, and breast feeding both babies. The staff are delighted with her, and she is very happy. She has just given me a letter to post home to let you know. I'm so glad you are here and I won't have to post it.'

'Give it to me,' Beatrice said. I know I should not do this, but I just want to see how she was telling Mum news like this.'

'Don't read it,' Ethel said. 'That might upset us more. Our poor mother might have died if she got that news. She would not have been able to keep that from Dad.'

The girls did not know how they were going to face Lydia, She was always so difficult about everything. Aunt Phyllis said,

'I'll make lunch and when you have eaten and let this news sink in you might be better able for her.'

'Don't make any lunch. We will just have a cup of tea, and then go and see her.'

'Do you want me to come with you?' asked Aunt Phyllis.

'Not at all, you have done enough for all of us. We are really grateful to you Phyllis.'

They drank the tea and left for the Hospital. On the way Ethel could not decide what to do about the babies. She would love the little girl and she could understand why Lydia would not separate them. But to take on two babies? She could not even think what that would be like. When they reached the hospital, they were worn out. They were still in shock, and hoped they would be able to have patience to deal with Lydia. When they opened the door to her room, there she was sitting up, her hair done beautifully, looking fantastic and delighted with how well she was, after bringing two babies into the world. The babies were in the nursery to give their mother a rest. Beatrice and Ethel burst into tears. Lydia was not expecting to see them, and for once in her life she was stuck for words.

Then she asked, 'How did you two get here so quickly?'

'We were in Dublin and called to see you. When Aunt Phyllis told us about the babies we got such a shock.'

'Not half as much of a shock as I got. The doctor told me I was having a big baby, but he never mentioned twins.'

Beatrice asked her if she had thought of names for them.

'Yes,' she said, 'I like Desmond and Doris, what do you think?'

'They are nice names, but not after anybody in the family,' Beatrice said.

'No, I hate family names.'

Ethel asked, 'Will we be allowed to see the babies?'

'I think so, I'll ring the nurse and check.'

'Great!' Ethel thought to herself,

'Just to get away from her for a few minutes.'

Lydia rang the bell and the nurse was in immediately. She was surprised to see she had visitors. Lydia introduced the girls to her and told her they just happened to be in Dublin today and how surprised they were to hear about the babies. Would it be possible for them to see the babies just for a few seconds? They are only here for the day and would not be in Dublin for some weeks. In that case.

'I will take them to the nursery for a few minutes and show off the beautiful babies to their two Aunties,' said the nurse.

The babies were small, but they were beautiful. They both had black hair, their eyes were closed but the nurse said they had brown eyes.

'I'll let you wait a while and they might open their eyes,' the nurse said.

She was a lovely nurse and let them stay longer than they had expected, but the babies did not open their eyes.

She said, 'Sorry about that but I have to take you back to Lydia's room now.'

They thanked her and left the nursery.

'Who do you think they look like?' Lydia asked.

'Well, it's hard to tell at the moment.

They are so young, they are really beautiful.'

Lydia said, 'I'm delighted with them. I hope Mum gets a chance to come and see them, I wish Dad knew about them. What do you think? Should we tell him?'

The sisters nearly died.

Beatrice said, 'No way! After all the lies Mum told him about you doing so well in England, not coming home for Christmas and nearly killing her trying to keep it from him.'

Ethel said, 'Don't you ever even think about telling him. That could be enough to break up their marriage. For once in your life, think about somebody else besides yourself. We'll have to go now to make it back in time for the train. It's great to see you looking so well. We have a lot to talk about, not today we will take another trip up in a few days.'

They left, before both of them lost it with her. They

made it in time for the train. They travelled the whole way to Wicklow without speaking. They could not believe all that had happened. Just as they were getting off the train Ethel said to Beatrice, 'We won't tell George about the babies tonight. I am so tired, it's been such a hectic day. I need time to think things out.'

'Yes, sure. Leave it. There is a solution to every problem. George is better at finding them than we are. He is not as involved as we are.'

They both put on a brave face, when they saw George. They said they were very tired, and thought they would never get home.

Ethel said, 'I am getting fed up going to Dublin so often.'

George said, 'I thought you loved the capital city.'

'Not anymore. Especially in winter it is not so interesting and I have been there so much lately.'

'Well,' George said, 'I'll get you home as quickly as this animal will allow me to go. At the same time I'll be kind to him.'

The next morning Ethel woke up early, feeling a bit better about yesterday. When the boys were gone to school she told George to sit down. What she was going to tell him would shock him. When she told him about the twins he was not surprised.

'You are taking this very well,' she said.

'Well yes,' he said, 'you know when you said Lydia was as big as a house. I thought that knowing Lydia, she might just do that. I was going to say it at the time, joking. But then I thought, no. you don't joke about things like that.'

'What are we going to do then? If you want the girl, well, then you have to take the boy also. How would we explain that?'

'We won't explain anything. Lydia will be kept in hospital for a while. The babies may be kept a bit longer. That will give us time to make arrangements. Stop worrying! The two of you go down to your Mother tonight and tell her.' George said, 'I feel so sorry for her trying to keep all this to herself. Your Dad should have been told from the start. I know he would not have been very happy about it. It would have saved all this pussyfooting around. There is no way he can be told now. It would kill him.'

When the girls went to the shop their Mum and Dad were still working. They were delighted to see them.

'It's great that you came tonight, you can give us a hand here,' their Dad said.

'No problem Dad, what do you want us to do?'

He told them and they worked together very hard. They got a lot done in a short time.

Beatrice said, 'That's enough now Dad, if you overdo it you will get sick again. We don't want that now, do we? I'll make tea now, then Dad, you are going to bed.'

'See what I have to put up with?' he said to their Mum.

'They are right, it's time you were in bed.'

Their mother had realised the girls were there on a mission and wanted the Dad out of the way. In her wildest dreams, news like this was not what she expected to be told. Ethel assured her everything was going to be ok. Nothing was going to happen for a few weeks.

'It won't be easy for you Mum, but you have done a great job up to now keeping things from Dad. So don't stress about it. Carry on as best as you can let us do the worrying.'

'Easier said than done, but with your help I know we will get through it.'

'Sorry to have to bring such news. But there is never a good time. It's hard to get you on your own. It would have been so much easier if Dad had been told from the beginning. We'd better be going.'

They hugged and kissed her, it was hard to hold back the tears.

Beatrice said, 'What a great start to the new year!'

When they left their Mum, the two of them burst into tears. They were crying for their Mum, who was always so good to all of them. Lydia was their parents' pride and joy. It was awful. They never thought she would bring such trouble to them. It just was not fair. They walked home, in better form, the telling of that news had gone better than expected.

Chapter 14

The building work in the village was going up at great speed. The bakery was almost finished. The chemist was opening in about two months. The flour mill had taken on more men. Everyone was excited, there was so much work for men and women. Mr. Taylor had applied to the council for permission to build twelve houses. He thought the plans were a bit much, but if he got the chance to build even six, he felt that would be great. No houses had been built in the village for years. When people are coming from other parts of the country to work, getting a council house would be fantastic for a man who would like to live there. Travelling to work every day was hard for some people. There was no public transport. The sale of bikes went up. George was going to the station so often to collect bikes for people, the poor pony was worn out.

As the work was going so well people were coming up with more ideas as to what would be great to have in the village. The buzz around the town was brilliant. Mr. & Mrs. Cramp were very busy in the shop although they had taken on a lovely mature woman Patsy Clarke, and a junior Sheila Kelch, who had helped them before. Sheila really wanted to work in the shop full time when she was old enough and they told her the job was waiting for her. She was ideal for the work. Philip and Trevor were helping out when they could. They were so happy to be making money, they wanted to leave school and work full time with their grandparents. That was never going to happen. They had to keep up with their education. All the customers commented on how Trevor was so good and helpful, especially with older people. When he saw something to be done, he did it and never complained. He was a treasure to have around. He was so pleasant. Grandma loved him.

Philip was more of a dodger, a bit on the lazy side, only did what was necessary. He didn't enjoy dealing with the public as much as Trevor did. Grandma copped on to this and gave him plenty of jobs to do that were in the store, this was a great help. In those days there was no such thing as biscuits, sugar, flour, etc. coming in packets, everything had to be weighed. Trevor loved to weigh things, especially biscuits. Sometimes he even sang while he worked, Granddad thought he was a great kid, and he let him know it.

Ethel missed them not coming straight home from school. She missed the banter she had with them. When they came home now they were tired. They had to do their homework. Then it was time for bed. At the same time she knew they had to help in the shop. Beatrice and herself were so busy. They didn't get to help as often as they would have liked. She was beginning to think, she liked the old days better. Was it worth all the rushing around making money, and having no time to spend it? She had a big decision to make about these babies. George was adamant they were taking them. He was not going to have them separated. He was right, she would take them. She might get help if she needed it. She was not going to stress about it now. Plenty of time to make the arrangements. They could do nothing until they heard from Lydia. Her mother had a letter from her telling her she was home with Aunt Phyllis, and the babies were doing fine. She would write to Ethel when she decided to allow her to take them. She was not ready to let her have them yet. She was enjoying being a Mum. Her mother burned the letter as usual, and asked herself how Lydia could be so awful to those who are trying to help, she was so selfish?

The babies were now three months old. Ethel wanted to know when Lydia was going to make arrangements to part with them. She was afraid she would not give them to her at all. The longer she held on to them, the less likely she was to part with them. Why Lydia made everything so hard for everybody, Ethel could not understand. Ethel's biggest worry was that one day she would arrive home with them saying she was keeping them. If she could get George to go to Dublin and talk to her about getting her life back together and go to England as she had promised. That would be great, but would it work? Well, it was worth giving it a try. They could not leave things as they were at present, her whole life was being turned upside down. She could not plan anything until she knew when the babies were coming. She liked to have order in her life. So when the babies arrived she would have plenty of time to get to know them, as by now they would be getting to know their mum so well. It would be harder for her to part with them. That wasn't fair to them. She just wished she had them now and was able to get on with her life. At the moment she was up to date with the business side of things at least.

The girls in the workroom could go on without her a lot of the time. Sometimes they needed her, and she was delighted when they did. She loved the work. If she could keep making the patterns, that would be as much as she could do when the babies came.

Chapter 15

A week later both herself and George went to Dublin. Lydia got the shock of her life when she saw George. He was very calm and told her the effect her behaviour was having on her Mother was horrible. She is working so hard, she does not need all this extra worry.

'Please Lydia for once, do the right thing.'

She burst into tears and George felt sorry for her. He put his arms around her and said,

'You know the babies will be loved, and you will be able to follow their progress. You can come down in a few weeks and see them. If you really do not want to go to England, don't go. You are so needed in the shop at the moment. Your parents would be really pleased to have you. So, here's the deal.'

Ethel did not know what he was going to say.

'We will take the babies now. You write to your Mother when we are gone, tell her you are coming home from England. That you hate it and you miss them so much. She would be thrilled to be able to show a letter like that to your Dad. Instead of what she had always to do, burn them as soon as she reads them. That was awful for her. Your Dad would be over the moon with that news. We did not tell you but he has not been very well. I think for him to see you would clear all his ills. We just want to do the best for everyone, we know how hard it is for you. We are trying to make it easy for you. What do you want to do?'

The silence was deafening.

Now Phyllis, Ethel, and Lydia, were in tears.

George said, 'Now girls stop it, crying will get us nowhere.'

Lydia stood up and said, 'Take them now then. I will write and do what you said.'

Lydia loved George, he was a good man, and she knew his words were his bond. She was so happy, the fact that she could go home was what she really wanted. Aunt Phyllis gave her a big hug and said,

'Come on I will help you get the babies ready. That's the right thing to do, if that's what you want, it's ok with me.'

George said, 'Why don't both of you come down together in two weeks' time? Phyllis, I'm sure you could do with a break, and that would be good for Lydia to have you with her.'

Lydia was so excited, 'Please do,' she said to Phyllis.

'OK, I will,' Phyllis said and they both smiled.

It was noticeable how well this pair got on with each other. Ethel never saw so many things being sorted out in such a short time, it was a miracle. But George had that way about him. He commanded respect and he got it. Phyllis put the kettle on and said,

'A nice cup of tea is what we all need.'

They all agreed. The babies had been asleep through all this, and were now starting to wake up. Ethel asked Lydia if she could hold one of them.

'Of course, they are yours now. Here this is Doris.'

Ethel took the baby, she was beautiful, she loved her straight away. Lydia handed Desmond to George.

He said, 'He is so lovely.'

Ethel looked over at him, and saw the same expression on his face as she did when he held his first son. She knew then things would be fine. They held the babies while they drank the tea. It was as if they were the real parents. She thought she could not get home quickly enough before Lydia changed her mind.

Lydia said, 'Come upstairs and help me pack. There is so much stuff for babies. You would not believe it.'

'We'll take as much as we can. You can bring more with you. Come sooner than two weeks if you like. Just make sure you write that letter first.' said Ethel.

'I'll write now, you can take it with you, and give it to Mum tomorrow. Then I'll know she has got it for sure.'

Ethel answered, 'That's good thinking, she will be so excited. We will bring the babies home with us. It will be late when we get home and we will be tired. So tomorrow will be a great day in all our lives. Can you imagine the excitement in our house? The boys won't believe it when they see us coming home with two babies.'

George and Ethel made it back to the station as soon as they could. With a baby each, they could not believe it. It was such a shock, at the same time Ethel knew that Lydia was so homesick, when George said don't go to England, that was the ace card. The babies were on their way to Wicklow. When the boys saw the babies, they were fascinated with them. Especially Trevor. Philip surprised Ethel with his reaction. He wanted to hold one, so Ethel gave him Doris and he held her really carefully.

'Mum she is beautiful.' Philip said.

Trevor took Desmond from George and said,

'He is so cute.'

'Call Beatrice!' Ethel said to George, 'Tell her we have a great surprise for her.'

'We don't want the shock to kill her.' answered George.

When Beatrice came in she was shocked.

'My God!' she said, 'How and when did all this happen? I can't believe it.'

She sat beside Trevor looking at the baby he was holding. She asked him, 'Which one is this?'

'Desmond', Trevor said, 'Isn't he so cute?'

'He is, and so big.'

Beatrice then went over to Philip and asked if she could hold Doris. Philip gave Doris to her and she burst into tears. They were tears of joy and sadness. Beatrice would have loved to be a mum herself. She knew she was going to take over the rearing of this baby every chance she got. Ethel told her they came straight home from the station. Mum and Dad did not know they had the babies. What did she think? Should they wait until tomorrow to tell them.

'Oh God, yes!' she said, 'They really will get such a shock.'

'We are still in shock ourselves, and we are very tired so it's best to leave it till morning.' Ethel answered.

Everyone agreed. As they had no cots for the babies George went upstairs and cleared out two drawers. He shouted down that the babies' beds were ready. Ethel took Desmond from Trevor and carried him up, followed by Beatrice with Doris. They laughed when they saw the drawers. They laid the babies on the bed.

Ethel said, 'We can't put them in there. Wait till I put

blankets under them and make them cosy. You can have Doris on your side.' she told him.

'Oh, thanks a lot, I hope she is a good sleeper.'

When both were asleep they left the room. Beatrice told Ethel to go to bed herself, if the babies didn't settle down she might not get much sleep. It was nearly bedtime anyway.

'I am off to bed now, tomorrow is going to be exciting. We'll need to be very alert and careful, what we say and do to explain to Dad where these babies came from. I have my speech ready. I hate all this cloak and dagger stuff. It's not going to be easy. When we go to the shop, having Mum there will be a great help.'

Ethel gave Beatrice a big hug and said,

'You by my side to support me will be greatly needed.'

'You don't have to worry about me. I'll always be there for you. You are so good to me. I'll never forget your kindness when I lost my husband. We are so lucky to have each other,' answered Beatrice.

'That's what sisters do, when the chips are down. There we go again, picking up the pieces for Lydia,' added Ethel.

The babies slept until 6a.m. Ethel thought if this happens all the time we won't know they are here! She made the two bottles. When she went back to the room George was awake with Doris in his arms.

'Was she crying?' Ethel asked.

'No, I just wanted to look at her. She is beautiful.'

When they were fed and winded they kept them in their arms looking at them. They were still in shock. At the end of the day it all happened at such speed it was hard to take in. They were so happy. George had his daughter, and Ethel had three boys again.

The first thing Philip and Trevor did when they woke up was to come and see the babies. George and Ethel were surprised they were so excited about them. They expected Trevor to love them, but Philip was even more interested than they ever imagined.

Ethel gave Desmond to George for a second and allowed the boys in with their Dad. She gave Desmond to Philip. George put Doris into Trevor's arms and stayed in the bed with them. Beatrice came in for breakfast.

'Where is everybody?' she asked.

'All in my bed,' Ethel smiled. 'I think I'll give the boys the day off school.'

'Yes, of course.' Beatrice said.

'That's it then, no hurry on anybody. The workroom is closed for the rest of the week. We have to work out the best way to do things from now on. The babies come first. We'll work around them, if things get out of hand we will cut back on the sewing. Mrs. Solomons has offered to come to work and bring her baby with her. That might be a good idea, especially now, the nice spring weather, and summer coming. It would be lovely for her to have space to leave the baby outside. The twins would be outside also. I'm sure she would like that.'

Ethel agreed with everything Beatrice said. She was always so level headed.

'We don't have to think about that now. I'm dying to get down to the shop and get that over with, then we can get on with our lives.' Ethel said.

It took ages to get everything ready to go out. Nobody got a proper breakfast. Just tea and toast. The babies had to be carried. Bottles and nappies packed. It was just as well they had so little for the babies. It meant they could not stay very long in the shop. The Mum would give them small things that she sold in the shop for now, but George was going to go to Dublin with a list for bigger things. Get them delivered to the house. A big pram was the most urgent.

When the Mother saw the pony and trap arriving at the shop, she got an awful fright. She called their dad and said,

'George is outside with the whole family, come here and see what's going on.'

The Dad said, 'Wait woman! They are coming in.'

George had all of them out in minutes. The mother nearly died when she saw the two sisters with a baby each. She knew exactly what it was.

'Oh my God!' she said, 'When did this all happen? Who owns these babies?' she asked.

Trevor said, 'We do.'

'No you don't,' she was about to continue when Ethel said,

'Yes, we do mother.'

'Since when?'

'Last night.'

'How come?' asked Mum.

'It's a long story. Let me introduce you to them. This is Desmond.'

'A boy?' her mother said.

'Well, yes. And this is Doris and she is a girl.'

'Well, let's hope so. You have not adopted two babies have you?'

'Well, Mum we only wanted a girl, but the mother would not separate them, we agreed she was right. So we have two babies now.'

The Dad just stood there looking at them as if they were all mad. A customer came into the shop and the mother told him to serve her. When he was busy, Ethel filled her in on a bit of what had happened, gave her the letter and told her she could pretend it came from England, and show it to him. She put the letter away, and she started to admire the babies. When the Dad came back he looked at the babies and said,

'You did the right thing. Twins should never be separated. Now you will have double trouble, and then of course double the joy.'

The shop started to get busy and Ethel said,

'We won't stay Mum, we'll come when the shop is closed. We just wanted to let you see the babies first. It took us a while to make up our minds to take them. That's why we said nothing until we got them.'

They left the shop and called to see Mrs. Solomons. Ethel and Beatrice were the only ones that went into the house with the babies. The whole family was there. They could not believe it when they saw two babies. Ethel told her their names and allowed everyone to look at them but not hold them. They wanted to make one more call before the babies were due to be fed. As they left Ethel told Mrs. Solomons they were not working for the rest of the week. Next Monday if she wanted to, she could come to work and bring the baby. She was delighted, and would be looking forward to it. They didn't stay long.

Next they went to Thelma's house. She was shocked. She could not believe they had two babies. They didn't go in. They showed the babies to her and told her their names. She did her best to get them to come in, but she understood they were in a hurry. Then she was told she was to take the rest of the week off work. Unless she wanted to do some work for herself?

They left and went home. They spent the rest of the day trying to get some kind of organised system going. It was difficult. It was going to take a long time if it ever happened.

After the family left Mrs. Cramp was dying to read the letter. Ethel told her it was good news. When she read it she thought it was brilliant news. The post had not come yet, so she had to wait until it did before she could show it to her husband. This news was going to really lift his spirits. Having Lydia home was all she ever wanted.

Mr. Taylor got permission for the twelve houses. He could not believe it. He came into the shop and told Mr. Cramp the good news. Mr. Cramp was dumb founded.

'Well,' he said Patrick, 'I have to admire you, for sticking your neck out in the first place and applying for permission for twelve. When you would have been really pleased with six. But to get what you asked for is unheard of in this town.'

I always say John, 'Ask for a lot and you might get a little, ask for a little and you will get nothing. To be honest I didn't

94

think they would answer the letter. I cannot believe it, and to get a reply so quickly.'

'Patrick you must have promised a free house to a big shot on the council.'

'You know me better than that John. Not my way of doing things.'

'No, of course not Patrick, only joking.'

'There will be a lot of discussion, consultations, and conditions, before I can get started. As soon as that happens the diggers will be in and I'll put as many men as possible working on that site. Those houses will be built in jig time.'

'That's the best news I've heard in a long time.'

'You can tell all your customers. Anyone wanting work can get in touch with me or any of my sons. That would be a great help to me. I'm so busy these days. Any help I can get is greatly appreciated.'

'You are welcome Patrick, you are the best employer around here and deserve all the luck in the world.'

'We are a very lucky family, so why not share it?'

'You are perfectly right.' John said.

'Sure you don't want anything?'

'The only thing I really want, and don't laugh, is a motor car.'

John did not laugh, but asked,

'Sure, where you would get one of them?'

'I am making enquiries at the moment. Ann and I were in one in Dublin last week. We went to a garage and had a drive in a beautiful car. It was so comfortable. I loved it. In fact we both loved it. We will be celebrating a big wedding anniversary next year. I'd love to surprise Ann and have one at the house on that date. Wrapped up in silver paper, tied with a big red bow on it. When she opened the door, she would love it.'

'That would be lovely Patrick aren't you a real romantic at heart?'

He leaned in close to John and whispered,

'Not really, I want it for myself. But if I said I was buying something that nobody else had she wouldn't hear of it.'

'So give it to her as a present, and she cannot refuse.'

'Good thinking, that's a great Idea. Patrick, I won't tell anybody.'

They laughed and he left the shop. John was still laughing.

Mrs. Cramp asked, 'What was that all about?'

 He told her the good news, she was shocked and said, 'That man works wonders. Nobody else would have got that application passed.'

'Now,' he said to Mary, 'There is big important news that you can tell Mrs. Moore. News we want her to be the one to tell. The whole village will know before the day is out.'

Chapter 16

Mrs. Cramp had held onto Lydia's letter for a few days. She had to pretend it had just arrived, now she thought it was an excellent time to tell him. He was in such good humour.

'Now John,' she said. 'Here is something that will keep you smiling.'

'What's this?' he asked.

'Read it and see what,' she said.

'Take it inside and sit down, it's great news.'

He took the letter. She stood at the door peeping through watching him open it. The expression on his face while he was reading was so joyful, then he burst into tears.

She rushed through the door, 'Oh John.' She asked, 'Are you not pleased?'

He lifted his head and said, 'Mary, I am so happy. These are tears of joy. I've been so afraid I'd never see Lydia again. I think I'm going to burst. I'm so happy.'

A customer had come into the shop.

Mary said, 'I'll get it.'

When she saw who it was she was delighted. Mrs. Solomons was very diplomatic and pretended she did not notice Mrs. Cramp's tear stained face. Giving her a chance to collect herself, she pretended she wanted apples and started to pick some from the box. When she brought them to the counter Mrs. Cramp asked, 'Do you really want these apples?'

'Oh,' she said, 'I really wanted apples to eat, I made a

mistake. I'll put these back.'

Which she did. She knew by the time she picked the right apples, Mrs. Cramp would be ok and ready to serve her. She bought the things she had come for and after a little small talk about the weather and left the shop. Mrs. Cramp called John and asked him to stay in the shop while she washed her face. That would make her feel better. Maud would soon be in to work, she did not want her to think they had a disagreement. When she came back, he could tidy himself and be ready for the shop getting very busy. They were both back in the shop just in time when Maud arrived. She was such a good time keeper. Never a minute late or a minute early, always on the dot. You could set your watch by her. She was very particular, neat and tidy and kept the shop spotlessly clean. After a busy rush, instead of taking a rest, she would tidy, dust and keep going looking for work. Mrs. Cramp told her many times that she would stick her bum to a chair if she didn't take a proper break and sit down. Mary told John to have a word with her, he said,

'No Mary, if it keeps her happy, let her get on with it, say no more. If she was lazy you would have something to moan about. Stop worrying she likes what she is doing.'

Mary knew she was not getting any satisfaction from him, she was never going to win this battle. The three of them got on great and worked very well together, so why change anything. John couldn't understand why Mary was getting so upset.

He said to himself, 'That's women for you, always looking for something to worry about. Never happy unless they are worried. Strange creatures. What we men have to put up with.'

The weeks were flying by and the twins were coming on

98

very well. Ethel and Beatrice were so wrapped up in them, getting a great system going and enjoying every minute of them when they suddenly realised Lydia had not come home.

'Oh God,' Beatrice thought, 'Poor Mum and Dad, they have not mentioned her lately. What's going on?'

She asked Ethel if there had been any mention of Lydia lately.

'God,' Beatrice. I have to be honest, I never thought about her coming home. Since the twin's arrived I've been so busy, I've no excuse. Poor Mum and Dad, they must be so upset. We'll have to go down to them tonight and see if she has written to them. They haven't mentioned her lately. It's not like them to keep us in the dark if they know something. If they do, whether it's good or bad news they should tell us.'

The sisters felt so bad about not mentioning her to the parents. What excuse were they going to use for being so selfish?

Beatrice said, 'Leave it with me, I'll come up with a plan.'

When it was near closing time for the shop they arrived. The first words out of Beatrice's mouth and with a big wave of her hand she said, 'Just a flying visit, so busy and hard to keep up with everything. How are things?'

'Never better,' Mary and John said in unison.

Beatrice knew they were telling the truth. They were very happy about something, but she was not going to ask. She talked about everything except Lydia.

Then John said, 'What do you think about Lydia's great news?'

'Oh! That is great news,' they both said.

99

'Thank God,' Ethel said, 'There seems to be good news everywhere lately. I told you Mum the New Year would be great and so far it is for a lot of people. It's great that you are on that list. The shop is doing so well, but don't overdo it. We will all have to take a break soon and catch up on the family and friends. We will have to go now. Sorry for the short stay. We will have a longer one next time we promise.'

They left the shop, walked a while, then stopped, looked at each other, then Ethel said,

'What the hell is going on with Lydia? They must think they told us, who could we ask? There's nobody we could ask? That's really very annoying, after all the trouble we've been going through with Lydia. Something good happens, and we are not told.'

Beatrice said, 'I'll call in during the week, I'll get Mum on her own and I'll ask her out straight. We have to know. How could they not have told us? Hold on a minute, George is there so often why don't we get him to find out. He is very diplomatic, he won't ask he will scoot around until he gets the right answers, that's a better plan. Maybe he knows already, and was told not to tell us?'

'Don't be silly, if he kept something from me I'll go mad and he will be very sorry. I can't wait. I'm going to ask him when I get home tonight.'

Patrick Taylor came into the shop.

'John, I've got so much good news I don't know where to start.'

'At the beginning is a very good place,' John said.

'Oh, you are very smart now. What did you have for breakfast? Smart beans?'

They both laughed.

'Seriously though, I do think you should slow down a bit. Mary and I were just thinking about these houses. How are you going to decide who will get one?'

'Well I'm going to give nine to married couples with children. Three to couples who are engaged and haven't a hope of ever getting a house, simple.'

'What makes you think that will be simple? There are so many decent people.'

'I would like to give all of them one. Not possible, so I'm going to put all the names of those who apply into a draw. The draw will be held in the church hall and will be very fair. I was thinking of asking you to draw the tickets.'

'Oh no you don't! I will not, thanks very much.'

'Joking, here's what we will do. We will get the Jewish family to pull all the tickets.'

'Have you asked them yet?'

'No, but I will be having plenty of scrap for free that the father might be interested in, so he will owe me one.'

'Oh my God Patrick! How do you think of such things so far ahead?'

Tapping his head he said, 'Up here for dancing. John, that's how.'

'Seriously, can you imagine the excitement in the village the day the draw will take place? On that day, we could make it a festival day. A lot of hard work and planning. My girls would be delighted to help out.'

'It would be a great day to remember. The winners of the houses would be thrilled to celebrate with the whole village.'

'Let's do it then.'

'John, I came in to talk to you about something else. You waylaid me.'

'The shop is getting too busy now. I'll call some night when the shop is closed and we'll sort things out.'

'Patrick, you are more than welcome anytime, but after hours is the best time.'

He left without giving John his shopping list. John knew most of the things on his usual list, but then he decided to wait. He will put it together when he comes back. Mary could call out to him what was on the list and that would be quicker. The two men got on very well but being so busy John knew Patrick would keep talking while he would be trying to concentrate. It was as much his own fault, he should have asked him for the list. Mary always told him to take the list from him before they started talking as she knew what he was like.

'Well, it won't happen again, I'll make sure of that.'

George called in many times but found out nothing about Lydia. Then one evening they were just about to close when George called.

'Just the man I wanted to see,' John said. 'Come in. I wanted to shift some furniture in Lydia's room before she comes next week.'

'What day is she coming, John?'

'On Wednesday, she is coming on the evening train.'

'Do I have to collect her at the station?'

'Oh no, James' father is picking her up.'

'How come?'

'Oh, they are coming together so he said he would do it.'

'Which of Patrick's sons is coming with her?'

'I think it's the eldest lad.'

George asked Mary, 'Which of the Taylor's is Lydia coming home with?'

'James,' Mary answered. 'Remember him George? Lydia went out with James for a long time, on and off. We liked James, and his parents loved Lydia. We thought she was going to marry him. John would have loved that. Patrick Taylor Senior is one of his best friends.'

'Oh, that's right, I remember him. Trevor was always hanging around with them. He was only a child but he must have driven them mad.'

'Well, I'm delighted.' George said. 'I'm glad I do not have to go to the station. I seem to be going there a lot lately. I'll soon have to replace the pony at the rate things are going.'

'George, there are plenty of people in the village now that can afford their own transport. You should take a break, you have done it long enough.'

'You know me John, I would never see anybody stuck. Is there anything else to be moved?'

'No, that's it, thanks a million. I had better get going. The girls will be expecting me.'

'Did you want anything from the shop?'

'Oh yes, butter, biscuits and sugar. That's it, thank you.'

'Which kind of biscuits?'

'I can't remember.' George just wanted to get out of there.

'Just give me the ones nearest to you there John.'

He said goodbye to them and left. He could not get home quick enough with his news. When he came in, Ethel asked, 'Is there news?'

'No,' he said.

'What kept you then?'

'I had to help your father to move furniture.'

'Furniture? Where?'

'In Lydia's room.'

'Move it to where and for what?'

'To make room I suppose.'

'Where's Beatrice?'

'Why?' Ethel asked.

'I want her for a minute?'

'For what?'

Ethel thought he was acting funny. She called Beatrice and when she came in, George said.

'Sit down.'

The girls looked at each other and wondered what was going on.

'He said, Are you ready?'

'Ready for what?' Beatrice asked. 'The news I'm going to tell you.'

'Oh George you big tease, you said there was no news.'

'I was kidding you.'

Ethel got very annoyed.

'This is not funny.'

'Sorry, I still can't believe it myself. Lydia is coming home next Wednesday.'

The sisters were just about to say that's great but George said, 'Wait! Who do you think is meeting her at the station?'

'Now come on George, we are not playing a guessing game here. Who?'

'Patrick Taylor.'

'The father of James Taylor? Taylor with all the money?'

'She is coming home with all three sons. Patrick the father is collecting them.'

'What's going on here?'

'I don't know, but your Father seems very pleased with himself. I was so glad I didn't have to go to the station, I put no more thought into it.'

'Is she coming home with James Taylor as a boyfriend?' Beatrice asked.

'I don't know, but that's the impression I got.'

'If that's true, Mum must know all about it. Why did she not tell us?'

'James Taylor,' Beatrice said.

'I think Lydia was going out with him, at Easter time last year when he was home from college. Am I right?'

Ethel said yes she was right.

'We thought they were mad about each other. We all loved him, he was a lovely guy. Trevor was always hanging around him. Lydia couldn't get rid of Trevor. She loves Trevor and wouldn't hurt him by telling to get lost. James also liked him, but not enough to have him going round with them as a threesome. He had not long gone back to Dublin, when she started going out with that awful guy we all hated. It was soon after that she announced she was pregnant. She must have met James in Dublin and started going out with him again. Mum and Dad would be delighted if that was the case, they both were very fond of him.'

Ethel said. 'But why not tell us? What's the big secret? What's that all about?'

Beatrice said. 'I'm very annoyed about this and I'm going to let Mum know how I feel.'

Ethel said, 'Don't be. If this is good news let's enjoy it. I am annoyed but if Lydia is doing well we won't knock it.'

'OK.' Beatrice said. 'We will wait until after Wednesday then go down to the shop when it's closed and get all the info.'

Beatrice left the room and went to bed. Ethel said, 'Well done!' to George and they went to bed.

The next morning after breakfast Beatrice sat at the table for ages.

Ethel asked her, 'What is it?'

'Don't laugh but I was awake all night and I started to count.'

'Count what?'

'Months.'

'What do you mean months?'

'James Taylor was here for weeks at Easter. That was Springtime. Lydia gave birth in January. That would be exactly right for him to be the father of the babies.'

'Now that you say that, they are beautiful. Let's take a real close look at them.'

The two of them went upstairs and looked very closely at both babies. 'He is the father! He is the father!' Ethel exclaimed. "Look even in their sleep, the black hair, they have ebony eyes. I often looked at them and thought how could such an ugly man as that guy be the father? She should have told us the truth. If it was James, we could have told Mum and Dad. They would have been very annoyed and disappointed with her.'

The disgrace of having a baby outside of marriage in

Ireland at that time was horrible. It was considered the worst thing to happen in a family. This happened many times, but was swept under the carpet. Girls just disappeared, sent to Dublin or England. There was no way a girl pregnant outside marriage would be allowed to go around in the village. The solution was to get her out of sight. Put her on the boat as soon as possible. Tell the people in the village, she has gone to England to be a nurse. Somehow people always knew the real reason. So it was silly trying to cover it up. The saddest thing of all was if a family could not afford to send her away she was sent to a mother and baby home. It was a disgrace the way girls were treated. Some girls died in those homes. Some were there for the rest of their lives.

'Our parents would never have done that. But she would have been sent away from the village. As bad as it was, if she had told the truth then, things could have been so much different. Our parents and the Taylor family have been friends for years. Between them and they would come up with some solution. Everything would have been much easier for Mum.'

'Nothing is easy when it comes to Lydia. Dad would have insisted she go away. But only as far as Dublin. Mum would not have been so stressed. All the unnecessary lies she told Dad nearly killed her. I'll never forgive Lydia. Why did she do that?'

'They might have planned that between them. This was his last year in college and oh, I don't know. Let's not get carried away.'

Just then Desmond opened his eyes.

'Look, look,' Beatrice said. 'He is the image of James Taylor.'

She lifted him up and brought him down. George had just come in from the workroom and was about to have breakfast. Beatrice asked him to hold the baby for a second. When he had him in his arms she asked him,

'Do you think that baby looks like James Taylor?'

George looked and looked then he asked, 'What brought all this on?'

'Answer the question'

'He is very handsome, but why should he look like James Taylor?'

'Because we think he is the father.'

Ethel came in with Doris.

She said, 'Look George, she is the image of James Taylor. We have been fooled again by Lydia.'

George said, 'I'm not so surprised really, I often thought how could such an ugly guy father such beautiful children?'

'Great minds think alike,' Ethel said.

'I used to look at them, and think the same thing.'

George asked her, 'Are you happy about this?'

'I am happy if he is the father. But if she had told the truth in the first place it would have made things much easier.'

Ethel said, 'I have had it with her now. She hadn't got the decency to write and let you know she did not need you at the station. I have changed my mind now. I'm not going down to my parents asking any questions about her or her boyfriend. I'll wait and see how long it takes her to come and see her children. I'll never ask about the father and I'll never be the good sister I always was to her. I'll tell you something else, she is never getting these babies back. We'd better get them legally adopted, as soon as possible I don't trust her. If it suited her she could walk in here, take them and walk out with them, there would be nothing we could do about it. She wouldn't care who she upsets.'

'Oh' George said, 'She would never do that ever. Surely she has a bit of decency in her. I can tell you now she will never do that while I'm here. We'll wait and see.'

Ethel said, 'I'm not so sure, she is capable of anything. We'll play the fools and see what happens. We won't ask questions, we won't speak until we are spoken to and we'll just carry on doing what we always do, enjoying the babies.'

It was a beautiful day. They fed and dressed them and brought them out into the garden. Ethel went into the workroom, greeted the girls as if she was the happiest person in the world. Everything had been going so well, she felt Lydia's homecoming was going to be a disaster. She looked at Beatrice and thought how unfair life was to her compared to Lydia. Beatrice was a beautiful, kind, helpful, generous and loving person. She was married to a wonderful guy for such a short time, when he was taken from her. If she had been pregnant, she would have a baby to love and remind her of him. But she was denied all that happiness and never moaned or complained. Ethel loved her so much. She would never survive without her.

The next day there was a long letter from Joseph, He didn't write often. When he did it was always a great letter. He was now in England. He was training very hard but he loved it. He could have come home before going away, but he did not want to see his mother cry again when he left. He would have loved to have seen the babies but that would have to wait until next time. Not far off he would be coming home for Christmas. He loved their names and thought calling them names starting with the same letter was a good idea. He mentioned the business. Told Mum not to work too hard now that she was looking after two babies. He was delighted that there was so much going on in the village. The shop seemed to be making a fortune. He was happy for all of them, but he still did not want to be back there. He had a big paragraph for Dad, about the army. Ethel wasn't interested in that, but George was delighted. He had a bit for Philip, Trevor and Aunt Beatrice. He had gone to a lot of trouble thinking about everybody. Funny thing Ethel thought he did not mention the grandparents. She didn't say anything to George. She got a sinking feeling that he knew something about them or Lydia, he did not mention her either. Why did she always feel something was wrong? Because she was always right. What could it be? She was not going to worry about that now. If it's bad she will hear about it time enough. She read the letter again, and said to herself, 'Well at least Joseph is doing ok.'

It was a good letter.

Chapter 17

The Taylor family were excited, because the three oldest boys were coming home from college. Lydia was in her element travelling with them. They all liked her and she always had great fun with them. It was going to be a great summer for her. After a week of holidaying at home and taking it easy, the boys would be working on the building sites. Lydia would be working in the shop during the day time. In the evening they would go to the Taylor's house or meet over the shop, go for walks, or play sports. Mrs. Taylor loved the boys being home and bringing in their friends. She loved Lydia and wished James would become engaged to her. She thought they would have last year. When they didn't and James had gone back to college in Dublin, she thought they had broken up. Because Lydia was seen with an awful looking stranger. He was not from around the village. Nobody knew him. Her parents hated him. Then suddenly she was gone to England. James hadn't mentioned her since he went back to Dublin. Mrs. Taylor thought she was in England. She wondered how long, and when they were together again. She would never ask James, and she knew she would never be told. It was a bit of a mystery, but if they were together again that was good enough for her. She hoped they would become engaged this year. It would be great to announce the engagement the day of the draw for the houses. When everybody would be in great spirits and it would be a great end to the summer, before all the youths went back to college in Dublin. There were a few more girls in the group. She liked all of them, but none of them were going out with her other sons. She wished they were, especially Linda Clinton. She was a beautiful girl, full of fun and a nice singer. The younger members of the family loved it when the boys brought all their friends back to the house. They were allowed to stay up late and join in the fun. It was a really happy house with nice vibes in it. Mrs. Taylor was brilliant at playing the piano. The twin boys played the fiddle. They were ok. The youngest girls played recorders they were learning to play in school and thought they were great. They were brutal, but everyone got a chance to do their party piece and then get lost and leave the older ones to do their thing. They finished around midnight because they all had to go to work the next day. The sun seemed to shine every day in those summers. The evenings were long, warm and wonderful. The river that ran through the town was very clean and they could swim in it. All their entertainment was free. When they went for a picnic. The girl's parents supplied all the food. The boy brought all the drinks. Lemonade, orange juice. No alcoholic drinks in those days. That did not stop them from having a great time. The summers flew by. When all those young people were gone again, they were really missed. Lydia was staying home now. She was such a good worker. Her Parents were delighted to have her. James wanted to stay here also. He had got his degree. He was sure what he wanted to do. He knew it would be hard to find a teaching job locally. But he also knew he could not leave Lydia, if he had to go to Dublin without her it would kill him. After all she had done for him when she was pregnant he would never ask her to leave home again. Lydia living in Dublin although she was pregnant, was a great help to him. They spent a lot of time together. She was helping him, making sure he never fell behind. She wanted him to achieve all he needed to follow his dream. A teacher was what he always wanted to be, and she was going to make sure he gave it his best shot. He was crazy about her. She felt the same about him. He would have married her when she told him she was pregnant.

She said, 'No, it's not going to be easy for me, but I'll do anything I can to keep you in college until you qualify. I'll follow you in a few weeks to Dublin. I have arranged to stay with my aunt Phyllis, as long as we are together we will get through this.'

He was only a few weeks in Dublin, when Lydia came to join him. They had a great time under the circumstances. A lot of the time he stayed overnight with her. Aunt Phyllis was very fond of him and he sometimes helped around the house. Lydia never gave a thought to her family. All the stress she caused her mother. She was doing her thing, that's all she cared about. If Ethel ever found out what went on in Dublin she would tell her father, and disgrace her and him and never speak to her again. But Lydia knew if Ethel ever found out, she would do nothing. She would never do anything that would hurt her father, and that would kill him. She wouldn't care if Ethel never spoke to her again and she knew that wouldn't happen either. Because the babies still belonged to her and James. Ethel had to be nice to her all the time. Well, at least until the adoption papers were signed. That could take a long time, then again she might never sign them. Lydia could be really awful at times. Even for her to be thinking like that was scary. Then again she could be so nice. There was nothing wrong with her brain, she was just very bold.

At the moment Lydia was racking her brain, trying to think of a way for James to get work, so he wouldn't have to go back to Dublin. She wanted to stay home, but if he had to go she would go with him. Then she came up with a great idea. If he could get enough pupils to come to the house for grinds, and they did very well as a result of his work with them. He would have a good chance of getting work in the local school. The headmaster hadn't long to go to retirement. That was the job he wanted to get. In the meantime, he could stand in if a teacher was out sick. He would love that. He really wanted to stay in the village. He had some time to decide. He would have a chat with his dad. Tell him he had an idea. Ask him what he thought of this idea, hear what he had to say then decide. His dad listened to all he had to say, then he said, 'That is a great idea, give it a go. If it doesn't work after a year, start looking for a proper job. Dublin is not that far away if you have to go.'

He would make sure he didn't have to go. He would do his best to make it work. At least his dad thought it was a good idea, and he was no fool.

His brother Michael, when he qualified as a civil engineer, had work already to go to when he left college. It was in Dublin, he liked living there, so that was good for him. His father was proud of Michael. James wanted him to be proud of him also. Although his father was a very wealthy man, he was not going to allow any of his children to be lazy. They would all get a good education. He did not mind how long it took them to qualify for whatever they wanted to do, as long as they worked hard and didn't become *dossers*. They had to do their best. That was all he asked for, from all his children. He was very fair, a great dad, and his children wanted him to be proud of them too.

Mr. Taylor had influence everywhere in the country.

He could let schools know James had finished in college. He could ask for favours, but that was not his style. He liked to think they got what they wanted by the quality of their work. Make a good career and earn plenty of money. It also had to be enjoyable. Life is short, no point in being rich and miserable. You can't buy happiness.

Chapter 18

George and Ethel had to go to the church hall to prepare for tomorrow, the draw for the houses was to take place. She was not looking forward to celebrating anything. Lydia would be there, and she hadn't been in touch with her since she came home.

Ethel decided not to go tomorrow, that would be the best thing to do. She couldn't face her parents and Lydia.

The draw for the houses would be exciting. The party after would be great. She might nip in after the babies went to bed, if Beatrice came home early enough. She wouldn't ask her to leave early, because she would want to stay home to babysit, so Ethel could take the day off. Beatrice was not a party person. Ethel loved parties, singing, dancing and mixing with people, which made her really happy. She hadn't done these things for such a long time.

On Sunday 2.30pm. There was a queue outside the hall. People were so excited about the draw of the twelve houses. Nothing like this had ever happened in the village before. Only three engaged couples applied. That left nine houses for married couples. There were thirty applications from married couples. So now the three engaged couples were sure of getting a house. That brought the number of houses for married couples to nine. They would say nothing to the applicants, and put all the names in the hat. Then call the names as they were picked. As the tickets were picked out, the silence was golden. Then a big cheer went up. When the twelve houses were won Mr. Taylor congratulated the winners, then told the people they only had three requests from the engaged couples. If they had been told they had got a house before the draw it would have taken the element of surprise out of it for them. That was how there were nine houses for married couples. The houses would be given out as they were won, one to twelve. Because they were two blocks of six terraced houses there would be four with sidewalks. Numbers 1, 6, 7 and 12. They really were the lucky ones. He made a few jokes and said he was sorry he hadn't applied for semi-detached houses.

'Then everyone would have had a sidewalk.'

Maybe next time he would do better when making a planning application. He laughed. The audience clapped and clapped. He got a great kick from all this. He was not used to doing things so publicly. All the good things he did were done anonymously. He thanked all those who played any part in getting this project off the ground. He said the houses would be built as quickly as possible. They were badly needed. He finished wishing all the winners the best of luck in their new homes. Somebody shouted three cheers for Mr. Taylor, they screamed the cheers as loud as they could. When the noise stopped. He said, 'No need for that, but thank you,' and left the stage.

Then the party started for real. It was fantastic. Everybody that could be there was there. Big, small, young, old. Anyone who could play an instrument brought it along. It was what we call in Ireland a great session. Then Mr. Solomons started to play his balalaika. He was brilliant. The whole room fell silent, even the youngest children sat down and were quiet. Every time he tried to finish the crowd roared for more. He thought the Irish were mad, but he loved them. When he played all the tunes he knew, He put

117

the balalaika down, and sang a Russian song. He had a big powerful voice, he was a lovely singer. When the crowd screamed for more, he shook his head and said a few Russian words. The crowd got the message, he was not going to do any more. But they clapped and clapped to show their appreciation. It was the best day ever. Then the Irish fiddlers started playing again. Those with young children left early. Older people began to move out. The crowd diminished bit by bit until George came in to lock up the hall. He had to tell the fiddlers to stop playing as it was after midnight and he wanted to go home.

One guy said, 'Go ahead George, sure we'll lock up.'

'In your dreams,' he said. 'Come on lads.'

They knew he was serious. They stopped playing, put the fiddles away and left. George locked the doors, sat on a chair for a few minutes, then put the lights out and went home. Ethel stayed with her first decision and didn't go. When George told Ethel Mr. Solomons sang and played at the party, she was sorry she had missed that. Lydia and James were there for a short time. He was glad when they left.

'They were making a show of themselves. Close dancing, kissing on the dance floor. Acting like teenagers. In fact the teens were better behaved. I'm sure your parents were mortified. If they had stayed any longer than they did I was going to ask them to leave.'

'You would not.'

'I would, it was not an adult dance we were running. This was a family party day not a place for the way they were behaving.'

'God, were they that bad? With Mum and Dad there?'

'Yes and his parents and their young children.'

'I'm so glad I wasn't there. I would like to tell her to go away from here forever.' Ethel said. 'I've been on tenterhooks since she came home. Did she speak to you?'

'No, she didn't. I didn't see her talking to anybody. She only had eyes for James.'

'What's she playing at? She was always so prim and proper, people thought she was a snob.'

'Well, they won't think that after today. They were disgusting. I don't know what's come over Lydia. She was never like that. I was glad when they left, I did not want to have to ask them to go. I hoped they wouldn't come back. Thank God they didn't. I was sorry you missed it. You would have enjoyed watching our boys dance. They are great movers. They were giving it socks and they stayed on the floor all night dancing. I wonder who they are copying! They were very popular with the girls. They were delighted with themselves. I think they forgot I was backstage watching the goings on. It was not like any other party we've ever had in the church hall,' George told Ethel.

'Now I am sorry I missed it. There will never be another one like it.' Ethel answered.

Chapter 19

It was late the next morning when James came down. In fact it was lunch time. His mother told him off for his behaviour at the party. 'I was surprised at Lydia. I had a different opinion of her.'

'What are you saying, now you don't like her?' asked James.

'No, I'm not saying that I don't like her but, but...'

'What?' he asked.

'Both of you could have behaved a bit better, that's all I'm saying.'

'Well I've news for you. I had just asked her to marry me and she said yes. We were so excited we forgot where we were for a moment. Then we left.'

'Oh!' she said. 'That's fantastic! I am so happy for you. Congratulations! Your dad will be pleased, he likes Lydia. You should have told us before you left.'

'I had not planned to do it there, but when they played our special song, and I had my arms around her I just blurted it out. I was going to wait until Christmas, but now it's done.'

His mother said, 'If you want to keep it a secret till then, I won't tell anybody. Not even Dad. If Lydia hasn't told her parents then we will wait till Christmas to tell. Then she will have a ring to show off. Come here to me!' she said. 'Give me a hug! Our first son to take the plunge.' She was so excited about the engagement, she forgave him for yesterday. He didn't eat much. He was in a rush now to get down to Lydia and tell her not to say anything to her parents until Christmas.

Everybody in the village was looking forward to Christmas. There was so much more money than any other year it was wonderful. Mrs. Cramp decided to give all the local customers a hamper this year as well as the usual box of biscuits. Profits had been so good. She didn't buy any fancy containers. She just put the things in cardboard boxes she had kept from deliveries. The box of biscuits took up a lot of room. She gave an Oxford lunch cake, half a big glass jar of sweets, the ones that each customer bought throughout the year. She knew the type of tea people drank. She put as many dry items in that would be useful after Christmas. She went to a lot of trouble to get things right. She was really enjoying putting everything together. This was going to be a big surprise to her customers. She had never done this before. They could not have afforded to do it before. She felt like Santa and was looking forward to seeing the look on the faces when she gave them out. She asked John if he would agree to allowing the people who were getting hampers to come into the shop after closing time to collect them. He had no problem with that. But he thought it would be better if George would bring them to their homes.

'Yes,' she said. 'I'm sure he would do that for us, they are heavy. Older folks would appreciate that.'

Then she thought she would not see their faces, so she would tell them they were getting a surprise this Christmas as business was so good. This surprise was only for loyal customers. She loved giving presents and was so pleased to give something back to the locals. They kept the shop going when things were not so good. This was going to be the best Christmas ever. Not like last year. Joseph is coming home,

Lydia is home. The twins are with us now. Although they are very young, Santa will be coming to them. John was so looking forward to it. She was so excited, because when John was looking forward to something, it was so pleasant to be working with him. He was never as happy as this, when Lydia was away. She hoped Ethel's family would all come to them for Christmas dinner. She must check with her, they only agreed to go to Ethel's last year because Lydia, and Joseph were away. This year they will get back to normal. She suddenly realised she had not made arrangements with Ethel and Beatrice to go to Dublin on the 8th of December to do her Christmas shopping. They went every year. She loved that day. The girls made it so special for her. They went to all the big department stores. Clery's was the store she liked best. They always left her for one hour, so she could buy the things she wanted to give to them for Christmas. She wanted to surprise them and not let them see what they were getting. She had a great memory, if either of them mentioned anything during the year they might like for Christmas, she would get it that day. It would be exactly what they wanted. Right size, right colour. They would have forgotten they ever mentioned whatever it was, but Mum never forgot. She did the same with all the family. Shopping for everybody else was her favourite part of Christmas.

They never bought anything, it was her day. The only day in the year the three of them got to do this. It was her very special day with them. She could go to Dublin other times with Dad or the grandchildren, that was different. Nothing meant so much to her as this day. They did enjoy some parts of it. They always came home in rag order. It took days to recover. It didn't bother her. She would be up the next day, back in the shop working, as she would say herself, 'Working like a white man.' This year she had so much money she was going to spend, spend, spend. She was so happy, like a child going to see Santa for the first time. She went to Santa during her free hour, and bought four parcels for girls. She gave them theirs on the train going home. They were allowed to open them and she opened her own. She thought this was great fun. They didn't think it was that funny. They knew she was reliving the time when they were little girls brought to Dublin every year on the Holy day for Catholics, the 8th of December. Going to Santa was their big treat, they loved it, that memory was for herself. They pretended it was great, but they were mortified.

George, Ethel and Beatrice had tried to make plans for Christmas. One of them was going to have to go down to the mother and see what she wanted to do. Ethel was mad about so many things she did not want to go.

George said, 'The two of you go. That's easier for everybody. You can't keep leaving with it, wondering who is doing what, and where. Decisions have to be made, and stop changing your minds. Make a plan and stick to it. Time is running out. Both of you have to go to Dublin with your mother for her shopping on the 8th of December and that hasn't been mentioned.'

'Oh God!' Beatrice said.

'I completely forgot about that. We'll make a date and tell her we have to go that day.'

Everything was going to be very different this year.

'No.' Ethel said. 'If she can't go on the 8th she will not go at all, I know that. She loves the buzz of that day. People from all over the country go to Dublin that day every year. She talks about it in the shop forever. She is still talking about last year. I'll make arrangements to go on the 8th no matter what happens. We'll ask her what her plans are for Christmas dinner. Tell her what we've planned, see what she thinks.'

'Don't come home with anything left hanging. Whatever you decide is final, no more time to keep going over things. Stay there as long as you have to get it right. Then we will know where we are going and what we are doing,' said George.

'I am not changing anything once a decision is made, that's what I'm doing.' Ethel agreed.

Ethel hated this kind of messing. Somebody is always going to be disappointed. That's Life.

George said, 'You know what's best for you this year, Ethel, so suit yourself. Stop thinking about everybody else. With the Twins, and Joseph coming home. It would be too much to drag all the things we'd need for the babies with us.'

She might suggest to her mum that herself Dad and Lydia come to her house for dinner like last year. She was going to ask the Solomons again. If Lydia said she did not want to come she knew the parents would not leave her on her own. It would be better if the three of them had dinner in their own house and then came up to them later. It would be more comfortable for everyone. She would leave it to her parents to decide. Lydia had not come once to see the babies since she came home. They didn't care if she never came. It would be hard to put up with her at the dinner table, for the parents' sake they would have to be pleasant to her. Ethel was not going to stress anymore about it. Things had a way of working out completely differently from the way you expected.

The Taylors were really excited about Christmas. Not because of money. They had that every Christmas. Michael was bringing his girlfriend home from Dublin. He had never mentioned a girl, Mrs. Taylor hoped it was one of the girls from the group that were in the house during the summer. She asked James if he knew who it was?

He said that he knew Michael liked one particular girl from college and she had passed her exams. She had got work in the same office as Michael. If it wasn't her he had no idea who it was.

'Well, the important thing is that they love each other. I'm looking forward to meeting her. She must be from around here. He didn't mention having a bed made for her, so she must be staying with her own parents. I'll have to make a few inquiries. Do a bit of Detective work.'

James said, 'Stop Mum! Have patience, you will know, when you know.'

He would ask Lydia if she knew, then he would tell her. Apart from that he was not going to ask anybody else. What was it about mothers and their sons? No girl was good enough for them. Michael was the eldest son, James felt sorry for the girl whoever she was coming to their house, for the first time. His parents were lovely, but she would have to pass the *Taylor Test*. He was so lucky they knew the Cramp family and they liked Lydia. But if their secret was ever leaked he knew they would never forgive him. He was always sorry they didn't tell them at the time. They would have been furious, but they would have gotten over it. When they saw the babies they would love them. After all, they were their grandchildren. They loved children and they wouldn't be able to ignore these children. There were two sets of twins in their family already. Two boys and then two girls. Imagine the excitement when he had twins. One of each. What a mess they had made of things? They could never go back now and tell the truth. Lydia didn't want to even look at them, since she came home. She would not talk about them to him. Such a change in her. She was so happy with them in Dublin. He couldn't understand it. Maybe she was afraid she might let something slip and wanted to block them out of her mind. He couldn't go to Ethel's house and ask to see the babies, she would think he was mad. He should never have listened to Lydia. But he was so much in love with her, he could not go against her wishes. She had said if he told anybody it would ruin her life. She would never speak to him again. He felt their lives were ruined anyway. Maybe it would be better for everybody if they went away from here, and made a new life in another country. When they get married and start a family, things might get better. He would pine for those babies for the rest of his life. That was the price he had to pay. Lydia didn't seem to feel the same as he did. Maybe she was pretending she didn't care, and was getting on with life. Deep down he knew she would love to tell her dad. If her mother was dead she would tell him. He would forgive her for anything. She didn't care about anybody else. If he knew those babies were hers, he would make her take them back, forget the past. Bring them up knowing their true parents and be a proper family. James was a lovely guy and her dad would forgive all and things would be great. As much as she'd love to do it. She knew she never would.

The girls called down to their mother, the first chance they got.

'Now Mother,' they said. 'This is not a social visit. We are here to make final decisions about Christmas dinner. Where we are having it. What we are having etc. No messing. With the babies we just can't drop everything and decide on the spur of the moment to do anything. Everything has to be planned. You understand that Mum? So, what we decide tonight is final, no going back. Let's do this now so we can all get on with everything else that has to be ready for Christmas. We can't please everybody. We'll do our best to please most, what do you say?'

'Well, I was not expecting this tonight, tell me your plans, and we'll see. If I don't agree with some of them, can I say so?'

'Of course you can, but what we agree on here now will not change. It has to stay as planned. OK Well, let's get started then. You first Mum.'

'I was thinking of having everybody here. We have the whole top of the shop. Plenty of room, how's that for starters?'

'That's a great idea but, think of all the trips George would have to make to bring all the stuff we'd need for the babies.'

'Yes,' she said, looking disappointed. 'That's a thought.'

'We have to make a decision now.'

'What were you thinking, Ethel?'

Ethel felt so sorry for her mother, she did not want to hurt her, she kicked Beatrice under the table and said,

'Well, that's what we'll do.'

'Oh,' their Mother said. 'I'm so pleased, I know George will have to make a few trips, but it will be well worth it. Do you want to invite the Solomons?'

'Yes if that's alright with you?'

'Yes, yes, but he must bring his music and his beautiful

voice with him.'

'He can't leave his voice behind him,' Ethel said. 'He will be delighted to come.'

'I will get Lydia to clean the rooms upstairs and then Beatrice you can come down some night and decorate them.'

'It will be my pleasure,' Beatrice said.

'I'll do all the cooking then, and whoever wants to can do the washing up.'

'We'll all help, don't worry about that.'

'Can you imagine your dad with those babies? He will be beside himself with happiness. It will be a Christmas he will never forget. Having such a crowd here in his place will be right up his street. He did enjoy himself in your place last year. But, as he gets older I think he likes to be in his own home at Christmas.'

'That's all good then, are we all happy?'

'Well, I am anyway. I am so happy I think I'll burst,' Mum said.

The girls looked at each other and thought George might not be so happy. At least they were coming home with a plan.

'The other thing Mum is, your day in Dublin. We've decided we will go as usual on the 8th of December. No change there.'

'Oh girls, that's too much to ask this year, how are you going to manage that?'

'Don't you worry we have everything arranged. You have to go this year above all years, you have so much money to spend.'

'Oh girls! You are so good, I would love it. Thank you both so much.'

She called Dad and just said, 'Christmas is in our house this year.'

'Sure, that's where it should be, in the family home.'

He could not take the smile off his face.

'Get the glasses!' Mum said to him. 'This calls for a little drink.'

He said, 'I couldn't agree more.'

He came back with the glasses. All four of them drank Sherry, told a few jokes, had a bit of banter and then they left. They never drank Sherry before. It went straight to their heads. When they left the house, they felt a bit funny. They stood up against a wall and laughed and laughed at nothing.

Beatrice said, 'I think we're drunk.'

'I hope so,' Ethel said. 'It feels great, put Sherry on the list for Christmas!'

When George saw the state of them he laughed. He knew the smallest drop of Sherry would have gone to their heads. He was delighted to see them so happy. He made them a cup of coffee and then decided bed was the place for them. Ethel muttered, they had celebrated with their parents. Everything had gone very, very well, all finalised. 'I'll tell you the bad news tomorrow.'

Ethel slept well. When Beatrice came down for breakfast, they looked at each other and started to laugh. Beatrice asked Ethel if she'd slept well?

'Never better,' she said, 'And you?'

'I had a very nice sleep. Thank you for asking.'

They started laughing again. They were still very giddy when George came into the breakfast room.

'Still having a good time I see. You two were drunk last night,' he said in a serious voice. 'I didn't know the man who brought you home. Drunk and disorderly.'

'We were not drunk. We came home together. No man brought us home.' Ethel said. 'Nobody brought us home,' he repeated after her.

'Stop being silly George.'

'I'm not being silly.'

'You are being silly.'

'You two were being silly. I had to put both of you to bed. I never saw either of you in a state like that before, and I don't want to see it again.'

'Oh getting bossy are we? You might see us like that again. We had a great time.'

'Would you both stop being silly? Beatrice said. 'Mum gave us a small drop of Sherry. It went straight to our heads. We never drank alcohol before. But we could get to like it couldn't we, Ethel?'

'That's enough nonsense from all of us. When you hear our news, George you won't be smiling.'

'What news?'

'We made all the arrangements for Christmas last night. We are all including the Solomons, going to our parents for Christmas dinner, over the shop. Lydia is doing the cleaning. Beatrice is doing all the decorations. Mum will do all the cooking. You, me, and the boys will do the washing up. After dinner everybody is coming here. All of that is set in stone, no changes whatsoever. Do you want to hear more or will I stop?'

'Oh don't stop. I want to hear more.'

'This is the good part. Before Christmas, Mum is giving hampers to the regular customers. You have to deliver them. Our boys will help her put them together. She will pay them of course. The boys will go with you, so that will save you getting up and down. They will knock at the door and ask the man of the house to come and take the hamper. No carrying involved. What are your thoughts on all that?'

'Well, well, well, didn't you do well? I agree with everything you said. That was a great night's work. It was worth seeing you drunk if you achieved all that. How did you do it?'

'Charm,' Beatrice said. 'We told Mum, all decisions had to be made, and no changes. Whatever was decided last night was final. We don't have time to mess around. When she told us her plan about the top of the shop. We were dumb founded and said yes immediately. We knew she had put a lot of thought into it. We couldn't say no. We never mentioned what we had planned. She was so excited we couldn't disappoint her. We pretended to be delighted, and said it was a great idea. She called Dad into the room. When she told him, everyone was coming to them for dinner, he said that it was proper order that all the family should be coming to the family home. We knew he was happy, he had a big smile on his face. He left the room and came back with four Sherry glasses.'

'Well done girls! Very well done,' George said. They knew he was pleased.

'You did do the right thing. It has been a tough year all round. Your parents are getting on a bit. We should do what they want on this occasion. It's a big deal for them, for us it's only dinner after all. We'll have lots of fun in our house before we go there. It will be nice to have a meal ready to eat when we arrive. If going there pleases them so much, and that's what they want, that's what we'll do, I really don't mind one bit. They have always been so good to us it's about time we did something for them. As regards the hampers, of course I'll do that. I'll offer to take your mother with me, if she would like to come.'

The two sisters hugged him.

Ethel said 'George you are so good, we all love you so much.'

'You are both so lucky to have each other, treasure every moment.' Beatrice said and left the room with tears streaming down her face. George held Ethel, sobbing into his shoulder.

'Don't follow her, she needs to be alone, and have a good cry. It must be so hard for her every Christmas, not having her husband, and she never complains. She is lucky to live with us. She will always have company. We all love her, just think what Christmas would be like for her if she lived alone?'

'No,' Ethel said. 'I couldn't imagine that for one minute. That will never happen while we are alive. She will always have a home here.'

Chapter 20

It had been a great year for the Solomons family. Mr Solomons had been very busy with his own business. Then there was so much building going on he was making more money right at his own doorstep. He was collecting the cut off pieces of wood from the building sites. One of the carpenters, Robbie Byrne, who he liked a lot, asked what was he going to do with them? He tried to explain, but he wasn't getting through to him. Then he drew on a piece of wood and showed it to him. Robbie understood him perfectly from the beginning. He loved pretending he didn't, just see the actions he did. He wanted to listen to his broken English accent. Now he was getting to know a lot more words. He was very funny to listen to. He was getting a strong Wicklow accent. That mixed with his Russian, made Robbie laugh. After a while Robbie with the piece of wood in his hand said to him,

'You want to make people?'

'No, no!'

He put his hands in the air and said,

'Mine God, mine God, what you know?' He gave Robbie a push. Robbie burst out laughing and said,

'You know Louie. He is my God too, your guys killed him.'

Louie tapped his watch and said,

'I go now.' He turned to walk away, and Robbie shouted after him,

'You want to make toys, is that it?'

He turned and made a run at Robbie. The two of them

laughed and laughed, Louie realised he had been joking with him. He said a mouthful of Russian words. Robbie would love to have known what he was saying, he knew it wasn't very nice.

'Wait a minute!' Robbie said. He went over to a shelf, took down a box of small pieces of new woodcuttings. He handed the box to him and said, 'There you go Louie, I heard you are making lovely toys, I kept these pieces especially for you.'

Louie felt bad he cursed and said sorry. Robbie didn't mind him.

'I make a nice toy for your little one. Yes?'

Robbie said, 'Thank you. That would be lovely. I'll keep more cuttings for you next week.'

Louie was so pleased. Messing around with Robbie had delayed him, but when he gave him the box full of wood, that made up for lost time. He liked Robbie a lot but he always made him explain before he understood what he was trying to say. He never copped on that Robbie knew exactly what he was saying. Robbie just wanted to hear him speak and watch his actions. It was only a bit of fun and Louie took it very well. The only thing was that Louie fell for it every time. He would love to catch onto Robbie doing this to him quicker than he did. Someday he would and the joke would be on Robbie. When he got home with the wood pieces, he started to work on a doll for Robbie's little one. He put a lot of time into making it, this one was special. He was very pleased with it when it was finished. It took a lot of time, so he decided he would stay with making things that were less complicated. Less curves and less time. They were usually only small toys, so he couldn't charge much for them. It started as a hobby, making things for his own children. Other kids liked them and wanted to buy them. He loved working with wood. In his spare time he made a few things, sold them quickly. He didn't have time to make any more for weeks. Mrs. Solomons didn't like him doing this at all. There was no room in the house and it made a mess. She was very house proud. They didn't need the bit of money he was making from them. It was driving her mad. She made him stop. He knew she was right and he stopped. But he kept the idea in the back of his mind. He could not let all those lovely pieces of new wood go to waste but what could he do? He told Robbie he had to stop keeping any more wood for him. Robbie felt so sorry for him.

He said, 'And I have a big box full of pieces I kept for you up there in No. 6, the end house. We were doing a lot of woodwork in that block all week. I got all the lads to put their waste into a pile in each house and then I collected it and put it in a box for you. What do you want me to do with it?'

'I'd love to take it but I have nowhere to put it.'

'I'll hold on to it for a while for you,' Robbie told him. 'If you don't want then I'll use it for the fire.'

'Oh no!' he said. 'Don't do that. I'll think of something. You can't burn good new wood like that. He said, 'I'll collect that box tomorrow and you can still keep the bits for me.'

'That was a quick decision. What are you going to do?'

'I don't know, there is money to make. I do not burn money.'

'Fair enough,' Robbie said. 'Laura loves that doll you made for her. You could make a good business working with wood. You are very good at it.'

'I know,' he said. 'Tell it to my vife.'

'I can't tell your *vife*,' Robbie jeered him. 'Louie you will have to start coming out with the lads for a drink. Start staying out late, go home drunk, then she will change her mind and let you do your woodwork.'

'Oh no!' he said. 'Not the drink. Drink not like me. My vife not like me in drink.'

'Ah Louie,' Robbie said. 'In Ireland that's what we call being henpecked!'

'No! No! My vife not picking hen!'

Robbie roared laughing at him, he laughed himself.

'It's up to you do whatever you want,' Robbie said and went on his way. When he was gone Louie got out his cart and went and got the wood. When he opened the box and saw all the beautiful pieces he nearly cried. He walked around no. 6, looking at the work of the carpenters. It was good he thought, if this house was for sale I would buy it. Why did he not put his name in the hat for the draw? He might have won one. His wife said 'No, they were only for the local people.' He thought to himself, 'That's it! I will buy a bigger house.' He should have done that when the baby was born. He was so busy making money he never thought of that. Olga loves the cottage, she might not like a bigger house. He would ask her when he got home. She was not home when he got there. He looked around the cottage. It was beautiful but very small, Olga would never leave it. She had a place for everything, and everything in its place. It was always so tidy. He loved it himself so he would have to think of something else. He would do nothing until after Christmas. What was he going to do with this cart load of wood now? When he came home he showed her the wood.

136

Told her what he was thinking.

She said, 'What about the scrap business? We are making a good living from it.'

'I know, but we could do much better if I worked with wood. Then why don't you rent a place to work with wood and see how it goes. Then give up the scrap business. You can't do both.'

He could not believe it. In one sentence she could solve a problem. 'Well,' he asked. 'Could I make things from this lot for Christmas?'

'Yes, of course' she said, 'and give some of the toys you make to the Christmas fair.'

'That's a great idea!' He said. 'Thank you, we will be living in a bigger house sooner than you think.'

'That would be lovely,' she said.

'There's another problem solved,' he thought to himself. She would move house.'

He will start tomorrow looking out for a bigger house for sale in the village. Maybe a little further out, depending on the price. Now that he had her interested he was in a hurry to find something suitable before she changed her mind.

Chapter 21

Mr. Taylor was very pleased with the way work in the village was going. The flour mill is fully operational. The bakery, chemist and the hairdresser are all open for business and doing well. The only thing he was a bit disappointed about was the houses. He had hoped they would be finished and the tenants living in them before Christmas. However, a few weeks more and they will have a big celebration opening party. That will be nice to look forward to in January, a cold, wet, windy and really miserable month. When there is nothing to look forward to. If the snow comes in January it will stay on the hills for weeks. January is not a very popular month of the year in Ireland. The day the people get the keys of the houses will be a fantastic day, regardless of the weather. It will be on a Sunday, when everybody will be off work, and are able to join in the excitement. The keys will be handed over in the parish hall. There will be people there from all walks of life. The council, the Catholic priest, the Protestant minister, The Taylor family, the builders and all the tradesmen who worked so hard to make this day happen. It will be a day to remember. Mr. Taylor was more excited about this day than Christmas day. He had done a lot of good things over the years at Christmas time for people, but nothing as big as this. He never wanted anything he did for charity to be made public, but this was different. It was a huge scoop to get the permission to build in the first place, from this council. They never gave the go ahead to anyone on a first application, even if it was only for one house. They objected to so many things, the toing and froing, could go on for years. The few things they objected to on these plans were sorted so quickly everybody was shocked, especially Mr. Taylor. He was going to give a speech on that day. Thank the members of the council a thousand times, for the great work they had done, and with such speed. He hoped to embarrass them, for the way they treat other applicants and hope they get the message. His houses were built now. The best of everything had been used to make sure they couldn't find any faults. They were built exactly as he applied for, and fitted into the surrounding area beautifully. Although they were two story houses, from the front they looked like bungalows.

They fitted in so well they looked like they were always there. He was so happy with them, he never stopped talking about them. One day he said to Mrs. Taylor, 'Ann, you know what these houses remind me of?'

She stopped him in his tracks and said, 'Patrick, stop you are talking about those houses every day. I know you are very proud of them, they are very nice, they look lovely but I have had enough of them.'

'Sorry,' he said. 'Have I been that annoying?'

'Yes!' she said.

'Well, I won't mention them again. I was only going to say, they fit into the village so well. They remind me of the way a baby fits into a family. When they are born, you can't remember not having them. It's as if they were always there.' He laughed.

'You can laugh if you like, but there are no more babies coming into this family, Mr. Taylor, I can remember when there were none of them here, and it was bliss.'

'Oh, you don't mean that Ann. Do you regret having them?'

'No, I do not. You know I love all of them, but they didn't come easy, that's what I'm saying.'

'Ah,' he said. 'Which one would you be without.'

'All of them,' she said. She laughed this time, when she saw the worried look on his face.

'Now go back to your work and let me get back to mine. You silly old man.'

As he walked out he said, 'Less of the old man,' under his breath.

She knew he hated her calling him old, she did it deliberately to annoy him!

She was fed up hearing about those houses. It was great he got the chance to build them, but he kept going on about them. She was more excited about what was going on with the family. Lydia was coming for dinner and she was looking forward to having her. She was going to ask her what plans she had for Christmas day. She wanted to have dinner at a time that suited everybody. After dinner they could do whatever they wanted. Then they would have the party they had every Christmas night. If Michael and James wanted to invite the girlfriend's parents over they would be very welcome. If any more of their friends wanted to come over that was fine. Mrs. Taylor loved Christmas night. The party went on very late, because they could have a good rest the next day. She was really looking forward to Christmas this year. It would be lovely for James to announce the engagement at the dinner table. Mrs. Taylor was dying for him to tell the family. She was so excited about seeing the ring. James had good, but expensive taste. But of course it would be Lydia's choice, and Lydia had some nice jewellery already so she expected it to be beautiful. He had saved a lot of money after working all summer on the building site. Lydia had been to Dublin and they bought the ring in Wests on Grafton Street. James had it in the house, but didn't show it to his mother. In fact, he had told her that it was very like her own. A solitaire set in platinum. Lydia had said, 'A diamond is forever'. James was happy she got the one she wanted. He was looking forward to telling everybody. It had been hard keeping it a secret.

The Boles family were so excited, George had gone to the station to collect Joseph. He brought Trevor with him. He wanted them to have a little time with each other before they arrived home. The train was already in and Joseph was the only one waiting on the station platform. Trevor was so excited when he saw him. They ran to each other. Joseph lifted Trevor off his feet, swung him around. George waited a minute before telling them to come on.

'Welcome home son,' he said to Joseph. 'You look great. Army life seems to agree with you.'

'Thanks Dad,' he said. 'I love it.'

George turned to Trevor and told him to stand back when they got home and give his mother, Beatrice, and Philip a chance to welcome Joseph home.

'If the babies are awake, Joseph will want to give some attention to them also. Now you have him all to yourself. Talk as much as you like. Tell him all your news and then give him a break. He is going to be home for a while so you will have plenty of time with him.'

George knew Trevor could be overpowering at times. He wanted Joseph to enjoy his holiday and not have Trevor hanging out of him all the time. Ethel was thrilled to see

Joseph looking so well. The hug he gave her was a hug that can only be between a mother and son. They held each other for seconds, but to Beatrice it seemed ages, so by the time he got to her, the tears were streaming down her face. She was his Godmother and when she saw him and Ethel together like this she wished she was his mother. She loved him so much. Philip was next, Joseph patted him on the head, told him he looked great. Philip couldn't care less. He just wanted to see if he brought him home anything. He knew he would be waiting for ages. Joseph had to see the babies, have a meal and talk to everybody, before he would even think of opening his case. Ether and George went upstairs and brought down the twins. George was going to hand Doris to him. She started to cry and held onto her father. Ethel gave Desmond to him and told him that in a while Doris would come to him. Joseph thought the babies were beautiful. He told his parents they were right to take the two of them. It would have been a shame to separate them.

Philip asked, 'When are we going to eat?'

'Right now.' George said. 'I'm starving.'

Ethel and Beatrice went into the kitchen and brought back plates of food. They smiled as they put them on the table.

Ethel said to Beatrice, 'This is going to be a great Christmas.'

After the meal Joseph went to see his grandparents and Lydia. He was amazed at the improvements in the town. The shop was very busy, so he helped to serve for a while and when it eased up he and his grandmother went into the back room and had a great chat. She went back out to serve to give Grandpa a chance to talk to him. Lydia was still busy so he told her he would meet her later when the shop was closed.

Chapter 22

Christmas morning and Mr. & Mrs. Cramp had everything ready. The only things she had to cook were the turkey and vegetables. Beatrice had set the table beautifully. The three babies would be fed first. The adults and older children would all eat at the big table. Lydia was going to James' parents for dinner. Her parents didn't mind, James would come back with her later.

Ethel and George were up early, having their breakfast on their own. They wanted to enjoy a quiet time before everybody appeared. They were looking forward to watching the boys' reaction when they saw what they got. It wasn't long before the babies woke up and then it was a free for all.

George said, 'No opening of presents until the breakfast is over.'

The boys didn't want to wait so they ate very little.

'We're finished!' they said.

'Hold on!' George said. 'Wait, you are not leaving the table until everybody is finished.'

Ethel asked George if she could give them one small present from the babies?

'They can open them at the table.'

The boys were pleased with their mother. By the time they opened them the breakfast was finished. Ethel and George cleared the dishes and then the presents were handed out. There was surprise after surprise and a lot of thought had gone into the choices people made when buying them.

When things calmed down Joseph came over with a huge box and handed it to Philip and said,

'That's between the two of you, no fighting, play with it together and enjoy it!'

They couldn't get the wrapping paper off quick enough. When they saw what it was they could not believe it. It was a huge amount of soldiers, lorries, cardboard buildings, flags etc. When put together it would make a huge army base. They were thrilled. They had never seen anything like it. They wanted to play with it there and then. But of course, they would have to wait until they came home after dinner.

Ethel said, 'Leave it until tomorrow and then you can take it out to the fitting room, play as long as you like, leave it there, no will touch it. Then you can play with it again and again, without having to put it away.'

The boys thought that was great. They had got lots of other things that morning to play with. Joseph suggested he would walk to the grandparents, Trevor and Philip said they would walk with him. They were dying to see what the grandparents had for them. Joseph wanted to see Lydia and talk to her before the others came. When they arrived and saw the way the place was decorated they were surprised. It was so beautiful. It did not look like the same place it was before Christmas. Where had they put all the stock? They gave the grandparents their presents. Only small things, but nice things. They were pleased with them. They were told not to give their presents out until everybody was there. But they couldn't wait. Lydia said she had a surprise for them, which she would give to them now. But they would have to wait until after she came back from dinner with James for their presents like everybody else. She had lovely hurling sticks and a slither for each of them. They had

145

wanted them for ages, but were never allowed to have them. Every boy in the village played hurling except them. Their parents thought hurling was not a nice game. They hugged and kissed her. They thanked her so much, now they could play it with each other even if they were not allowed to play on a team. This surprise and the present from Joseph made their day. They were so excited. They gave Lydia her presents. They were so pleased they had bought her one from each of them. They always gave her one between them. This year they had their own money and decided to buy everybody something. She was delighted with them and asked,

'Who helped you to buy these lovely things?'

'The girl in the new chemist shop.'

'Well, you are very good, they are beautiful, I love them.'

She told them she would be going out for dinner but when she came back she would have a nice surprise for them.

'Oh don't go out, we'll miss you!' they said. Joseph was surprised she was going out, but said nothing. She had just left when the Solomons arrived. A few minutes later everybody was there. Ethel called her mother out to the kitchen and asked where Lydia was.

'Oh she is gone to the Taylor's for dinner but she will be back with James before you go.'

Ethel was mad but said nothing. She gave Beatrice a look that said nothing, but Beatrice knew something was not right. Her mother looked very happy, so what could it be? The Granddad had Doris on his knee playing with her. Desmond and Sophia were on the floor, playing with each other. Presents were being passed around. It was chaotic. Mrs. Solomons started picking up wrapping paper. In

146

seconds she had everything in order. She asked Ethel if they would feed the babies first and put them down for a nap? They might have their dinner in peace.

'Sure we will, I have every intention of having my dinner in peace.'

Mrs Cramp was busy in the kitchen and was delighted with the way things were going. There was a great buzz from the dining room. George was disgusted with Lydia's presents for the boys. She knew well that he and Ethel hated that game.

He thought, 'Why would she do that? That was rotten. Why was she doing these things?'

It seemed she was deliberately trying to hurt them. Why, was the big question? He was glad she was gone out for dinner. At least they would enjoy the meal. Ethel, Beatrice and Mrs. Solomons fed the babies and put them safely in the bedroom that Mr. Cramp had put a double and a single together at the wall and a homemade safety barrier on the outside, it was brilliant. When the babies were asleep Mrs. Cramp told them to take their places at the table dinner was ready to be served. When they finished the first course. Ethel Beatrice, Mrs. Solomons and Mrs. Cramp carried in the main course. The meal was very nice, and they had a lot of fun pulling crackers and telling jokes. Nobody wanted dessert. Everybody had plenty, and just wanted to relax. The boys, their Dad, and Mr. Solomons cleared the table and washed all the dishes. Joseph was told he did not have to help as he was on holidays, but he insisted on joining the men in the kitchen. They seemed to be having a great time. Mrs. Cramp thought she heard Lydia's voice and she left the table. She was right. Lydia and James had arrived. Lydia held up her left hand and said to her Mother, 'Surprise!'

Mrs. Cramp nearly died.

She called, 'John!'

The girls knew there was something going on, but it wasn't something bad. It sounded like they were expecting something silly to happen. When their mother walked in. She had the biggest smile the girls had ever seen and said,

'Come on in.'

Who was she calling in? Then Lydia and James walked in. Their mother held Lydia's hand up and said 'Surprise!'

Ethel and Beatrice were dumb founded. They couldn't stand up. They never in a million years expected this. Lydia walked round to the two of them and said,

'Would you like to make a wish on my ring?'

Ethel said, 'Yes, of course. Congratulations, it's beautiful.' She passed it on to Beatrice.

She said, 'Congrats, it's magnificent.' She passed it on to Mrs. Solomons.

She said, 'Very wonderful, expensive yes?'

They all stood up then congratulated James, and wished them both the best of luck.

Mrs Cramp said, 'Everybody into the sitting room, this needs a big celebration drink.'

John, George, Joseph and Mr. Solomons carried trays of glasses of all sizes, all kinds of drinks and a special tray with two glasses and a bottle of champagne for the engaged couple. Ethel and Beatrice were very worried. What was this going to mean? This could cause all kinds of trouble. There hadn't been a hint or a mention of this happening at Christmas. Lydia had not spoken to the sisters or asked about the babies since she came home. It will be interesting to see what happens when the babies wake up. They had the toast and things quietened down a bit.

Mrs Cramp said, 'I have to make a wish on the ring.'

Lydia passed it over to her. She turned it round three times, closed her eyes, as was the custom and made her wish. She was so happy, Lydia was a very lucky girl. James was a very nice lad from a lovely family, they couldn't have asked for more. Mr. Solomons took out his balalaika, and sang a beautiful Russian love song. Ethel was nearly getting sick. Not because she was envious but because Lydia never did anything for anybody, yet everybody did lots for her and she never appreciated it. Beatrice was dying to see the couple's reaction to the babies. She hoped they would wake up soon. Lydia was a great actress but would she be able to act this one out? It was going to be hard for both of them to pretend they were seeing them for the first time. They hadn't seen them for ages. Now they were nearly one year old, with beautiful black hair, able to stand up almost walking, with lots of words, so cute, and very good looking, like their father.   Ethel was making sure she was in the room when they were brought in. Beatrice was thinking the same thing. Their first reaction would speak volumes. James might not do as well as Lydia, he was a softer person, and more used to babies. Lydia was as hard as nails. Although she loved Trevor, and was always kind to him. Whatever happened here today was going to be very important to Ethel. She excused herself and winked at George, he followed her out. She told him, 'When you hear a stir from the babies, make sure you get in there quickly and bring one of the twins out. I'll tell Joseph to take the other one, and leave Sofia for Mr Solomons. We don't want James or Lydia to see them, until

I have one on my lap and Beatrice has the other one. We want to watch their faces when the babies are brought in.'

George was as worried as Ethel, but didn't pretend to be. This was going to be a very delicate thing to do, but it had to be done. The sooner the better. Lydia and James could leave any minute, and a great opportunity would be missed. They might never have the two of them in a room together like this again. George called Joseph and they went into the room where the babies slept. They woke the twins gently, and lifted them up. Doris gave George a big smile, He handed her to Joseph and he lifted Desmond. He might not be so pleasant, but he was fine. George took a deep breath and said, 'Let's go.'

When they walked in, Ethel and Beatrice put out their arms, took a baby each and looked over at the couple.

'Well!' Ethel said 'These are our beautiful babies. What do you think?'

Lydia's face gave nothing away, but James went as white as snow. Ethel could see he was not able to cope. She asked him if he would like to hold the baby.

He said, 'Yes, but I must go to the bathroom first.'

Ethel knew he was going out to be sick. She felt very sorry for him. He was back in a while looking better, and he put his arms out to Ethel to take the baby.

'This is Doris, she is a very pleasant child, look at her smiling up at you. She never gets strange with anybody.'

'Oh!' he said, 'She is beautiful.'

He couldn't take his eyes off her. Beatrice stood up and walked over to Lydia, she put the baby in her arms, 'Desmond is different, he doesn't smile as much as Doris, but he has his good points. He is a better sleeper than his sister. They are both great babies.'

Mr. Cramp asked,

'Where is little Sophia?'

'Oh. she is still asleep, but I think I will wake her up.' Mrs. Solomons said. 'She will be awake all night if I leave her any longer.'

Mrs. Cramp was very uncomfortable with Lydia and James holding the babies. She was afraid John might notice how much like James they were.

'Will I give the babies a drink?' she asked. 'They must be very thirsty.'

Mrs. Solomons got up and said, 'I'll get the drinks for them and wake my baby.'

When Mrs. Solomons came back, she gave Sophia to Mrs. Cramp. Having Sophia in the room made things a bit easier. Philip, Trevor, David and Sybil got down on the floor and started to play board games.

Mr. Cramp said he was going to have a little nap, he was feeling a bit tired. Ethel said, 'You should have a little nap yourself Mum. George will come for you at eight.'

'That's great, we are looking forward to it.'

Lydia said, 'Hold on a minute Dad, I have to give out my presents.'

She went downstairs and came back with a big bag of the most beautifully wrapped presents. She had bought presents for everybody, including the Solomons. Luckily everybody had something for her. Nothing to compare with what she had for everybody. This was most unusual, for Lydia was not a giver. Maybe because she knew she was getting engaged she went overboard. She knew that after

Christmas, engagement presents would be coming in and she would want to show off to the Taylors how popular she was. Whatever her reason she had put a lot of thought into the presents. Maybe James was making her into a nice person. That would be great! She must have bought the presents in Dublin. She must have gone there before Christmas, to buy the ring! But their Mother never mentioned Lydia going to Dublin. The two sisters looked at each other, something was going on, because Mum looked very happy. Ethel turned to James and said, 'You will have to come to our house tonight James with Lydia.'

'Oh,' he said, 'I'm sorry but my mum is expecting us back, a lot of friends are coming to the house and they don't know about the engagement. She is more excited than we are. So we have to go back.'

'That's fine, maybe tomorrow, if you feel like calling up you are more than welcome anytime.'

He thanked her. She was giving him a chance to call, she was very aware of his feelings for the babies, and she hoped he would call up on his own sometime. She was going to question him about the babies' adoption papers. She wanted to get things sorted, they were nearly one year old and it had gone on long enough. They stayed about another hour.

George said, 'I think we should all go home, we have a big night ahead of us.'

The Solomons came home with the Boles. The children wanted to show David the things they got and especially the present from Joseph. When it was set up he could come over and play with them. Not tonight though,

152

they had lots of other things to play with. The adults sat around. Just relaxing and having a drink. Nobody wanted food. A couple of hours more and Christmas day would be over for another year. It had been a very successful day considering what might have happened. But Ethel was still very worried about the babies. She did not trust Lydia, she couldn't tell the truth now and take back the babies or could she? Those papers must be signed as soon as possible.

When Lydia and James arrived back at the Taylor house it was full of people. Lydia loved parties. This was a very special party because she was the star of the show. The most important person in the room and that was what she loved to be. Everybody is making a big fuss of her. James was very quiet and never wanted to be the man of the moment. All the women wanted to try on the ring and make their wishes. When all this was over the party got going full swing. It was brilliant. Mr. Taylor was so pleased, he was very fond of Lydia. He loved dealing with her in the post office. She was so good at her work and so obliging when he wanted anything done that would take a lot of time. When he was a bit unsure of anything, she would say 'For you Mr. Taylor, nothing is too much trouble.'

He always wondered why she went away after James went back to college but he never asked James. He thought they had fallen out, but they had been so close. Now they are engaged and that's great. He missed her and he knew John was never as happy as he was when she was there. When she came back John was his old self again. Now she was going to become part of his family. He couldn't ask for more. She had all the get up and go that James lacked, if opposites attract then this was the perfect match. He liked the girl Michael brought to the house this year. She had been there in the summer but he did not think they were a couple then. He was happy about Michael's choice. Linda was very nice, very attractive, beautiful big ebony eyes and long black hair. She did not look Irish, she was from the village but he didn't know her family. He sat back in his chair, looked at the way the party was going and thought how lucky he was. It had been a beautiful day. A Christmas to remember. He was very tired now and wished they would all go home. It was after midnight and he wanted to go to bed. The rule of this house was, he was last to go to bed, lock up and make sure everybody was safe. This might have to change, he admitted to himself. This was the first time in his life he felt like going to bed and letting them all get on with it. He must be getting old!

Chapter 23

Saint Stephen's day was a really lazy day. Adults took it easy. Ethel was delighted to have Joseph to talk to on her own. She didn't get much time to talk to him on Christmas day. It was lovely having him home. He only had one more day and then he would be gone again. Life really was hard on mothers. The children were busy with all the things they got as presents. Joseph helped them to set up the toy army base in the fitting room. It could be left there for a while. Nobody was due for fittings for a couple of weeks. After that they would have had enough of it anyway she hoped!

This year was different for the Boles. The fact that Lydia had decided to marry James Taylor the father of the children could be a big issue. If Lydia decided to take them back it would cause terrible trouble.

George decided to ask both of them to come to the house and talk to them. Put everything out in the open. Ask them out straight what was going to happen. They wanted the adoption papers signed and to get on with their lives. They came to the meeting, and said they would sign and seal everything as soon as Christmas was over. Ethel and George would have to go with them to Dublin. That was no trouble as long as the date was made and kept. It was not easy for both of them to be away for a day without making arrangements early. Lydia agreed she would make the arrangements and give them plenty of notice. Ethel didn't want plenty of notice; she wanted it done as soon as possible. She didn't trust Lydia at all. James said very little, but Ethel knew that Lydia was the boss and whatever she said was done. She was very sorry for him. She felt he would love to have the babies but that was impossible now. She trusted him to do the right thing and hoped he would be strong enough to get Lydia to do the same. It was a pleasant enough meeting but Ethel found it hard to forgive Lydia for all the trouble she caused. She was as polite as she could be with her and when they left George gave her a big hug and told her she did great. George said he felt Lydia could not go back on her word now. She would never let Taylor's down. If it had been anybody else who was the father she would have done whatever she liked. He felt they could trust James, he was a gentleman. He wouldn't want to let his parents down either.

Ethel said, 'I hope you are right. I will not be really happy until the papers are signed and sealed. Please God it will happen early in the new year rather than later. Once that's done we will be able to relax and enjoy our lives.'

In the new year when Ethel's work had to start again. She got up very early and worked at getting things ready for Beatrice and Mrs. Solomons. She wanted to mind the babies herself to give Mrs Solomons a break. She did a great job minding them. Ethel felt Mrs. Solomons needed to get her back sewing. She was a quicker worker than Ethel herself, and it was a while since she spent full days sewing. She never complained but Ethel felt she was missing it, and it was time Ethel spent more time with the three babies.

The babies were great company for each other. When they went for a nap Ethel could do lots while they were asleep. She liked the break from the workroom. Beatrice loved the babies but she was not able to manage three of them. She was good with them in small doses, enough time for Ethel to have a tea break, and she would babysit once they were asleep. But to mind them for a whole day? No, she couldn't do it. When Lydia told Ethel the date to go to Dublin was the third Friday in January she was thrilled. She told Mrs. Solomons she wanted her on that day to mind the babies all day in the house. Beatrice and Thelma could stay in the house with her and help her. They could take the day off from sewing and enjoy the babies. This was a very important day in their lives, and they didn't want anything to go wrong. Ethel was excited to have a date, but she would not believe it was true until it was here and gone and she had the papers in her hands signed and sealed. George thought she was a terrible doubting Thomas. Little did she know he was just as worried as she was. All his faith was in James. He hoped and prayed that he would keep his word.

Chapter 24

Mr. Solomons was looking round for a house that might suit him for doing his woodwork. After many weeks, a house in the town came up for sale. It had no front garden but it had a huge back garden. It had three bedrooms, a sitting room, a dining room, a kitchen and a bathroom, and he liked it. He also liked the price. He was not going to get excited until his wife saw it. The next day he brought her to see it. She thought he was mad, she hated it. She had other ideas on her mind. She was looking out for something for him to rent. Like a big shed. She was never going to leave this beautiful place, or this lucky little cottage, her *paradise* she called it. She was not sure about the woodwork. It was great when he was getting all the wood for nothing. But when he had to buy it and started to make bigger pieces, how was he going to do it? She knew he was very good at it, but she couldn't see the demand being good enough for him to give up the scrap business.

He wanted to do both, she said 'No.' She was earning good money and there was no need for it. If he worked any harder he would kill himself. She had said all this to Ethel, who told her there was plenty of space at the back of her parents shop. If he wanted to, he could ask her dad if he could rent the space and put his own shed on it.

'That sounds great but I'm hoping he will get fed up with the idea and forget about it. But I'll keep that in mind. Imagine if we bought a house and then it didn't work out? I'd lose my mind. No, we are not buying a house. He can rent somewhere or forget about it altogether.'

Although a couple of weeks in the new year had passed Lydia never mentioned a word about getting married. Her mother was dying to know the usual. What? Where? When? There was a lot to think of and plans to make. James was a Catholic and Lydia was a Protestant. The Cramps didn't mind and the Taylors were as easy about whatever the couple wanted to do would be done. James' sisters were hoping it would be a big wedding. They wanted to be flower girls and bridesmaids. Mr. Taylor asked James one day, 'Will the wedding be this year? Or is it going to be a long engagement like the rest of them in this area?'

James said, 'It depends on Lydia, I'd love a summer wedding but she can't make up her mind.'

His Father said, 'Make up her mind for her. Your mother is looking forward to a big wedding. Her first son, getting married.'

James said, 'I'll do my best to get a move on her I promise.'

His Dad laughed and said, 'Your Mother and I met each other, became engaged, got married in eight months. Then had Michael, you and Patrick within five years.'

'Well Dad, I don't think Lydia would like a big family.'

'So what's the point in getting married then?'

'We love each other, that's the point.'

'Come on son, we need a big day out, you are not getting any younger,' he laughed!

'Her dad is dying to give her away! I know that for a fact.'

'Go away Dad, her dad does not want to see her going. She is his favourite child.'

'No such thing son, all children are their parents favourite.'

He walked away from James, saying as he went, 'Don't leave

it too long then.'

The wedding was the last thing James had on his mind. He wished with all his heart he could tell his father about the twins. He did not know how he was going to keep it a secret. More excuses were going to be made in January, when they had to go to Dublin. Friday is a very busy day in the shop. How is Lydia going to work that one out? How was he going to give those beautiful babies away? He had not slept well since holding Doris on his knee at Christmas. Lydia wouldn't speak to him about them. If only she would tell him how she was feeling, it would be a big help. Nothing was easy with Lydia. She loved drama and every time she did something that started out simple, it ended up complicated. Now her latest thing was she wanted to become a Catholic, before they got married and not tell anybody. She wanted a big wedding in the beautiful little Catholic church, with lots of flowers, candles, and a red carpet. With music, a singer. The whole works. James was willing to go along with her wishes as long as she told her parents everything she was going to do beforehand. He never asked her to become a Catholic. If she was going to keep it a secret, he was having none of it. He was going to tell everybody. Why was she doing this? Who was she trying to hurt? She had so much going for her. When the word of the engagement got around, presents came flowing in from everywhere. She was very popular. He couldn't understand why she wanted to go on with all this intrigue. This time, he was going to sit down with her parents and tell them their plans. His parents had no problem with him marrying a Protestant. Her parents had no problem with her marrying a Catholic. Why was she making a big deal where there was no need to? If she was going to change her religion, she would have to tell her parents and at least give them the respect they deserve by letting them know her plans. He had made up his mind he was never going to do anything again in secret, no matter how small. Everything they did was going to be out in the open. He had been brought up with some rules, one was never to lie. The truth might hurt, but if you lie, it always comes back to haunt you. A liar needs a good memory. His father hated lies. When they were growing up no matter what they did, how serious it was, once you told the truth, you never got into trouble. How did he ever give into Lydia and lie about the babies? There was nobody he could talk to except Ethel and George, but he never got a chance to go to their house on his own. Things had to stay the way they are.

Chapter 25

The third Friday in January had come quicker than they expected. The four of them went to the station together. They sat in separate carriages on the train. Ethel and George were on a high, but Lydia and James were down in the dumps. When they reached Dublin they walked to the adoption agency together. Nobody said a word. It was a desperate situation. When the papers were signed, George went to shake James by the hand and James burst into tears, and put his head on George's shoulder. George was mortified. In those days men never cried. Ethel put her arms around Lydia and they both cried. Sobbing uncontrollably. It was horrible. It took ages for them to get their act together. Ethel put the papers in her bag. The most important papers she would ever have in that bag. They left the agency and went their separate ways. Whatever happened from now on the babies were theirs. It was a day she would never forget. In spite of all the tears she was happy it was over at last. Her heart was breaking for Lydia and James, but it was their own fault. If they had told her the truth in the beginning, everything would have been so different.

When George and Ethel arrived home the babies were in bed. Thelma and Mrs. Solomones were gone home. The boys were in the fitting room playing with the toy army base. Beatrice was reading a book. The peace was glorious. Beatrice had a lovely supper for them. They were starving, they had forgotten to have dinner in Dublin. They told her how upsetting it was and she was not surprised.

Beatrice, as always sensible, said, 'That's the past now. Enjoy your meal and go to bed. I'll give the boys their supper in a few minutes. You don't need to see them tonight. What you both need is a good night's sleep'.

She was right, they finished their supper and just as they were about to go to bed. Ethel remembered the box of lead soldiers they had bought for the boys. Beatrice told her to leave that until tomorrow. Ethel agreed with her and they went to bed. Beatrice wanted to go to bed herself. She called the boys, told them their parents were asleep and if they didn't want anything to eat, to go to bed quietly. They tip-toed up the stairs, and got into bed. They were so good, Beatrice loved them. She treated them as if they were her own. She spoiled them in a good way. They would do anything she asked them to do for her. Likewise she would always be on their side. She was the best Aunty ever.

Chapter 26

James and Lydia stayed the night in Dublin and had dinner with Michael and Linda in her flat. She was a great cook and the meal was lovely. After a few drinks, Lydia told them they were getting married in August. James nearly fell off the chair, it was the first he heard of it.

He said to Lydia, 'You might have told me.'

She laughed and said, 'I'm telling you now.'

James was annoyed he felt foolish in front of his brother and Linda.

'What's her game?' he thought. Then he tried to make light of it and asked her,

'On what date?'

'Oh the 7th,' she said.

'Great, the 7th is a nice date.'

He had one more drink and then said, 'We should be going, we don't want to keep Phyllis up too late waiting for us.'

They thanked Michael and Linda and told them they would be in Dublin again soon. Next time dinner would be on them in the Shelbourne Hotel. 'That's great,' Michael said, 'We'll keep that in mind.'

They left having said their goodbyes. They walked in silence for a few minutes. James decided not to mention what had just happened. It had been a horrendous day and he needed sleep badly.

Lydia said she was tired and she was going to bed when they got to Phyllis'. James didn't answer her. When Phyllis saw the state of them she pointed upstairs. She expected them to be upset, but they looked dreadfully worn out. She would talk to them in the morning. She was not looking forward to it. She had asked them so many times to tell the truth before the babies were born. Lydia was as stubborn as a mule. She would never give in.

James and Lydia left Dublin on the morning train on Saturday. James asked her when she was going to tell the parents about the wedding?

She kept looking out the window and said, 'Whenever!'

James said, 'That's not an answer. If you have decided the 7th of August is the date then I am telling both our parents when we get home today.'

'That's OK, we'll both do it together.'

'Then we will tell them everything.'

'Are you changing your religion? Are we getting married in the Catholic church?'

'Yes! Yes! Yes! she said, nearly taking his head off.

He held her hand and asked her to leave all that for another day. They both needed to get over yesterday. He was feeling as bad as she was.

'Maybe tomorrow we will feel better.'

He was just sorry she had said anything to Michael and Linda. Now they were going to have to tell the parents, before Michael wrote home and said something about the wedding. His parents would be mad if they were not told first. She put her head on his shoulder and cried more than she cried yesterday. How was he going to stop her.? It took a long time before she lifted her head. She looked desperate. She combed her hair, put on some makeup, and looked a bit better. When they reached Rathdrum, George

165

was not there. Most unlike him to be late. They were so glad he was late. It was a very cold day and waiting in the wind could be blamed for the state of Lydia's face. When he came they asked him to take them to James' mother's house. If they went to the shop Lydia would be expected to help out. There was no way she could do that today. George felt so sorry for both of them. What a mess they made just out of one mistake! It had destroyed both their lives. But they were a lot better off than some other couples, who had a baby outside marriage, had to give it up and would never see it again. They at least could see the babies every day if they wanted to. They were still in the family and they would be there for all the big days. Starting school, growing up, big birthdays, all the special days in their lives. That was a lot to be thankful for but it was still a heavy secret to have to carry.

Mrs. Taylor was delighted to see them and started to fuss over them. She wanted to make them a big meal. That was the last thing they wanted. They just wanted a cup of coffee, nothing to eat. James told his mother to sit down and talk to them. They never get a chance to talk to her. They never get her on their own.

'That's true,' she said and sat down. 'Now talk to me,' she told them.

Lydia said, 'Well the big news is, we have set a date for the wedding.'

'Well, that's great news.'

'We are not going to tell the others until tomorrow. We want both our parents to hear at the same time. So we'll have lunch here with my parents or in my parents' house with you, or we go out for lunch.'

'Oh!' she said, 'I would love to have lunch here. Tell your parents to come to our house tomorrow. It is about time we got together. We have a lot to talk about. James' dad has plenty of chats with your mum and dad in the shop but I never get a chance to talk to them. That's settled then.'

Lydia said, 'I had better get home and tell them, they don't like being rushed anywhere. They like plenty of notice when they are going out.'

'This is not going out for goodness sake.'

'If they agree to come here.'

'They have been here before many times. Sure when you get married we will be related. They are very welcome here anytime.'

Lydia said she would tell them, she was sure they would come and James would let her know tonight. They got up to leave and she asked if they were going to walk? They said that they needed some air after sitting on that train from Dublin. They hugged her and left. When they got to the shop it was busy. Lydia used her hall door key and went straight up to bed. James went into the shop and waited until Mrs. Cramp finished serving a customer. He told her about lunch tomorrow and she agreed to come. He told her Lydia was very tired. She had gone to bed. He was sure she would be fine after a good rest. He would not come back tonight. He would see her in the morning. He left and walked home. He was going to go to bed himself when he got home. He did not know what to make of Lydia's behaviour. He hoped she would go back to being her old self. Always smiling, happy and a pleasure to be with. Since

167

Christmas she has been a nightmare. He was fed up with her moods when she should be looking forward to getting married. What if she has changed her mind? 'No,' he told himself, 'she would never do that, or would she?'

His mind was playing tricks on him! What he really needed was twenty four hours of sleep at least. At this moment he felt so awful he didn't care if he went to sleep and never woke up. That would be the best thing for everybody. Just as he got near the house he saw his father was home. How was he going to face him? Trying to pretend to him he had a great time in Dublin, when it was the last thing he wanted to talk about. While he was wondering what to do, the hall door opened and Mark was coming out. James greeted him, walked in and went straight to bed. He slept until midnight. When he woke he came down to make a cup of tea. His mother heard him in the kitchen and asked him.

'Where did you come from?'

'Bed,' he said.

'We were waiting for you to come home. We thought you were with Lydia. Are her parents coming for lunch tomorrow?'

'Yes,' he said.

He drank the tea, said 'Good night Mum,' and went back to bed.

Mr. Taylor and James went to collect the Cramps on Sunday for lunch. Lydia was in much better form Thank God. James was happy to see her smiling. He was dreading her being in a bad mood and making everybody uncomfortable. All the Taylor children were there. The table was set beautifully and ready to start lunch immediately. The girls were dying to hear the date of the wedding. They

168

were not allowed to ask questions and were fed up with all the small talk. When everybody had finished the main course Lydia said, 'The 7th of August girls is going to be the day of the wedding. You are all going to be part of the bridal party.'

They were thrilled with that news.

'Mary being the eldest will be the main bridesmaid. Anne-Marie and Margaret will be flower girls. Your best friend Paul would be ideal for best man with Mary.' James agreed. Mary was delighted with that. She really liked Paul.

'We'll have to find two nice boys for you girls, or you could walk down together. What do you want to do?'

'Walk down together.'

'That's settled then. Is everybody happy with that?'

'Yes, yes, that's great,' the girls said.

'Usually the groom's brothers are the best men, but I'm sure you girls don't want to walk down the aisle with your brothers!'

'No we don't,' they said.

'The bride will be in white. Would you girls like to be in autumn shades or just a plain colour?'

'Plain colour,' they both said together.

'Well' that's good. We will all go to Dublin before Easter and decide what colour you like best. We'll have a great day choosing the materials. Ethel and Beatrice will do all the sewing. The dresses will be beautiful.'

John and Patrick had sat through all this girl talk and had had enough. Patrick thought he would never get John on his own. He had a big secret he wanted to share with him. When they were in the sitting room he told him,

'I've ordered the motor car and I will have it in time for the wedding. I want to drive the bride to the church.'

'Oh my God Patrick! You will be the first man outside Dublin to have a motor car. Can you drive?'

'No, but I'll learn.'

'It must have cost you a fortune.'

'It did, but I've never bought anything for myself. Now, nobody knows. So don't say a word. If Ann knew she would go mad. I told you before what I'm going to do is, have it delivered to the door and tell her it's hers. An anniversary present so then she can't say anything. What do you think?'

'I think it's fantastic. I wish you the best of luck with it. I'd love one myself but I could never afford one.'

'I won't have it for a while yet, but it's ordered.'

'You will cause a great stir when you start driving around in a motor car. Everyone in the village will be delighted for you.'

'Don't say a word to anybody. You are the only one I've told. I had to tell somebody I can't believe it myself. I have wanted one since the first time I sat in one. They are a real luxury.'

'You deserve a bit of luxury.'

'You are dead right Patrick.'

'If I could afford one I would buy one myself, I'll be long gone before there are many of them on the road.'

'Well when I get mine and I know how to drive you will be the first man in the village to get a ride in it.'

'That's very kind Patrick, but I'd like you to be driving a long time before I'd get into a motor vehicle with you. If you drive anything like you drive that pony and trap I'd never get into a car with you that had engine power.'

'I am not that bad, am I?'

'No, you are not. I'm your friend so I would say that. There's a lot of people around here that will run a mile when they see you driving a real motor car. The whole town will be empty in a flash.'

The two of them laughed so much Ann came into the room to ask what the joke was?

'Ah!' Patrick said, 'You would not think it was funny!'

'Try me,' she said.

'Woman,' he said, 'could you not let two men have a joke between themselves without wanting to know what they are laughing at?'

She knew when Patrick called her woman, she was not going to be told.

John had enjoyed the afternoon. He liked Patrick's company. The girls, their mother and Mrs. Cramp had a lovely time. James and Lydia had gone for a walk. The afternoon went so quickly they stayed for tea. As was usual in the Taylor house the evening ended with Mrs. Taylor at the piano. The girls played the recorders. Mrs. Cramp sang without being asked.

John said, 'It's time to go if my wife is singing that means she has had a few drinks. Come Mary, it's past your bedtime.'

The girls thought he was very funny, the way he spoke to his wife. He asked for their coats, it was time to go. Michael insisted on driving them home. John was not looking forward to that drive. Patrick was a bad enough driver in the daytime. It was dark now and John would prefer to walk. Mrs Cramp said she could do with a bit of fresh air

171

and loved walking. So when she got up to leave John was very pleased. It was very dark, not a sinner out, which was just as well, because Mrs. Cramp sang all the way home. He never heard her sing like this, especially outside. What had she been drinking? He didn't ask. He was delighted to see her so happy, it was time she got a chance to let herself go. It had been a great end to a perfect day.

Now that the wedding date had been set, James was going to ask Lydia, about her plans to become a Catholic. She would have to start taking instructions soon, if she was serious. He felt telling her this might put her off. But when she got something into her head that she wanted to do, it was very hard to get her to change her mind. This was going to be a big shock to her parents. They knew George would be thinking he was the one going to perform the service. James wasn't going to leave this any longer. People had to be told now. He was meeting with Lydia later on when the shop closed, and before they went anywhere he was going to tell them. When she opened the door he kissed her feeling really brave and said, 'I've decided to tell your parents tonight.'

'Tell them what?'

'You are changing your religion.'

She said, 'OK. Let's do that then.'

He was not expecting that.

'How will we start this conversation?' he asked.

'Oh,' she said, 'I'll just say it out straight.'

Which is exactly what she did. Her father and mother were stunned. James was stuck to the floor. She put her coat on and walked out the door. James didn't know what to do. He looked up to heaven, put his hands in the air and ran after her.

When he caught up with her he said, 'That was so cruel Lydia.'

She cut him off and said,

'I don't want to talk about it.'

James said, 'Well I want to talk about it. You could have killed your parents. My God, the look on their faces. They knew you were serious and then just walked out the way you did. Why are you being so cruel? I was going to tell them in a proper manner, not blurt it like that.'

'It's done now and that's the end of it.'

'Oh no, it is not the end of it. You have to make arrangements to have instructions. You don't walk in on the day of the wedding and expect the priest to allow you to use his church when you are not a member of it. There is a lot to do before you are received into the Catholic Church.'

'Like what?' she asked.

'I'm not going to go through that now. I was hoping we could tell your parents and at least asked them how they felt about it.'

'It doesn't matter how they feel. It's my choice.' she said. 'And, by the way, how do you feel about it?'

'At this moment I don't know how I feel about anything. I'm wondering if you want to get married at all?'

'Well, that's a coincidence because I was wondering the same thing myself.'

'Then if that's the way we both feel maybe we should call the whole thing off.'

'Yes,' she said, 'I think we should take a couple of weeks'

173

break and then see how we feel.'

He kissed her on the cheek and left her. James was heart-broken. He had planned to do so much tonight. How had it all gone so wrong? He walked home thinking, what could have happened for Lydia to change so much. All this being nasty was now going on a while, but he couldn't think when it had started. He was almost home when he turned back. He wasn't going to sleep on this stupidity. When Lydia opened the door and saw him there she was shocked, but delighted. She put her arms out and they hugged each other and all the old passion was there. They stayed that way for ages before letting go.

When they parted, he told her, 'This has to be settled right here and now. Tell me what's going on?'

She whispered in his ear,

'I can't live here anymore.'

'Where?'

'In this village.' she said.

'Where do you want to live?' he asked.

'I want to live in Dublin.'

This was music to his ears.

'Why did you not tell me?'

'Because I was the one that made you come back here to live. I can't see you ever getting a full time job here. Waiting for someone to retire. Getting a few days' work every now and then is soul destroying and I know you want a real job. I'm willing to live in Dublin.'

'Why didn't you tell me, for God's sake Lydia?'

She said, 'I don't know there is so much going on. I know I love you James. I'm so confused.'

James said, 'If you are sure you love me everything else we can work on. I don't care where we live as long as you are happy.'

'Are you sure?'

'Yes, of course I'm sure. So, we are still engaged then are we?'

No more needed to be said. James left looking forward to tomorrow. First thing he was going to do was make Lydia tell her parents the truth. She was annoyed last night and what she said about her religion was stupid. She was sorry if she had upset them. Then James was going to start looking for a teaching job in Dublin.

James thought, 'What a change! I wanted to stay in this village and now I can't wait to get out of it. I think I know the real reason for Lydia wanting to leave is that we can't stay here and watch those babies grow up. It would be too painful for both of us.'

Chapter 27

Easter had come and gone. There was not a word from Lydia about going to Dublin for material for the wedding party. Ethel and Beatrice were getting worried. What was going on? Surely she was going to get them to make all the clothes. The two of them called to see the parents one night and asked what was happening about the wedding.

They said that Lydia never spoke about it. The mother was afraid to mention it. Lydia was like a prickly pear, she was afraid to ask her the time of day. She was OK in the shop with the customers, but she never spoke to them the way she used to. The parents never told the sisters about her change of religion prank. That was all it was. She never intended to change her religion. Why she said that they would never know. She had done many strange things lately but they wouldn't say what.   Ethel suggested to her Mum,

'Talk to Mrs. Taylor and see if she could get any information from James. He must know what her plans are.'

'I wouldn't like to do that, if Lydia found out I was asking questions about her she would go mad.'

'Sounds to me she is mad already.' Beatrice said, 'It's not fair on those sisters of James. They were looking forward to going to Dublin with her, buying material, getting dresses made and being flower girls. She just can't let everybody down. Is she getting married or is she not? Mum you have to ask her.'

'It will take me some time to work up the courage to ask her anything.'

'No Mum, it's only weeks to the wedding date people have to know. Why does she take the good out of everything?'

'That's Lydia, everything is a big deal. How does James put up with her? He must really love her!'

The sisters left the shop no better off than they came. They decided they were not going to ask any more about arrangements. They knew they would get the dresses done in very little time. They would not pass a remark about anything. If she came with material and the girls without letting them know she was coming, they would welcome her as if she had an appointment. Ethel would have loved her boys to be page boys, but that was not going to happen. She hadn't told George what time she was getting married at or asked what time was best for George. In fact now that Ethel thought about it, she hadn't asked George to marry them at all. She hadn't mentioned having the reception in the church hall. Her behaviour was always a bit strange. This was really stupid. At the end of the day, she was going to have to tell somebody something. It was deliberate to upset everybody. But why? Was she getting pleasure out of being unreasonable?

The Taylor family knew everything about the wedding. Mrs Taylor took it for granted that the Cramps did as well. It was only one day when Mr. and Mrs. Taylor were in the shop and that she started talking about the wedding. Mrs. Cramp had to nod and agree with what she was saying as if she knew all about it. She said the girls had a day off school the following Monday. They were going to Dublin with Lydia to buy the material for the dresses. They were so excited, they loved Lydia. Mrs Cramp was so hurt she could hardly speak.

'That's right, next Monday,' she said, 'that will be lovely for them.'

She hoped it sounded like she knew all about it. She asked her if she had got her outfit yet?

Mrs. Taylor said, 'Yes, I bought it in Dublin two weeks ago. We didn't go there to shop for me, but when I saw this outfit in Switzer's Window I thought that's for me.'

'You are so right, your first choice is always the best. Do you mind me asking the colour?'

'Not at all, it's virgin blue, the girl told me. Though it won't be a virgin wearing it. It fits me perfectly and is so comfortable. I just had to buy it.'

'That's great. I haven't had time to go to Dublin yet. I'll make up my mind one of these days and make the trip. Whatever I buy I won't buy blue! It wouldn't be good for both mothers to arrive in the same colour.'

Ann said, 'No, that would not do at all.'

Patrick called her, 'Are you ready to leave yet?'

'Yes, whenever you are.'

Mrs Cramp said, 'Call down any time after the shop closes and we can have a good chat. Better still, come for lunch next Sunday and we'll have plenty of time to talk and plenty of things to talk about.'

'That would be lovely. Cheers for now,' Ann said, 'See you on Sunday.'

When they were gone and there was nobody in the shop Mary said to John, 'I am after hearing some things about the wedding at last. I've invited them for lunch next Sunday to find out more. Why didn't I think of that sooner? I should have known she would be up there telling them everything. Ethel had suggested I ask James. But I said no,

I would not give her the satisfaction knowing I was curious. Why is she treating us so badly? We don't deserve to be treated like this.'

John said, 'I'm very annoyed with her. Will I say something to her?'

'No, let it go. Her wedding present from us is getting less and less by the minute. I mean that John, if she keeps this up I'm not going to the wedding at all.'

'Don't say that! She is the only one we have left to make a wedding for. It will be a great day and we will enjoy every minute of it. Just think we will have the whole place to ourselves when she is gone. No more walking on eggshells or trying to make omelettes without breaking eggs or whatever it is they say about eggs.'

'You are right. We won't ask anything about the wedding. If we are asked for an opinion then we'll give it. If not we will pretend we don't care.'

'That will be hard on me, John,' she said. 'I would love to be in the thick of it.'

'That's why she is not telling you. She probably thinks you might interfere too much.'

'I would not, would I?'

'Not half. The best thing that happened today was Lydia was out of the shop when they were here. We won't tell her she will have to hear it from them. We'll see how she likes being ignored. Give her a taste of her own medicine.'

It was a pity Lydia had changed so much. She was always so pleasant and they loved working with her. It might be just pre-marriage nervousness. Whatever it was, it was awful and they didn't like it. If Mr. Cramp knew all

Lydia's troubles, he would have been much kinder to her but he could never be told.

Chapter 28

James had told his Dad he was looking for work in Dublin. He hoped after the wedding he would have a full time job ready to start in September. He had applied to all the advertisements for teachers in the newspapers his brother Michael had sent him. He had a few answers, and he had to go to Dublin next week for an interview with the one he really wanted to get. If he got that one he would be thrilled. It was in a big school on the north side of the city. If he got this one it would be a job for life. There was nothing here for them and once Lydia was happy to leave they could make a go of it there. His father was pleased, he knew James would make a great teacher given the chance. He could never get a proper job here for life. Lydia had already tried to get work. She was aiming high with all her experience. She could work in any big store in Dublin. She had sent a letter to Clery's in O'Connell Street. So far she had heard nothing, but they kept their fingers crossed, that it would be great if she got it. They both had a lot on their plates. Planning a wedding, moving to Dublin, and looking for work.

His dad told him, 'If you are offered work take it. Don't wait to start in September. By that time you would have experienced a lot in that school and if you were not happy there you can keep looking while you are working. It's better to look for a job while you are working. Then you are looking to change your job and you are not unemployed. That speaks volumes. So what if you have to go to Dublin before the wedding? You are getting married in the holiday time, you know when you come back from your honeymoon at least one of you has a job.'

'I never thought of that. I have an offer from one school. It's only until the summer. I could take that now and be in Dublin by next week.'

'Take it son, then you will be in the capital city and able to go for interviews if you have to. You are better off out of here while all the fuss about the wedding is going on. When you come back you will be very much appreciated. Think of all the trouble you will have saved yourself. Your mother and I will be making trips to Dublin now and then and we will meet with you for a meal. I have promised your Mother a trip in a motor car and she won't let me forget it. So to keep the peace, that is definitely on the cards. If we can arrange it for a Saturday then you could come with us for the drive. Have you ever been in one?'

'Yes, myself and Michael had a test drive once when the first car came to Dublin.'

'You never said a thing about that, why?'

'We knew we could never afford one so we never talked about it.'

'What would you think about me buying one?'

'Dad, you must be joking, nobody in Wicklow has a car.'

'Well, I'll be the first to have one.'

'You can't drive.'

'I can learn.'

'Where are you going to learn?'

'Oh, I will have lessons where I buy the car.'

'God Dad, you sound serious.'

'I am serious. To be honest, I am getting a bit nervous of

that pony and trap. Last week John Cramp told me I was a danger on the road with that thing.'

'Dad, if he said that what do you think he would say if you told him you were going to drive a car with an engine in it?'

'I thought I was a great driver.'

'Dad, you are great out in the country where there is no traffic, but since there is so much going on in the village you are a nightmare. I have heard it said that if you are seen in the village people keep their children indoors until you have left.'

'Is that so? Now, well tell me who said that about me?'

'No, I don't know who, but it is common knowledge around the town. Maybe you would be better off in a car at least you would be in charge with four wheels instead of an animal with a mind of his own. I'd say it sounds like a good idea, but there are a lot of questions you would have to have answered before you would buy it. Where would you buy petrol? How would you get it repaired if things went wrong?'

'I'm sure all those things can be sorted out, his Dad said. 'Anyway I am only thinking about it. I'm not in any hurry. I would love driving, not having to worry if the weather was good or bad. I'd like a bit of comfort in my old age. That's why I would like to get it now before I'm too old to drive. Mum's the word. I don't want your Mother to hear a word about this. If I do buy one I want it to be a big surprise for her.'

'I won't say a word.'

'She loves surprises and it's been a long time since she had one. Thank you James,' his dad said.

'Thank you dad for all the good advice and by the way, the best of luck with the car if you do buy it. That's it then I'm off to Dublin next week.'

He was sorry he had said anything about his driving. He loved his Dad, and hoped he hadn't hurt his feelings. He wouldn't hurt him for the world. The only thing he had to do now was tell Lydia he would be leaving next week. He wasn't sure how she would like this news but like it or not he was going. His Dad was right, this wedding was going to be a big affair. He would be better out of the way. A break from Lydia would be a good thing, when she was so busy.

Chapter 29

Two weeks later Lydia called up to the workroom and asked Ethel if she would come to Dublin with her, their mum and the girls to buy the material for all the dresses.

'Yes, of course. I'll be delighted to come.' Ethel said.

Lydia told her, 'The girls have a day off school next Monday. Would that suit you?'

'Perfect.' Ethel said.

'That's great! Thanks a million,' Lydia said.

Off she went as if Ethel was her best friend.

When she was gone Beatrice looked at Ethel and said, 'I don't know how you could be so nice to her after the way she has treated you and George.'

'It was difficult, but for Mum's sake I had to be nice. At last she has made some effort and now we can get something started. Thank God she wants Mum to come with us, her last daughter to get married. It would have been a shame if she kept behaving the way she has been for so long. Mum will love that day out. She still talks about the planning that went on before our weddings all those years ago.'

Both families were well liked. Everyone in the village was looking forward to this wedding. A lot of traders in the village would benefit from it also. Lydia had ordered her cake from the new bakery. Made like a royal crown. Beautifully decorated with angels and flowers, all edible. The girl in the bakery had been trained in a catering college in London and as this was her first order of a wedding cake it was going to be spectacular. As well as that, this was a very important order. It was going to be a huge wedding and there were lots of engaged couples invited. They might like what they see and want their cakes made by her. Mrs. Solmonos was going to give her advice on the food. She was a very good cook and had great ideas. She was bringing along some dishes that were popular at Jewish weddings in Russia. She knew what the guests liked, and they would have lots of their favourite food. She was planning on making a special starter for the bride and groom. They both loved it and it was going to be a real surprise for them only. They would not be expecting that.

Mr. Solomons had kept matzahs from Passover as a treat for the rest of the guests.

As it was a summer wedding, everything was going to be served cold. That made it so much easier for everybody. The wedding ceremony was at 11 o'clock and breakfast would follow. Then the music would start. In the afternoon when the bride and groom left, older guests might start to leave. But, not at this wedding, it would go as long as there was food to be eaten and drink to be drunk. This was the wedding of the year. Everybody in the village would be at the wedding at some part of the day. Some of the invited guests might leave after the bride and groom left. Then it would be a free for all. Anybody who had a fiddle, recorder, flute or accordion would bring it along. Singers would sing, dancers would dance and a great time would be had by everybody. It would be up to George at what time he would close the hall. It would not be before midnight, that was for sure.

Chapter 30

James was three weeks in Dublin when his Mum and Dad decided to go and visit him on a Saturday. James met them at the station. They went straight to the garage where his dad had arranged to have a test drive in a car. The car had already been bought by his dad months ago, but James and his Mum didn't know that. The salesman knew the secret and put on a great pretence of trying to sell the car to Mr. Taylor. The salesman drove them round the city. James had to admit it was a lovely car. Mrs. Taylor was delighted with herself. She hoped Patrick would buy it. She was getting very nervous going out with him in the pony and trap. The luxury of having a roof over your head and doors on each side was very nice. She could get very used to this. When they arrived back at the garage, the salesman asked if they had enjoyed the trip.

They all agreed they like it very much. The salesman asked if he could put Mr. Taylor's name on the order form for one.

'Dad,' James said, 'You should think a bit more about it.'

'Maybe I will but I'll take all the details you have on it.'

He thanked the man for the drive and said, 'You will be hearing from me. Not for a while, we have to get this fellow married first. Then we will count our money and see where we stand.'

They shook hands and left.

'Well,' the dad asked James, 'What did you think of that?'

'Oh, very nice and it looked very easy to drive.'

'I know I've driven a tractor that was harder than that to

drive. I think I could drive that car without any lessons. What do you make of that Ann?'

'To be honest Patrick, I know I could drive that car myself without any lessons.'

'Should I buy it then?'

'Of course you should. I would be thrilled driving around Wicklow in that car especially if it was raining.'

'Well, I'm so glad you like it. I'll do my accounts when we get home and see if we can afford it,' he said.

They left the garage and went to meet Michael and his girlfriend in a hotel near the station. They told him the lovely time they had driving around Dublin.

James said 'Dad is thinking of buying a motorcar.'

When Michael asked him if that was true Patrick answered, 'Oh I'm not sure, maybe next year.'

'I thought you were going to buy one now. With this big wedding coming up.'

'I'm not made of money you know.'

'Dad, if you really want to buy it you should. You never buy anything for yourself. You and Mum are always doing and buying for everybody. I'm delighted to hear you talking about something you would like for both of you.'

'That's great son, that you feel that way. I thought you were going to say I was mad. You've made my day. Thank you.'

Michael stood up and said, 'This calls for a drink and the drinks are on me!'

They lifted their glasses to their parents and wished them luck with their decision. The Dad could not believe the way they were all for him to buy the car. He thought they would be against it. He was so happy he had the approval of two of his sons and his wife. What more could he ask? In a week's time that exact motorcar would be at their front door. He felt a bit of a sneak not telling them he had already bought it. He wanted to have it in time for the wedding. Lydia would be over the moon going to the church in a real motorcar. He hoped he had done the right thing.

On the way home on the train he didn't said another word about the car. He was afraid he might let it slip that they had been driving around in *his* car. Ann asked him a few times if he was tired as he was so quiet.

He said, 'Dublin wears you out a bit, that's all that's wrong with me.'

'It was a great day!' Ann said.

'It's good that George is collecting us at the station.'

He fully agreed with her. When they arrived George was waiting. He was a careful driver and had them home in less than an hour.

Chapter 31

The day the girls went to Dublin worked out very well. Ethel was delighted with the material Lydia decided on for the wedding Dress. She knew it would be very easy to work with. The same with the bridesmaids' dresses. Lydia allowed them to decide on the material but she decided on the colour. A beautiful shade of apricot. Lydia wanted a very plain dress with just a lace centre panel. She was wearing a veil of French lace which she had sent from Paris. She bought enough lace to have the front panel of the dress matching. Lydia was very cute. She didn't want a real fancy dress, she wanted to look wonderful from the back as well as the front. The veil was wide enough to come right around her with plenty of material to spare and a four foot train. So when she stood with the veil falling round her you got the impression the whole dress was made of lace. She bought a beautiful crown, just one inch high and she was going to look like a princess. Ethel and Beatrice would make simple little head pieces for the bridesmaids with the same material as their dresses. They were not going to take anything from the bride. With all the material bought they had plenty of time to have a nice meal. Then mosey around the shops for any bits they wanted before having to leave for the train. Ethel and her mother couldn't believe how Lydia was so pleasant and easy to get on with the whole day. Then again, she could have been putting on a show for the girls that would soon be her sisters-in-law. Whatever it was, things couldn't have gone better.

When James came home from Dublin Lydia was in

much better form. She never stopped talking about the wedding. Everything was so different and her mother and father were in great form. It was a pity that things had been so unpleasant for so long. But the day in Dublin had gone so well at least now they could make the most of the short time that was left before the wedding day. It was amazing the difference that James made being home. He was such an easy going lad and just got things done as he was asked. At last all the dresses and all the arrangements were made. A couple of days left until the big day.

Chapter 32

Everybody was up at dawn. The sun was only peeping out, but as it was rising it felt that it was surely going to be a very hot day. The bride was very cool and calm. She went off and had her hair done. When she came home she did her own makeup, which she did not use much of at any time. When she got dressed and put her veil and crown on. She was so beautiful. She was ready when James' father called to collect her and her father. Everybody was in the church when they arrived. She walked up the aisle on her dad's arm looking fantastic. But her heart was breaking, because of the secret she had kept from him. She didn't know how she was keeping the tears from falling. When he gave her to James she felt a bit better, she didn't cry. George welcomed them with warm handshakes. That made her relax. The service and marriage vows didn't take very long. Now they had to come out and face the whole village.

This was what Lydia liked, but James hated attention and tried to avoid it but people were coming at him from everywhere. He was being hugged and kissed by so many strangers. It went on for ages. If he had thought it was going to be like this he would have got married in Dublin with just the two families. He was in shock, he thought weddings were all about the bride. Eventually, the people thinned out and they got to the hall. He sat down and waited for Lydia to continue what she was doing. When she sat down it was half past one. They were starving. Mrs. Solomons gave them their surprise starters and they were thrilled with them. Then they served the starters of the six course meal to everybody. All the food was very nice, and some of it very unusual. It was nearly half past five before the meal was finished. The bride and groom had a couple of dances and then they left. They were staying the night in the Shelbourne Hotel in Dublin and flying to London the next day.

After they left, the party really got started. It went on all night. There wasn't a human to be seen in the village the next day. The heat might have gotten to some of them. Maybe it was that Russian drink that Mr. Solomons kept pouring out so freely. It tasted gorgeous but it was very strong and the locals loved it. Whatever it was, some of those that drank it will not be seen for some time to come. The wedding was the best ever in the village and would never be forgotten.

Chapter 33

All the heavy building work was nearly finished in the village. At least the roof was on all of the buildings. A lot of work was still to be done on the inside. It was essential to get the roof on before the winter, when rain was guaranteed to fall every day. The shops that were finished had made a great difference. It was hard to remember how the old village looked and how difficult it was to have to travel for things that could now be bought in the village. A lot of young men that would have left had stayed. The result was there were now more engaged couples, neighbours' children marrying each other.

Thelma was not engaged, she was going steady and Ethel expected her to be getting the ring soon. Her boyfriend was a very nice guy and they made a lovely couple. Thelma who was great at pattern making and was fantastic at sewing and had just finished her apprenticeship. From next week her wages would increase greatly. The sisters always paid her well, but now she was qualified and would have to be paid as a senior. They were delighted she had stayed with them for the four years and hoped she would stay on working for them. They would give her more than she would earn anywhere else to hold onto her. She was a great worker and they needed her. The business had gone from strength to strength and now they could take on a new beginner to train. They did not want to expand any further. Now with Thelma as good as Ethel herself it made life easier for her. She had more time to look after the little people, as she had started calling them, and spend less time in the workroom. She would call in every day to see how things were going and have a few words with the girls, while the little people had a nap. Minding three children was not easy, but now they were older, able to walk and talk, it was more interesting. They were very good most of the time, and she had great fun with them. She thought at times Desmond was a bit rough with the girls and a bit vicious. She said nothing to George. After all he was a boy and two against one was hard for him at times. He got away with a lot. One day he really lost his temper for some reason that Ethel could not remember. But she knew it was something simple. He got so upset so quickly. She thought this was not just a temper tantrum at first. Then as it went on longer she got a real fright, this was different. He was kicking her, pulling her hair and screaming like she never heard before. She was terrified of him. No matter what she did, she could not control him. The girls were terrified of him. He didn't touch them, and now all three were crying. She hoped the girls in the workroom might hear the fuss and come and help. But with the noise of the machines they did not hear anything. Now she herself was crying and did not know what to do. In answer to prayer she heard the key in the hall door and, thank God, it was George. He could not believe what was going on. He took Desmond away from her and brought him outside. It took a while, but eventually he calmed down. The girls stopped crying once he was gone. Ethel could not remember what happened to cause this trauma. She got such a fright, she was in shock. Now, to be honest she thought Desmond was getting very upset for very little lately, but she had thought nothing of it. She had reared three boys and at times they were difficult. But nothing like this had ever happened. Now she would keep a diary and check if this ever happened again. She hoped and prayed it would never happen. She had never seen anything like it in her life. When Desmond stopped crying and George came in with him. He was perfectly normal.

'What happened?' he asked, 'to get him so upset?'

'I can't remember if it was something simple. I got such a fright I couldn't or didn't act quickly enough. It was out of hand in a flash. I tried to call for help nobody heard, and I panicked. Thank God you came when you did.'

George said, 'I only walked up and down with him whispering in his ear and he calmed down slowly.'

'Yes, George,' she said. 'But when he lost it, and the girls got such a fright, I couldn't handle it.'

'Oh!' George said. 'I'm not saying you are at fault, but it was not a normal reaction to whatever happened. It's a pity you can't remember so we won't let it happen again. We will have to keep a record of this behaviour. I feel there might be some little thing wrong with him.'

'Don't say that George, it would break my heart if there was anything wrong with him. I hope it was just a blip and it never happens again. He is normally such a loving child and likes being hugged and kissed. He seemed to hate me today, whatever happened, I was not his friend. It hurt me so much that I couldn't control him.'

'Stop beating yourself up. You did your best. Nobody could have control over a situation like what I saw when I came in. Look at him now you would not believe he is the same child.'

The three children played away as if nothing had happened. Ethel asked George to keep an eye on them for a while. She

196

had to go outside to get fresh air, to collect herself before the boys came home from school. When the boys came home there was the usual banter. They had a good day and plenty to say, funny and silly things. The family seemed to be normal again. Ethel was secretly still trying to recall what had upset Desmond so much. She couldn't let it go. It left her very nervous. If he hurt or injured Sofia, Mrs. Solomons would go mad. She would tell nobody including Beatrice. They would be starting school in a year or so and she would have more free time to do what she wanted. If she found she could not cope until then she would get some paid help. She hoped that wouldn't happen. She was so happy being a mum again and wanted to prove she could do it. She adored all three babies and was delighted they all got on so well together. All three of them would be in the same class when they started school. Desmond would start making friends with boys and the girls would have each other and make more friends. She was looking forward to that. She loved when the house was full of young people. Having a girl was so different. They played quietly with dolls and other toys. The boys ran riot round the field, the garden and the house. They never broke a flower, or walked on a vegetable, however. George had left plenty of room for them to play. They knew better than to break anything. George was very nice, but if you misbehaved in the garden you were never allowed in there again. All the kids in the area loved playing there. So they were always very well behaved and had a great time.

When George and Ethel were in bed that night, Ethel asked him what he thought might be wrong with Desmond? 'I don't know but it was very strange for him to be so upset.

Should we bring him to the doctor?'

'No, not at the moment but we will keep a close eye on him and see if there is anything else happening that we are missing. The Doctor would think we are mad if we brought him for having one fit, tantrum, bold episode, whatever it was.'

'Try to get some sleep and we will deal with it whatever it is.'

Ethel never slept a wink. She told George she did. When the boys went to school and the little people were fed, dressed and ready to play she asked Beatrice if she could spare a half day to look after them. She needed to sleep as she was awake all night. She told her George would be home at twelve thirty and not to let her sleep longer than twelve twenty. She told him this morning she had a good sleep and she did not want him to think there was something wrong with her.

Beatrice said, 'There must be something wrong if you are not sleeping. You don't sleep when you are worried. Come on Ethel what's going on?'

'No, there is nothing going on. Yesterday was a bit hectic and I'm so tired. Please Beatrice if you are very busy ask one of the others. I have to go back to bed.'

'Oh no! I will do it, but I will find out what it is bothering you some time!'

Ethel went back to bed. She slept until Beatrice woke her. She knew there had been no panic and everybody was happy. Beatrice went out to the workroom and when George came home Ethel was busy making lunch. The rest of the day was normal. Everything was normal for months. Ethel managed well and didn't have to get help with the children, in fact, she forgot about the terrible day. She wasn't worried about Desmond anymore. The three children were starting school in a couple of weeks. Philip and Trevor wanted to bring them, their parents said no. Maybe after the summer holidays they could. They would only be going for a few days before the holidays to settle in.

Ethel and Mrs. Solomons wanted to bring them. The three little ones were so excited they ran into the school. No tears and the teacher thought this was a good start. The mothers could not believe it. They might as well allow the boys to bring them. They hoped when they came to collect them they would be as happy as they were going in. They needn't have worried there were no problems. The rest of the week went well and then they got their holidays. The boys were so glad it was holiday time. They were promised trips to Dublin and Cork. Two weeks with the family on holidays in Wexford by the sea, which they loved. Swimming every day, playing with the twins and making sand castles. The sun was always shining in Wexford. They hated going home after this holiday. Away from the sea it was always raining in their village in Wicklow. The only thing they could do there was to help out in the shop and get paid. The money was good, but they would give anything to live near the sea. They were lucky to get a holiday by the sea and they knew it. They did appreciate it but they would have loved to have stayed in Wexford the whole summer.

However, the holidays went very quickly and it was back to school time again. Now they were allowed to bring the twins with them. This was great because the twins loved the boys. They were very good and well behaved with them and the boys were delighted with all the attention they got from everybody. They were the only family with young twins in the village and it was a great novelty. The twins were so beautiful, with their big ebony eyes and black hair. If you put a dress on Desmond he would have passed for a girl. It was unreal that they were so alike. It was just as well they were not two girls. You would never have known the difference. As they got older they became more and more like their father and that was a big worry. The people in the village were wise and not easily fooled. It would only take one person to pass a comment about them being like Lydia's husband to Mr. Cramp and if anyone thought there was any truth in a rumour like that it would kill him.

Chapter 34

James and Lydia were five years married now. James had got a job as a principal in a nice school on the south side of Dublin. He loved it and got on well with all his staff. He was very young for such a high profile job. He had been a great teacher and never expected to get this job. When he answered the advertisement he never thought he would be called for an interview. At the first interview, he felt they liked him but they thought he was a bit young. When he was called for a second interview he couldn't believe it. This interview went very well, but he was afraid to get excited in case he didn't get the job. A couple of weeks later he got the good news that he was successful and the job was his. Lydia had got a great job in the department store, Arnotts, which she got after a friend had recommended her. Because at that time in Ireland when a girl got married she had to leave work. She was the only married woman working in Arnotts. She was very popular, as she was a good worker and was well able to put on the charm. She was a buyer for children's wear. That was right up her street. She could buy dresses from her sisters, and they put the Arnotts label on them so nobody knew they were made by them. They would make one of each design and if a dress did not sell quickly enough she would return it. This drove the sisters mad. They would have to take the label off and sell it in their parents' shop for less than Arnotts paid. They never said anything to her for doing this. Because it was good for Lydia. It looked like she always made the right decision when buying. At the end of any season she never had a dress left that didn't sell. The sisters discovered at the end of the year Arnotts had bought a lot from them thanks to Lydia. Arnotts paid well and they bought the best materials. Lydia was very good at judging best sellers. She had a wonderful way of buying as far as little girl's clothes were concerned. As a result, her wages were fantastic.

She had everything in the world she wanted. Except the thing she most longed for was a baby. This was getting to them but they never said anything to anybody. Lydia pretended she loved her work so much she did not want a baby. Having a baby would mean giving up work. That was the only thing in the world she wanted to happen, but there was nothing she could do about it. Lydia always got what she wanted, and she thought this was something that would just happen as soon as they were married. The very first time she and James made love before they married she was pregnant, not with one baby but with two. After four years she began to worry, and now another year has passed. Now they had stopped even talking about babies. Every day she wished she had never parted with the twins. Now they are at school. The years had gone so quickly and they were beautiful little people. She never wanted to go back home again. She couldn't bear to watch Ethel and her family so happy with her children. Letting her have them was the biggest mistake she had ever made, and she would pay for it for the rest of her life. James never wanted to give them away. He would have told the truth from the beginning. So what if the neighbours didn't like it? There were very few of them that could say a word. Plenty of their daughters disappeared from time to time and not a word about them. Lydia knew she was the one that insisted it be kept secret, and she always accepted the blame. James never blamed her. He never talked about it, but Lydia couldn't let it go.

He did everything in his power to keep her from going on about it. No matter what he did she would stop for a time then she would start again. He was beginning to get fed up with it and stayed in school longer and longer. She never seemed to mind how late he came in and never asked what his day was like or why he was late. The only thing he felt that was going well was that when they made love she was as beautiful as ever, and he knew she loved him. If only once it resulted in a pregnancy life would be perfect. He felt so sorry for her, he would have loved to have had more children, but he didn't dwell on it like she did. Maybe it was different for a woman he didn't know. Lately, he had turned his mind to different things like motorcars. There was a lot more on the road now in Dublin. They were still very expensive. With both of them working, earning plenty of money, and lots of savings, he was seriously thinking of buying one. He knew how much Lydia loved arriving at the church in his Dad's car. He never thought he would ever be able to afford one. He wasn't going to say anything to her about it. He would buy it as a birthday present and surprise her. If that didn't do the trick nothing would. He made all the enquiries and eventually settled on buying one in the same garage as his dad. He had to wait for a while, because he wanted it in yellow, Lydia's favourite colour. There was one in the showroom, a beautiful red. He liked that but he decided to wait for the yellow one. It was getting near to her birthday and he went to find out about the car and there it was, looking beautiful and he loved the colour. He left it in the garage until the day of her birthday. On that day the post had come and there was no card from him. That was deliberate. He wanted her to think that he had forgotten. When she opened the hall door, she thought it was a joke.

There was the car with a big yellow bow tied across it and a big card saying, 'Happy Birthday Darling Lydia.'

She ran back into the house crying. He thought she didn't like it, but they were tears of joy. She loved it. She didn't go to work. She was so excited. She came back out and asked if she could sit in it.

He said, 'It's yours, you can do what you like.'

She sat in the driver seat and she said, 'It's perfect. Imagine I will be the only woman in Dublin driving my own car.'

He never thought she would want to drive it. He thought it would be hers in name only and he would be doing the driving. Now he realised he made a mistake. He would never be allowed to drive this car. It was Lydia's car and nobody would ever get to drive it. He had forgotten how possessive she was about her things. What a fool! His brothers would want to go driving in it. He could do nothing about it now. Lydia was a quick learner and James knew she would be driving in a very short time. You didn't have to do a driving rest at that time in Ireland. Anybody could buy a licence and drive anywhere they liked. Within a month Lydia had her licence and lessons from James sitting beside her telling her what to do. She couldn't wait to get that car on the road. He knew she would be a good driver, but she still needed practical lessons. She sat in the car every chance she got. She read everything she could about it. She knew every part of the engine by its proper name. She said she could take it apart and put it back together again. He believed her, but he told her not to do that. She thought she was God. James was regretting buying it. He told her if she drove without getting proper lessons he would be very annoyed. Lydia had decided that was exactly what she was going to do. She took two days off from work. She marked the ground at the two front wheels and at the back wheels. In case James realised it had been moved. She then started to move the car slowly in the garden back and forth. It was very simple. Each time she went a bit further forward and back. When she was finished she put it back right on the marks. She was so excited she knew she was a natural at this driving game. Tomorrow, she was going to take it out on the road. When James came home she was in the kitchen.

'What are you doing home so early?' he asked.

She was so excited about the car she forgot she hadn't gone to work.

'Oh,' she said, 'I left a bit early.'

James put no pass on it; he believed her. They had a nice meal and then she wanted him to get into the car with her again.

He said, 'Lydia just let me drive you round the block. I want to get a feel of how she goes. After one go you can drive it. If you don't let me that car is not leaving the garden except to go back to the garage where I bought it.'

She knew he was serious so against all her principles she gave in. He backed out of the garden and it was so comfortable he loved it. After one round she saw how much he loved it so she gave him another go.

'Now,' she said, 'It's my turn.'

She took the wheel as if she had been driving all her life. He couldn't believe it.

'Now,' she said, Show me how to reverse.'

He got back into the driving seat and showed her. Same again, like she had done it before. He had to admit she was a natural. Once she made up her mind to do something she excelled at it. Driving was going to be no different. She drove the car back to the house and straight through the gates perfectly. He nearly died. The gates were wide enough but he never expected that. Lydia was driving now and nothing was going to stop her. He told her she was a very good driver. He asked her if she was ever going to allow him to drive.

She said, 'Only if you don't tell anybody. You know what I'm like about my things. When we are going on long journeys I'll drive away from the house. When we get on the country road I'll let you drive some of the way.'

'That's very nice of you, thanks a million,' he said.

'I knew you would like that.'

'Yes, I would like it. Driving is a man's job. I feel a bit silly sitting beside a woman driving. I thought when I bought it you would only drive when you were on your own, or out with friends.'

'Well, I thought it was my car so I would be the driver all the time. OK then it's not my car, it's for both of us,' she said.

He didn't answer her. Nothing was easy with Lydia, he knew exactly what was going to happen. She would give the car back and say she didn't want to share a present or buy one of her own when she had enough money. That would take a long, long time and he knew she would never wait that long. So he made up his mind never to drive the car. He only travelled with her when they were going home to Wicklow. If they were invited to a friend's house or a party he would sit beside her and pretend he was enjoying the trip. He never thought she would behave like this. He thought he would be driving to all these places. Not sitting in the passenger seat. The car was supposed to bring them closer together, not cause such conflict between them. When all his brothers wanted to have a go at driving he was just going to say,

'You have to ask Lydia. It's her car not mine.'

They would laugh and think he was joking. He knew then she would give the keys to them and say, 'I'll go with you.'

They wanted to go out on their own for a drive but she would never allow that. They thought this a bit strange, but they never said anything. They thought James would say something to her about letting them go on their own but he didn't get involved. She knew James would never say a word to them about being privileged, allowed to have a go or say anything to let her down. She was so nice when she wanted to be. She could fool everybody with her charm. Sometimes he wondered if there was something wrong with her mind. Yet when she sat behind the wheel of the car, dressed up to the nines, she looked like a millionairess and acted like one. She was a fantastic driver and she knew it. She was only woman in Dublin driving her own car at that time. In fact, it was a most unusual sight to see a woman driving in any part of the country. That suited her very well. She was always a boaster and a show-off, having a car like this was the best thing she had to boast about. Fellows who couldn't afford a car stood in wonder looking at her. When she drove down the main street of Dublin, Sackville St., as O'Connell Street used to be called, the policeman on traffic duty held the traffic up longer on her side to make sure his eyes were not fooling him. *It was a woman driving, and she was a good driver.* The car and Lydia became known all over Ireland. Because she loved driving long distances. James did not always go with her as he felt uncomfortable sitting in the passenger seat. Especially when they drove home. He hated arriving at his parents' house with Lydia driving. He felt stupid. His father was a real man's man and if he thought James was not allowed to drive when they went out together, he would give him a hard time. Not only that, his brothers would never let him live it down if they knew he was not allowed to drive. He was getting fed up with the situation and made his decision to put a stop to it. The next time they were going home he was driving and if any of his brothers asked if they could have a go he was going to hand them the keys. Lydia would get the shock of her life, but he knew she would say nothing because all his family loved her and she would not let herself down by causing a fuss. It was about time he put an end to this codology. When you are married you are supposed to share everything. Lydia never shared anything, and he never minded before. But having only one car, and it was a luxury to have, she should have been happy to share it the odd time and allow him to drive. He never asked to take it out on his own. After all it was her car, but when they were together he loved to be in the driving seat. Lydia could be very mean with him at times. Then she could be very generous. She was hard to live with, and to understand sometimes. She was never short of people willing to go with her for a drive as there was so little traffic on the roads. She was very good company and her friends loved these trips. James thought she would get tired of doing this when she had the car for a while and the novelty had worn off, but she was still as excited as the first day she got it. She called it Betsy and she referred to it as if it was a real person. If she was going somewhere on her own, she would say to James, 'Oh, it's only the two of us going.'

He would forget sometimes and ask, 'You and who?'

She would look at him as if he had two heads and say, 'Me and Betsy of course.'

He wasn't happy about that. He never thought she would drop everything they were interested in as a couple and do nothing but drive. Buying the car as a present for Lydia was the biggest mistake he made in his life. James loved Lydia so much he forgave her every time she disappointed him. He had given into her every whim, now he was sick of it. This was the one time he was going to keep a promise he made to himself and do exactly as he said he was going to do and not go back on his word. He felt mean planning to be nasty. It was not in his nature. Lately she was stepping over the line too often. He felt he was being walked on. He didn't like the way things were going. It had to stop. The difference he felt when he went into work, people nearly bowed to him. He didn't want that at home but he did want to be respected. That was the big thing that was missing at home. He was sad about it. There was no need for it. He wished they could be as happy as they were when they bought this house. They both loved it, and he thought he would burst with happiness. Life was just fantastic. He felt like the luckiest man in the world. He could not believe things could have gone so wrong. He was convinced that Lydia had a serious mental illness. What could he do about it? Maybe it was him who had the problem. He would go to the doctor and have himself checked out. He could not mention mental illness to Lydia. She would go off the rails completely. If the doctor found nothing wrong with him, then he would live as best he could with Lydia and make the most of her good days. Her good days could be fantastic, he just wished there were more of them. He missed going to visit the couples they were friends with for years. He missed visiting his brother Michael who had married Linda. The four of them had great nights in both houses. Now when he invited them over to his house, just before they came Lydia would announce she was going for a drive. She could be gone for ages, and he'd get embarrassed trying to make excuses. When Michael invited him and Lydia over, she might go, be very pleasant and be quite normal. The next time they were there she could be so rude out of the blue, James would suggest leaving early. She might leave quietly or she might not. James never knew what to expect. So they stopped going. It was now at the stage James was going to have to tell Michael something was wrong with Lydia. When was he going to do that he asked himself, and what would he say? He was broken-hearted. She was still holding down her job, as far as he knew. She was going out with her friends. She kept the car immaculate as always, and referred to it as her baby. James thought if she was still regretting not having a baby, would he suggest adopting one? Where would he go first, and what would he say? He didn't know what to do. How do you tell somebody you think they are mad? Especially someone you love so much? He sat asking himself all these questions. He put his head in his hands and cried and cried. It was getting near ten o'clock and Lydia would be home soon. She never stayed out later than that. You could set your watch by her. No matter who she was out with, she was home by ten. He better tidy himself up before she came in and wanted to know what was wrong with him. He always waited up for her. Sometimes she would be in great form and they might stay up for ages talking. Tonight he was not in the mood of staying up. He wanted to be anywhere but here when she came in. He would go to bed and pretend to be asleep when she came in. He was very upset and did not want anything to do with her. He went to bed and fell asleep immediately. He woke about midnight and she was not in bed. He was a bit confused and not sure where he was. He got out of bed and looked out the window. No car in the garden, it was dark. He looked at his watch twelve fifteen. After midnight? It couldn't be. He put on his gown and went down to the kitchen where there was a clock that never went wrong. It was now seventeen minutes past midnight. The clock was right. God where was she? He had enough on his plate without this. What could he do but wait? Shortly after one o clock, the doorbell rang. Two police men were standing there when he opened the door. He fell backwards into the hall. The police stepped in and closed the door. James was out cold. They looked after him and made him comfortable. When he came to, they told him about Lydia. She was badly injured but she was alive. She was in the Meath Hospital. They could take him there but he would not be allowed to see her. She was having emergency surgery and it could be some time before it would get to see her. He said he wanted to go now. They waited for him to dress and they left for the hospital. When they got there were absolute panic stations. A very nice nurse took him to a small private room. She explained some of the details of what was happening with Lydia in the operating theatre. She made light of it and said that he would be allowed to rest there and to get some sleep if he could. He sat in the chair staring at the wall not able to take in what had happened. He must have fallen asleep because now it was day time. He looked out the door and the place was so quiet. He walked down a corridor and saw

211

nobody. He did not know what part of the hospital he was in. He stopped at a window and when he looked out he realised he was not on the second floor. He saw a stairway and walked down. There was a nurse sitting at a desk and he asked her if she knew anything about a patient who was brought in last night after an accident. She couldn't answer his questions but she told him where to go and who to ask for. He did what he was told and found the person he was looking for. She brought him into another room and told him to wait there. She came back with another nurse and a surgeon and they introduced themselves. James asked if he could see his wife?

The surgeon said, 'Yes, but we are so sorry she didn't make it.'

James screamed, 'What? Are you telling me she is dead?'

'We are so sorry. We did our best but she was very weak. She had lost a lot of blood and there was nothing more we could do for her. This has been quite a shock to you. Take all the time you need, and then you can come and see her.'

'I want to see her now.'

'That's fine,' said the surgeon and they went to see the body.

James fell apart. He held her hands, he touched her hair. He kissed her lips. The nurses stood one each side of him and held onto him. He started to cry. He was distraught. He had no control of any of his emotions. The nurses felt so sorry for him. He was like a child crying over his mother, not a husband crying over a wife. Nurses are well used to sadness, but this was different. He was so alone. They asked if there was somebody they could get in touch with who could come and be with him. He said his brother didn't live very far. They took his address and said they would have him there in a while. James would not leave Lydia. The nurse got him a chair and he sat down. He couldn't take his eyes off Lydia. He sat there like that until Michael and Linda came. They were as upset as he was, but at least he wasn't on his own now.

Michael asked what happened? Where? When? How? All the questions James never thought of asking. He said they told him nothing and he never thought of asking. He didn't think she was going to die. When she was in surgery they told him he could see her when they were finished. He heard no more until now and she was dead.

Michael said, 'We can ask all those questions later. There is a lot to be done now. When you are ready, come home with us, and we'll make a start letting her parents know first.'

James said he would call Lydia's parents. They could tell the sisters and George could tell James' parents. Michael knew he would be better at this kind of thing than James and told him that was all that needed to be told for now. Michael told James to try and get some sleep. He could sleep in their house and then they would go back to the hospital and ask what had to be done next. Michael thought a small private funeral would be best to have and he discussed this with Linda. She agreed with him. Because the two families had so many friends and relations, Linda thought a funeral in Dublin would solve the problem.

Michael said, 'No, James would never have that. We will have a private funeral in the village. The church is very small and people will respect the wishes of the families. George is the minister so whatever he decides, that's what will be done. We won't mention any of this to James. He will have his own ideas and we'll have no say in it. Mr. and Mrs. Taylor and Lydia's parents might drive up to support James and go to see Lydia. It's all ifs and buts now we will have to wait and see. It would be great if they came and stayed the night with James. He has plenty of room for all of them and it would be good for all of them to be together at this time.'

James did sleep in Michael's house for an hour. When he woke up he said he would go home and tidy himself up, shave and wash and then meet them at the hospital in about three hours. When James opened the hall door, it dawned on him he would never have Lydia here again. He would never get over this. He would never live here on his own. He couldn't think what he was going to do. He got ready to go to the hospital. When he came down the stairs and went into the front room, there was his father's car coming in the gate. He could not believe it. He was so delighted to see them, and Lydia's parents with them. When he opened the door his mother wrapped her arms round him and cried into his chest. That set him off. Then Lydia's mother did the same. Now three of them were crying. The two fathers put their arms round the mothers and it was a big circle of five adults letting their feelings out at the same time. When they let go of each other, they sat down and started talking about what had to be done now. Lydia's parents wanted to go to the hospital first thing.

James said, 'Yes, that's the first thing we will do. Michael and Linda will be there. They will be pleased to see you made it to Dublin today.'

John said, 'We've closed the shop for a week at least. We'll stay as long as you want us James, if that's any help to you.'

'That would be great,' James said. 'I don't know anything about where to start in a case like this.'

'As far as I know when the hospital releases the body, the funeral directors will arrange everything,' John said. 'We can do nothing until then. George, Ethel and Beatrice will be coming up tomorrow. George will talk to funeral directors, and as he is the minister of the Church he can arrange times and whatever he has to do with them. That will take a lot of pressure off everybody.'

Mrs. Cramp said, 'I don't know what they do in Dublin when there is a funeral. But this is not going to be the usual funeral when we get home. I don't know how you feel James, but we would like it to be private just the two families. We would never be able for all the people that will come. The church would never hold the crowd. The graveyard being beside it will be a help. That would hold plenty of people. Then after the service we will go back to the rooms over the shop, have a meal, and leave it at that. The locals will understand. There will be no Irish wake, in such tragic circumstances as these.'

James said, 'Whatever you want you will have.'

Mrs. Cramp never expected James to disagree with them. He was always such a gentleman, even in the height of his sorrow. Her heart was breaking for him. She knew he would never forgive himself for buying the car for her. He was going to need a lot of looking after when all the fuss was over. His parents were great, and would make sure he was coping OK. She would have a long chat with him when all this was over. He was in no way responsible for what happened. He bought the car in good faith. He must remember all the great times Lydia had in it. How happy she was driving around in it. All the places she went to, from one end of the country to the other. Although she got the car years after her father-in-law, there were a lot more miles covered on hers. The car had made her the happiest she had ever been. They were very thankful to him for buying it at the time. Nobody knows what the future is going to bring. If we did we would never do anything, buy anything or go anywhere. What kind of a life would that be? No, James was not to beat himself up for doing the right thing at the time he did. Mrs. Cramp knew how upset Lydia was at that time. When she was coming up and down so often buying from her sisters. She always called into the shop and poured out her heart to her mother, saying how sorry she was for not telling the truth about the twins. She thought God was punishing her for her sins. But why punish James? He never wanted to give them away. The mother always praised her for not separating them. They were with Ethel's lovely family. George was a great father to them. They would never want for anything. Her Mother would have her smiling before she left. But she worried so much about her. She had no idea what she could do to make her appreciate all she had. She could see her falling apart, and being more depressed every time she came to see them. After she got that car, there was a dramatic change. She was on top of the world. Her mother never saw her feeling down again. She thanked God every day for James, loving Lydia so much. What husband would think of doing such a thing? James never knew how grateful Lydia's mother was to him. That car brought more joy to so many people. She would one day tell him how happy it made her and Lydia's dad. They thought she was on the verge of a nervous breakdown or leaving James. That would have been a huge thing for them to cope with. No, James had done the right thing at the right time, and he should be told by them. He deserved to have peace of mind and get on with his life. Mrs.

Cramp was surprised at herself. Thinking so much about James. Lydia was dead and she had no feelings of sorrow towards her. She just felt numb. All these things were going through her mind while she was looking at her dead daughter. She looked beautiful. There was not a mark on her face from the crash. She wanted to get out of that hospital now. But she couldn't move at first. She had to wait until James decided it was time to go. A minute later Michael and his mother went outside and when they came back, Michael whispered to James.

'We should leave now. Everybody is very tired and hungry.'

James took his mother by the arm and walked her out. The others followed.

Michael said, 'We are all going back to my house. When we've had a meal, James you can drive Dad's car back to your house. Mum said all of them are staying with you. Are you OK with that?'

'Yes, I want them to stay with me.'

"If you want our Mum and Dad to stay with me that's fine.'

'No,' James said, 'I do want them all with me.'

James' parents wanted to stay with him. His house was huge. There was plenty of room for all of them. They all needed a good sleep. Tomorrow would be a very busy day George and the sisters were coming from Wicklow, on the early morning train. The mothers knew people would be calling to sympathise with all of them. There was shopping to be done. Food to be prepared. Sandwiches to be made. Mrs. Cramp knew Ethel would bring tons of food. Mostly prepared by Mrs. Solomons, no doubt. But when they arrived, she would like to have a meal ready for them, they would be hungry. James had not been in touch with anybody from his or Lydia's work. Some of his and her friends had called, and when James wasn't there they left notes. They would most likely call again. It was going to be a very long day. They were not looking forward to it, but it had to happen. The girls coming would be a great help. Especially Beatrice, she was so calm in these situations. Her coolness seemed to rub off on others. People never made a scene around her. One of her looks was enough to frighten the daylights out of you. It always amazed her mother, how she had this effect on people. She wasn't a big person. She was very timid, but she seemed to have a sternness about her, that people either had great respect for her or they were terrified of her. Yet the children loved her and she was very kind to everybody behind all her strictness. The boys were dying to come to Dublin, but one look from Beatrice, told them not to attempt to ask, and they didn't. Trevor was very upset. Ethel was worried about him. He was so sensitive. He had been very upset when his eldest brother left home to join the army. Now his young aunt is gone. It was a lot for him to take in. Ethel would have brought him with them. She was encouraged not to do that. Let him remember her alive. If he saw her in the hospital it might play on his young mind and that would not be fair to him. He was so soft, it upset Ethel. She tried to toughen him up. She was wasting her time.

George always told her, 'Leave him alone, give him enough time and the world will toughen him. He has a kind nature, but he is not stupid. He will survive, don't you worry.'

She would always worry about him no matter what anybody told her. Today was not about Trevor. Today she had to face James. She didn't know how she was going to do it. She felt so sorry for him not having any more children. What a mess it was now. It is such a strain on her to keep from talking about them. Her Dad had never been told the truth of who the children really belonged to. Poor James being the father and having to keep it a secret. Ethel thought even in death Lydia was causing everyone to be full of guilt. None of it is their making. She hoped the funeral could be organised soon. She just wanted it over, and some kind of normality back into their lives. George would do his best to get things moving. But it may not be up to him. He would have to wait until they got permission to have the body removed by the undertakers. Then the service and burial arrangements were up to him. He would make it as beautiful as a funeral can be. First of all, he would give a short sermon, then a little talk about her life. After a few prayers they would go to the burial plot. More prayers and finish. The families would leave. Then the locals could do whatever they wanted to do. George knew they would respect the wishes of the families and go home. There was sadness all over the village. Lydia had been very popular when she worked in the shop. When she got the car she would bring the lads she was friendly with from her youth for a drive around the county. She never allowed any of them to drive it. She would let them sit in the driver seat. That was as far as they got. But even that was a treat with so few cars around at that time. She loved all the attention she got as a result of owning a car. This was why it was so sad that she lost her life in the car she loved so much. She would be missed by a lot of people, and for different reasons. She had lots of good points. Her family knew nothing about it. She often gave poor people credit, and when they left the shop, she would pay for some of it out of her own money and not put it on their bill. This meant a lot to some people that were very poor. A few groceries for nothing was a great help. Lydia enjoyed doing this when her father was not in the shop. So the people thought she was not paying for it. But she never took a biscuit or a sweet without paying, unless she was told she could have it. That was one thing good about her. She firmly believed in not letting her right hand know what her left hand was doing when giving to charity. She was dead now and people could say what they liked about her.

In Ireland there seemed to be an unwritten rule, *never speak ill of the dead*. So nobody ever spoke ill of anybody who died in this village. Only good people lived in this village. But you were only good after you were dead. When the only man in the village who was horrible to his wife and children died, the locals could not believe the distress of the whole family. The talk around the village was now that he is gone they will all have a bit of peace. But no, from the eldest to the youngest, all they did was praise him and say how good he was and how he would be missed. One neighbour had to go into their house many times when he was drunk and stop him from killing his wife. She actually walked out of the church. She could not listen to the praises like how wonderful he was. When everybody knew how horrible he was. It would have been better if they just buried him, and said nothing about him. Everybody for miles around knew what he was. The wife and the family made fools of themselves.

Chapter 35

Lydia's body was brought home. George, Ethel and Beatrice left on the first train. Michael, Linda and Phyllis went on the same train. Mr. Taylor drove the rest of the family half way and James drove the rest of the way. When they got to Rathdrum station, Lydia's funeral hearse was waiting for them. The train had arrived, and all the relatives were there. Mr. Solomons took Ethel, Beatrice and George in his pony and trap. Mr. Brady was waiting to take Michael, Linda, and Phyllis with him. Mr. and Mrs. Taylor were meeting their daughter Mary and the twin boys in the village and taking them with them. Mr. and Mrs. Cramp and James went with Mr. Murphy in his beautiful brand new carriage and big black horse with wonderful black plumes. He had just bought it for weddings and funerals. This was the first time he used it for a funeral. The Cramps were so pleased they had cover over them. They did not want to be in an open pony and trap. They were so upset. The thought of having to go through the town with people looking at them was very daunting. The carriage was ideal for them today. They really appreciated it.

The funeral cortege started to move off slowly. When they got to the village, every shop was closed. The street on both sides of the road was crowded with people. Everybody was crying. Big men who never cried in their lives, were not ashamed to cry. Mr. and Mrs Cramp knew Lydia was popular in the town, but this pouring out of grief for her was beyond all expectations. When they were near the church, the Catholic priest rang the bells of his church in respect for the Taylor family. This was very touching. But Mrs. Cramp found the tolling of the bells very upsetting. The tears she had held in all day began to flow and she sobbed into her chest so as not to upset anybody else. When the carriage reached the church the bells stopped and she got control of herself.

George had promised nice prayers, a short talk, and then the body would be buried in the church grounds. As requested, the local people stayed away until the families left. Then they went to the grave. The flowers were placed on Lydia's grave, and there were so many flowers they put some on every grave. Nothing like this had ever happened before. When the sexton of the church saw it he was so moved. He put a note with the keys when he dropped them into the letter box in the hall door of the shop. When George picked them up and read the note he told Lydia's parents and he said he would take the girls to see it on the way home. The Cramps and The Taylors said they would go and see it tomorrow early in the morning when nobody was around.

The next morning Mr. & Mrs. Taylor and James called for Lydia's parents. When they got to the grave site George was waiting for them. They couldn't believe what they saw. It was a magnificent sight. They all cried. James was hysterical. Nobody could console him. Eventually his mother took him back to the car and while they were on their own, she allowed him to cry as long as it took.

When he stopped he just said, 'Mum, I'll never get over it.'

'No, son,' she said, 'None of us will, but we will learn to live with it."

222

When the others joined them James was OK. They all went back to the shop. Beatrice was waiting for them. They had a nice breakfast and then James and his parents went home. Beatrice stayed all day. She was very upset at the state of her parents. She was afraid they would never open the shop again. That would be awful. Being busy was the only thing that would keep them going. She never mentioned opening the shop. She just suggested to them to put a big book inside the door of the shop for people to sign when they came in. They could write as little or as much as they wanted to. That would save having to talk about Lydia to every customer. They could also put one in the Catholic church as lots of Catholics knew Lydia very well. James had always been involved and was very active in the church. He was very well liked, and sometimes Lydia went to mass with him. She was as well-known there as she was in her own church. They could check with James if he would like that. She knew the priest would have no objections. The Taylor family were very generous to the church and the priest liked James and Lydia. Her parents seemed to agree with her, that was a nice idea. She didn't say a word about opening the shop. They both looked so distraught. She was afraid they would break down, and that would be awful. Her Dad was usually very strong, not this time. Her heart was breaking for them. It was good that Lydia had been living in Dublin. They had gotten used to her not being with them, working in the shop since she was married. Beatrice was tired and had waited for a chance to say she was going. Then George called and asked if she was ready to leave. She asked her parents if they wanted anything done. They said no, she could go and she left with George. Ethel and Aunt Phyllis had a nice supper ready and they sat and talked for ages. There was nothing they could do about their parents. Just wait and see when they mention going back to work. Phyllis was staying for a few more days. They were glad of her company. Things would not get back to any kind of normality until the shop was open again.

On the following Monday, George went down to see the parents as usual and the shop was already open. He was delighted. John was on his own and told him Mary was asleep. He woke early and decided to get up and make a start on trying to get something done. Lying in bed every morning had to stop, it was getting him down. He needed to be working. He missed the locals coming in. If he got through today for a few hours, he would open tomorrow for a full day. People would start coming in again. They could make a start getting back to normal. George told him to keep opening the shop even if Mary didn't come into it for another while. It might take her a bit longer to face the people.

'She will come around when she is ready, don't rush her. Everybody grieves in a different way. There will be good and bad days, just go with the flow. Try and make the most of the good days and on the bad ones don't be afraid to say that you are having a bad day. People are very good at understanding. Losing a child no matter what age they are is very sad. It's against the natural order of life. We don't expect our children to go before us and when they do we find it hard to accept. There is nothing we can do about it. All you can do is remember the good times you had, and you had plenty of them. It won't make up for your loss but it might help a little. Both of you will have plenty of support. Don't be ashamed to ask for help if and when you need it.

You know John, we need you to take care of yourself and Mary for the sake of your other children and all the grandchildren.'

George gave him a big hug and a pat on the back, no more needed to be said. He left the shop and rushed home to tell the good news to Ethel and Beatrice. That would give them the push they needed to get back to work.

Chapter 36

Thelma was getting married and the girls decided to give her a present of her wedding dress and all the dresses for the bridal party. She thought that was a very big present, but they insisted. Ethel would take her to Dublin next week to buy the materials. Aunt Phyllis would go back home with them as she felt she had stayed long enough. If she left now they would get back into the workroom and start being busy again.

They had plenty of work to do but it was so hard to get back into the old routine. Mrs. Solomons and Thelma had kept things going, they were great workers. Beatrice and Ethel found it hard to face them, and tried not to be miserable. Lydia's death had affected them very badly. Being younger than both of them, it wasn't fair that she had died before them.

When Thelma had the material and decided on the pattern she liked, they could start to work on her dress from time to time. If they were feeling down it would give them a boost to be doing something so personal. Having Thelma there to try it on when necessary was good. They had great laughs making her watch her weight. Pretending they might not have enough material if she put on any more pounds. Beatrice would be holding a handful of material behind her back, telling her you have put on more weight, what are you eating? When she promised she had not been eating more than usual. Beatrice would turn her roud and show her in the mirror all the material she had in her hand. Thelma always took the joke well and they all enjoyed the simple fun they had. Thelma was having two bridesmaids, and Doris and Sofia were going to be the flower girls. They hadn't been told yet. They would want their dresses made now and would drive everybody mad trying them on. Two weeks before would be time enough to tell them. It was a few months until the wedding. They were all invited, and were looking forward to it so much. Mr. and Mrs Cramp, Mr. and Mrs. Taylor and James were invited. It would give them something to think about and a nice day out, to get dressed up for. The invitations had not gone out yet. Beatrice told her parents they were on the list and they were going, no excuses. The priest would be paying them a visit and they would never say no to him. A wedding in the parish was exactly what was needed. Because in the evening, anybody who was not invited to breakfast could come along. Bring a musical instrument if they have one and play for hours. This was the most enjoyable time. Everybody did their party piece, without being asked. There was no shortage of volunteers to show off their talents.

Chapter 37

Six weeks after Lydia's death, Ethel got a letter from Arnotts. A new buyer was starting in the children's department. She would like to call on them if that was not too soon. She told Beatrice, and asked her what she should do? Beatrice said, 'Yes, she is to call. They have been very good customers and life must go on. She will not have the privileges that Lydia had. We will advise her and tell her what sold well. None of this bringing back a dress after weeks if it didn't sell. Lydia got away with murder, we are not going down that road again.'

It was nice to have heard from Arnotts again. Ethel would reply to the letter and tell them yes. A new buyer would be most welcome. It was weeks before the new buyer arrived. She introduced herself as Miss McDonald. She didn't give a first name. She was very young and seemed very nervous. She was polite and was willing to listen to the advice the girls gave her. They told her to buy just one of each size. If they sold quickly she could reorder and have whatever she wanted by post the next day. She was happy to hear that. Ethel and Beatrice liked her and made her very welcome. They told her to call in to see them anytime she was in the area. She didn't have to buy, just a social call if she had time. They wanted her to be successful. Although she didn't say it was her first time as a buyer, they knew she hadn't a clue. They thought it was a bit unfair to have her out buying with so little experience. At the end of her visit, she bought three dresses and asked if they didn't sell, could she return them?

Beatrice looked at Ethel, and said, 'No.'

They were not going down that road again. It was not worth the trouble. They were very busy with their private clients, and the dresses were not very important to them now. They liked making them, but the profit was small compared with their private clients. They never thought the dresses would sell the way they did. Making them was great training for Thelma when they were not so busy. Now they were busy, they were becoming a chore more than a novelty. So they were going to give up making them for a while. Maybe stop making them altogether. Ethel and Beatrice never seemed to get back into the business the same as they were before Lydia died. Their whole attitude to life had changed. They thought it would get better as time passed but no, they became less and less interested. Only for Thelma and Mrs Solomons they felt they would give up altogether. They couldn't do that to them, they were so loyal to them through all the ups and downs. They helped out on every occasion when they were in trouble. They would never have gotten through without them. They decided to offer them a share in the business. They both said 'No.'

They were disappointed. But understood they loved the work, but did not want the responsibility. They thanked them for the offer. Left things the way they were, and got back to doing what they were doing. Ethel and Beatrice knew they would have to get their act together soon and they did.

Ethel recovered quicker than Beatrice. That was understandable. As she was the eldest she thought she had to be the strongest all the time. The finishing of the wedding dress was keeping Beatrice going. The rest of the bridal party dresses were finished. The excitement was beginning to build and the time was flying. Thelma was leaving on Friday to have a few days before the big day to put the finishing touches to last minute things. She needed a few days away from work to rest, as she had worked very hard when the sisters were in trouble. She was having a week on holiday in The Isle of Man for the honeymoon. She was really looking forward to it as she had never been out of Ireland before.

The sun was shining beautifully on Thelma's wedding day. She looked stunning. The church was decorated with beautiful flowers and lots of candles. Red carpet from the altar to the front steps of the church. Thelma's Dad was so proud with his beautiful daughter walking up the aisle. Proud to give her away to the gorgeous guy she was about to marry. Everything was perfect. The reception went on until midnight. Everybody had a great time. Even Lydia's and James' families, for the time they were there, did enjoy it more than they expected they would. It gave everybody a little boost. Ethel had a few good weeks after the wedding. Things seemed to be going well. Just as she was feeling so good, Desmond had a breakdown. This time it happened in school and the teacher got an awful fright. It happened so suddenly she didn't know what to do. Poor Doris tried to help to calm him, but he was so strong she couldn't. She ran for the headmaster, and then home for her parents. They ran for the doctor. It was a pity it happened in school. Now everybody in the village would hear about it. They had never told anybody before. It had been a long time since this had happened and they thought it had passed, whatever it was. The doctor gave him something that calmed him down after a while. He told them they would have to take him to Dublin for tests right away. He might have to stay a few days so be prepared to stay with him. They brought him home and got the things he would need to stay in hospital for a few days ready and packed in a bag. Desmond was in such good form now, you would think there was nothing wrong with him. It was very strange, whatever it was. He was so violent and after it had passed he was so calm. However, they had to obey the doctor's orders and bring him to Dublin right away. The four of them left for the station. Ethel was very upset. Desmond was in great form, happy as if there was nothing wrong with him. He gave Doris and George a big hug. He took Ethel by the hand and walked along the platform as if he was going on holiday. The train was already there. As they were about to get on Desmond looked back and waved. Doris and George waved back. Ethel didn't look back, she was distraught. Doris started to cry and she asked George if she was ever going to see her brother again, and she never did.

George could not get her to stop crying. On the way home he bought her a small toy and that helped to comfort her for a while. When she was in bed George heard her sobbing and asked Beatrice to see if she would sleep with her. She refused and cried herself to sleep in her own bed. The next day George kept her home from school. He took her with him everywhere he had to go. She loved going out with him on her own. She enjoyed driving with George and he liked having her with him. For a child of six, she had a great personality. He hoped she would not change, or fret a lot if Desmond was seriously ill and had to stay in Dublin for any length of time. He would worry about that later, for now she was happy, and it was great to see her smile. She went to school the next day and seemed OK. The following day Ethel rang the shop and told her mother she was coming home alone. Desmond was having more tests and Aunt Phyllis would stay with him.

'Tell George to collect me and don't tell Doris I am coming home. Tell Beatrice to have her in bed and asleep before we come home. I would not be able to deal with her tonight. When she sees me in the morning and Desmond has not come with me she will be very upset. How are we going to console her? They are so close. Sofia will miss him also, the three of them are always together.'

When George met Ethel he knew it was not good news, Desmond was a very sick child.

The doctors were not sure why he was taking these turns from the tests they had done so far. A brain specialist was coming to see him tomorrow and having his brain x-rayed. That was the only way they could be sure of what was wrong with him. The tests done so far showed nothing serious. If he had to have surgery, this man was one of the top brain surgeons in Dublin. They hoped it would not come to that, but if it did, he was in the best place. The whole family, the Solomons family, Thelma's family and all the children in his class would hear about him having to stay in hospital and would be very sad. When James Taylor heard he was in hospital he asked if he could go and see him.

The Boles said, 'Yes, of course. If he was allowed visitors.'

Aunt Phyllis thought James should tell the hospital he was the child's biological father and he would get in to see him. James said he could not do that to George and

232

Ethel, it might cause problems for them. He was legally adopted and there was nothing he could do. It was a very sad situation for him. If he were allowed to visit him he would be happy with that.

When Doris woke up the next morning and saw Ethel home she knew Desmond was not there. She didn't ask, she ran back into her bedroom and cried so much Ethel thought she would have a fit or something worse. All three of them tried to comfort her but they couldn't. George went for the doctor who came at once. He gave her something, and when that started to work she stopped crying and went to sleep. He told Ethel to stay with her until she woke up. She was not to go to school for the rest of the week. She was in shock and it would take time for her to recover. The fact that he was her twin might hit her harder than if he was just her brother. Being so close was another problem. She would get better in time. Being so young would help a little, this was the first time they had been apart since they were born. If she was allowed in to see him that would also help. At the moment they have to be careful with her, plenty of tender loving care will work wonders. Ethel knew it would take more than TLC. 'Please God, let Desmond get better without having surgery, and come home soon.'

That wasn't to be. The x-ray showed an inoperable tumour on Desmond's brain. There was nothing they could do. That was the most awful news they could imagine. Aunt Phyllis, James, Michael and Linda were in the hospital every day, at different times so he would not be alone. Although he was asleep a lot of the time when he was awake he was not interested in anything. Ethel and George were making the trip so often Ethel decided to stay with Phyllis in Dublin.

She stayed in the hospital for hours at a time and she knew he was fading away. She decided Doris was not going to be brought to Dublin to see him. She would have to remember him leaving on the train. That broke her heart at the time, if she saw him now it would kill her. She was such a sensitive child, and so kind when anybody was sick. She had a lovely soft nature. It was not fair that her brother, who she loved so much, was going to die. How do you tell a child such a thing? George would have to be the one, but how and when?

Three weeks after the awful news Desmond passed away in his sleep. Ethel, Phyllis and James were there at his bedside. James took it very badly. Aunt Phyllis was no help to him, she was very upset herself. Ethel was trying to hold it together but she couldn't. The hospital staff were great, and looked after all three of them. When George came he couldn't believe how upset they all were. He suggested they all go back with Phyllis, and do all their crying there. He felt so sorry for James, after all, he was his real father. He asked James if he had anything special he wanted to do with regards to the funeral. James said he would like to have him buried with Lydia if that was possible. George and Ethel agreed it was the right thing to do, and they would be very happy with that. He is a Protestant and would be going to their church and graveyard. James being at the service and burial would not be unusual as he had married a protestant himself. They would bring the body straight to the church and after a short service he would be buried with his mother Lydia. The fact that Ethel was Lydia's sister made this acceptable. The locals would show their respect by staying away. It was hard enough for the family to cope without the whole parish turning up to offer their condolences. The Boles knew how everybody felt for them and they appreciated them staying away. Doris was allowed to go to the church and the graveyard. She was very good and did not cry at all. This really surprised the Boles and they hoped Doris was going to continue being as good as this in the future. She tried to be really grown up about it. She did have an odd down day but recovered quickly. She was an amazing child. George had thought she would never get over it. When he was in Dublin he had bought two beautiful dolls. One for Doris and the other for Sofia, in case they couldn't cope with the loss of Desmond. When he told Doris he had bought her a doll she never expected what she got. It was the most beautiful doll she had ever seen in her life.

'That's not all,' he said to her, 'I have another one here for Sofia.'

'Oh, my God,' she said.

Her eyes were out on sticks.

'Now,' he said to her. 'Which one do you want?'

'Oh,' she said. 'The first one is dressed in my favourite colours and Sofia likes the other colours. So I'll keep the first one.'

'Don't tell her,' he said. 'We want to surprise her.'

'Does she like surprises?'

'Yes, she sure does.'

George was thrilled with the way she reacted and he was looking forward to seeing Sofia's face when she saw the doll. The dolls were expensive but it was worth it to see how happy it made Doris. She hadn't smiled like this for a long time. When Doris showed Sofia her doll she couldn't believe it. Doris asked her if her Dad would buy her one like that and she said, 'I don't think so.'

'Well he doesn't have to because look at this one for you.'

Sofia started to cry when Doris nearly let the box fall.

'Oh Sofia,' she said. 'My Dad thought you would like to have one the same as mine.'

'I do like it but does my Dad know about it?'

'Yes, he does and he is allowing you to have it.'

The two of them were so happy. It was a great idea to have done this. If this happiness lasts for any length of time, it will be fantastic. It was hard enough for the family to get over the loss of Desmond, without Doris breaking down and having to be looked after as well. Now, when Doris was looking a bit out of sorts Beatrice made new dresses for both dolls, Sofia always came home from school with Doris. So when they came in the dolls would be dressed in the new clothes and the girls would be delighted. This kept them interested in the dolls for a very long time, and the huge amount of clothes they had kept them interested in playing with them. Then one day Mr. Solomons came over to Ethel and said, 'I have a surprise for the girls today when they come home from school.'

'What is it?' she asked.

'Well,' he said. 'You and Beatrice will have to come down to your parents' shop and bring it home before they come from school.'

'Could George not bring it home in the cart?'

'No,' he said. 'I need the two of you to walk home with it.'

'What is it? she asked. 'Surely, you can tell us.'

'Well, OK.' he said. 'I have made two prams for the dolls. You will have to wheel one each home.'

'Oh, my God Louie!' Ethel said. 'What are they made from?'

'Wood.' said Louie.

'I don't believe you could have made two prams without Sofia finding out.'

'I made them in your mother's place and Olga doesn't know about them either. She will be surprised also. So if you and Beatrice could sneak out now, and bring them back with you, that would be great.'

'OK, I'll get Beatrice now and come with you.'

When they saw the prams they could not believe it. He had made them beautifully. Just like a baby's pram, with a hood and apron. Padded base, pillow and cover.

'Who made the soft furnishing for them?' Ethel asked.

'That's a secret, Ethel.' he said.

'No secrets!'

'Thelma in her spare time,' he laughed.

'She did a great job.'

'It was hard going for her, she nearly got caught a couple of times. Doris nearly caught her once, another time Olga asked her why she was staying back so much. She had to tell a lie. Now, it can all come out in the open. You can wheel them all the way home, before the girls come in from school. I'm sure you won't get a chance to wheel them again once they get their hands on them.'

Ethel and Beatrice were stunned. These prams must

have taken him months to make. He was so talented. Where did he get the idea of making prams for the girls? When they asked him he said, 'Whenever he saw them playing they were always walking with the dolls in their arms. I thought if they had prams they could take them out, and walk to our house or to the shop like two real little mammies.'

This would keep them interested in the dolls for longer, and Doris may get over the loss of Desmond, a bit quicker if she is kept busy.

'How kind of you,' they both said. 'We will have to pay you for all the work you have put into them.'

'No,' he said. 'Are you forgetting? Sofia misses Desmond as much as Doris. The three of them were always together. We have to keep an eye on Sofia, so that she doesn't go down for some time. Making the prams was a pleasure and I think they will like them.'

'You can be sure they will love them. We are so grateful to you, how can we repay you for all your goodness?'

'Just get these prams home! No more talking about them.'

Ethel and Beatrice walked home, so proud with the prams. They never had a pram for their dolls when they were small. They wished they were little girls again and that these prams were theirs. When they got home, they put the prams in the fitting room, not saying a word. Thelma hadn't seen the prams before now. Mr. Solomons gave her the measurements and the material and told her what he was doing but not to say anything to anybody. Beatrice had made new dresses and put them on the dolls and put the dolls in the prams. When the girls came home she would ask them to go out to the fitting room for her. She left a parcel there and it would take two of them to carry it.

'Or maybe you would like to go. Mrs. Solomons? In case they need help.'

She said, 'Come on girls, let's see what this parcel is all about.'

She thought there was something funny going on. The three of them went out at once. Then Ethel, Beatrice and Thelma sneaked quietly after them, stayed outside the door to hear what they said when they saw the prams. The first to spot them was Sofia. She was very calm. Then Mrs. Solomons realised that was why she was sent out with them, to see their reaction. Doris let out a scream, then the others came in and Thelma started to cry. The tears were of joy. Thelma never saw anything like them in her life. The covers she had made were perfect on them. The girls could not believe it. When Ethel told them Sofia's Dad made them, Mrs. Solomons started to cry. The excitement was a bit too much for everybody. There was no more work done that day. Now Sofia could wheel her doll home every night and keep her in her own house. Doris could bring hers over to Sofia's house and play there for a change.

Ethel said, 'You can both wheel them to your Grandma's shop. You can bring them to your other friends' houses sometimes maybe, we'll see.'

The girls thought they would never get outside to wheel them. Mrs. Solomons said she would walk with them as far as her house and back. She wanted a go of the pram herself!

Thelma said, 'Ah here, give me a go,' and she walked round the house with Sofia's pram. They were lovely to push.

239

Ethel said, 'Thelma, pushing a pram really suits you. Maybe this time next year you will need one for real.'

'God forgive you Ethel, give me a chance to get used to being married first.'

Now Beatrice started to cry.

'Ah, for God's sake! When are we going to stop crying and being upset? Let's just enjoy this time for the girls. Now Doris you have to thank Sofia's Dad for this lovely pram. So off you go with her and her Mum and bring your pram. And tell him how pleased you are with it and that you will treasure it forever.'

'Oh I will, come on Sofia, let's go.'

All three of them went off, Mrs Solomons said,

'I will come back with Doris and finish what I was doing before all this excitement happened.'

Ethel told Thelma to go home, she could finish what she was doing in the morning. Beatrice and herself sat there in the fitting room. They said nothing for a while, then Ethel said, 'I wonder did George know anything about this? It's funny he is not here now.'

Beatrice said, If he did know and was told not to say anything, then you know George, he wouldn't say a word.'

'The Solomons coming here to live has been the best thing that ever happened to the village. I know I have said it so many times. When I think there is nothing more they can do for us, something like this happened and here we are again in their debt. They never expect anything in return, I know, I would love to do something really nice for them. We will have to think of something we can do for them, when they are not expecting it.'

'I'll think of something,' Beatrice said. 'I'll even surprise myself, if what I have in mind comes to fruition.'

When Philip and Trevor saw the prams they asked, 'What did *we* get?'

George asked. 'What would you like to be surprised with?'

'Anything would be nice.' Philip said.

'What would you like, Trevor?'

'A surprise would do me too.'

'Ok.' George said. 'We'll see what we can do.'

Ethel said, 'Will you stop George, they are not getting a surprise. They are big enough to cope without having to be surprised.'

'Don't mind your Mother boys. I have a nice surprise for both of you lined up for next Saturday.'

'Tell us Dad! What is it?'

'No, I'll tell you on Friday.'

'That means making us wait until Friday. Tell us now.'

'No, you will be delighted when you hear what it is on Friday.'

They were mad at their Dad.

'What could it be Trevor?' Philip asked.

'I don't know, we'll just have to wait.'

'I hope it is worth waiting for.'

When they went out Ethel asked him what was he talking about?

'It's a surprise. I'm not going to tell you either,' he said.

Ethel got really annoyed, she hated it when George carried on like this. She knew he would never tell her. When Friday came George didn't mess about, he told the boys when they came home from school. Tomorrow they were going to Dublin with him and Mr. Taylor in Mr. Taylor's car and George was driving. They couldn't believe it. They were never in that car, and their Dad was driving. This was the best news ever.

'How did you swing this one?' they asked.

'Never mind, just make sure you enjoy it, it's costing me a fortune.'

'Don't take the good out of it now George by telling them the cost.' Ethel said.

'Just joking, it's going to be a great day. We have a lot of things lined up for you. You will love every bit of it. You deserve it. You were so good during all the trouble we've gone through. We are giving you money, so you can buy whatever you want. Mum and I are giving you five shillings each. Beatrice is giving you five shillings each. Grandad and Grandma Cramp are giving you ten shillings each. That's a lot of money to get something you really like. It will be a long time before you have that much money again.'

'Oh, thanks Dad the trip would be great even without spending money. You are so good.'

'Off with you now, you've to go to bed early. We are leaving here at nine o'clock sharp in the morning.'

The boys were so excited. They would never have thought they would get to sit in that car. Going to Dublin is a great treat. Their Dad was the best in the world. Ethel didn't know a thing about this trip. When the boys were gone she asked George when all this had been arranged.

'Weeks ago, Patrick Taylor suggested it to me after Desmond died. He thought the boys might be more upset than was noticed. He thought they should get some attention. A trip in his car would cheer them up. Something they would remember forever and tell their friends.'

'That's very nice of him. He has enough to do without thinking about our children, taking the day off and allowing you to drive. You must be thrilled.'

'I am, at the same time I would have preferred if he had given me the car for the day. When we get to Dublin, he is going to see James, Michael, and Linda. While he is with them, he is giving me the car to take the boys wherever they want to go.'

'That's great for you also. Make the most of it and enjoy yourself. I will love that car, I wish we could afford one. It makes life so much easier to get around. We would have to win the Irish Hospital Sweepstakes First Prize before we could afford a car like that.'

'That won't happen if we never buy a ticket.'

'Maybe we should buy one, we might be lucky sometime.'

'Shoulds, mights and maybes are not going to do us any good. Let's get real and enjoy the fact you are going to travel in the car of your dreams. All the way to Dublin and back.'

Chapter 38

Beatrice asked Mr. Solomons if he could take her and Ethel to the station on Saturday. She was going to surprise Ethel with a nice day out in Dublin. Ethel had looked after everybody. She never wanted anything for herself. She would have no excuse this Saturday with George and the boys gone for the day. Ethel was pleased when Beatrice told her the plan. A day with Beatrice on her own would be lovely. They would do no shopping, just mosey around. Have a nice dinner in the Gresham Hotel and a climb up Nelson's Pillar, 168 steps if they were able to, and get the best view of the city and surrounding area. Take a trip on a tram to Howth if they have enough time or do nothing at all but sit in St. Stephen's Green with a big ice cream cone and people watch. Whatever Ethel wanted to do, the day was for her. She was always rushing around when she went to Dublin, but not today. This was to be a real treat so Ethel knew she would love it. Beatrice had a great calming effect on her and it had been a long time since they had time like this together. They would leave Dublin on the last train home. Mr. Solomons would collect them at the station. There would be great excitement when they came home. If the boys were there when the sisters got home, they would listen to their news before telling them theirs. If they were home before them they would say nothing about their day until tomorrow. They would want to give the boys all the time it would take to tell them everything. Having something nice to talk about after all the awful times they had gone through lately would be lovely. If it took all night to hear their news, so be it. The boys never had a day out like this before. So Ethel and Beatrice were prepared to sit up all night and listen to them. The next day being Sunday they would all go back to the shop with the Grandparents after church. The boys would have to tell them about their day out. In school on Monday they would have to tell their friends, the teachers, and anybody who would listen. They would get great mileage from this trip. It was understandable. Any young lad would envy them. A motorcar was such a rare thing at that time. No doubt they would exaggerate, but this time that would be allowed. If George was as excited as they were, he would pretend to take it all in his stride. Ethel knew exactly what George would say. She would listen and pretend she was hearing it for the first time. She knew this man so well.

Everyone in the village was doing well. Most young men were working full time, getting married to local girls from different families and settling in the area. Only two lads from the same family left to go to America. Three girls went to England to become nurses. Two girls went up north to a convert, to become nuns. All those could have stayed, they didn't have to go like some years earlier. They left because they wanted to go. They had a choice to come back, if they were not happy. They didn't have the Irish wake, it was not like olden times. There might be a party, but no collections, there was nobody short of money. A few couples had additions to their families. But huge families were not the norm now. If there were six in a family now, that was considered a big family. The younger ones of the bigger families were going to college, and having a great time. What the older ones could never have done. Most people were much better off, and could even have a holiday. The mode of transport now was a horse and coach and a lot of the locals had one. There were three motorcars in the village now. Still expensive to buy, George to his regret could not afford one. Beatrice was saving all her money. Without saying a word to anybody. She would eventually tell Ethel. Her and their parents were going to surprise George. They were going to buy him a car. Not as expensive as the Taylors. But a car with four wheels and an engine. That was what he had always wanted, and he was going to have it. Doris had two more years at primary school. She was very clever but didn't know what she wanted to do. Sofia was much better at everything than Doris was. She was brilliant, the best in the class, but she was very shy, and hated being made a fuss of. Sometimes she would answer wrongly just to give somebody else a chance to answer. She was always prompting other children with the correct answer and never got caught. Everybody in the class loved her, she was so helpful and her English was perfect. She was good at Irish, but not as good as she was at English. Doris was better than her at arithmetic and helped Sofia with hers. They loved school and were very popular with all the teachers. They were happy that they still had two more years to go in this school. They had some nice friends in school, but their friendship with each other was unique and different. From the first day they started to play with each other, they never fell out. They sometimes did not agree, but they did agree to disagree. They were very funny and always happy. Both sets of parents could not get over the way they treated each other. They shared everything. If Doris was in the shop and had a bar of chocolate, she bought one for Sofia. The same with everything she had, there had to be one for Sofia. Sometimes Mrs. Cramp would show her something she knew she would like and tell her she only had one Doris would not take it. If it was something she really wanted, her grandmother would tell her she would explain to Sofia she could only get one, she would not allow her to do that. So sometimes Doris missed out on something she really wanted. There was no point trying to change her, she was a true friend. Sofia was the same, she would never take anything unless it could be shared or there was one for Doris.

Chapter 39

The past couple of years had been good for Ethel and George. The girls in the workroom were always very busy and could have taken on more work and more staff. But Ethel always refused to get any bigger. She was very happy with the amount they did. She loved her life the way it was and did not wish to change anything. Joseph was getting on very well in the army. Philip was doing great at college. He was growing up very nicely. Wrote lovely letters very regularly, always good news. He included a special page for Doris and Sofia and addressed them as his beautiful baby sisters. They loved that and wrote back to him. Trevor was working in the shop and was very happy there. That was what he always wanted to do. Ethel always thought he might follow in his father's footsteps and become a minister. He did talk about it one time, then he changed his mind. Beatrice was delighted about that. She loved Trevor and was glad he was not going away to study. He was such a pleasant person to have around the house. He was always in good humour. He saw the funny side of everything. No matter what went wrong, he never got upset. He used to say everything can be sorted, and he was right. When anybody said they had to do something, his answer was, the only thing you have to do in this world is die. With everything else you have a choice. Nothing is worth getting upset about. The things we worry about most of the time never happen. So why worry? When he put it like that you had to agree with him. That was why he got along well with people. He had the perfect personality for working in the shop. He was going out with a lovely girl. Everyone liked her, and hoped they would get married. They were so well suited, and got on so well together. Just as everything was going so well Beatrice started to lose weight very quickly. She went to the doctor. He couldn't understand why she was losing weight so suddenly. She had never been sick in her life. He took blood samples and sent them to Dublin. It would take a while before he would get results. While she was waiting, he recommended she take a tonic with iron that would help her eat better. She took the medicine but it made no difference. When the results of the blood tests came back, it wasn't good news. She had cancer. The silent killer, she didn't have long to live. Beatrice took the news very well. The only thing she said was that she hoped it would be quick.

Everyone else was distraught. She told her parents herself. She gave them the money towards the car for George. Told them to look after Ethel. Ethel would miss her a lot. Always being together for so long. Then she said, 'Now we can all have a good cry.'

Which they did.

Two weeks later she was dead. She got her wish. The funeral was huge. Something Beatrice would not have wanted. Everyone felt so sorry for Mr. and Mrs. Cramp losing another child. The shop closed for three days. Trevor insisted the grandparents go to Dublin with Aunt Phyllis and stay as long as they needed to. With the help of the staff he had, he could look after everything. They knew he was right. He was well able to take care of everything. Aunt Phyllis would love having them, so that's what they did.

Ethel didn't cry. She was so shocked she couldn't take in what had happened. She was on an automatic pilot and carried on as if nothing was wrong. George was so worried about her. He didn't know what to do. He waited for the time she would start talking about Beatrice, then hoped she might cry. She didn't. She got up very early in the morning. Went into the workroom and worked until near the time the girls would be coming in. She came back to the house, had a cup of tea and started to clean, cook, wash clothes, and keep busy all day. This went on for months. George said nothing, but he was finding it very hard to live with. Then one morning when she came back from the workroom she sat down at the kitchen table. She put her head into her hands and the tears flowed. George left her there in the kitchen, he was crying himself. When he got control he went back, and lifted her away from the table. He took her in his arms. Put her head on his shoulder and kept her there until she could cry no more.

This was what was needed to start her on the road to recovery. When Doris came home from school she felt a difference in the house. Ethel spoke to her and Doris started to cry. She had become so used to being ignored by her mother, she was frightened by her. Ethel put her arms around her and told her she was feeling better. Things would be back to normal from now on. Doris was so pleased and told her how she missed her hugs and how awful life had been. Ethel told her she was so sorry and that it was awful for her also. It is over now, and must be forgotten. That evening when Trevor came home from work and saw a smile on his mother's face he knew things were going to be fine from now on. He thought for a minute and then decided to tell her his good news.

He put down his knife and fork and asked her, 'Do you want the good news or the great news?'

She said, 'Let's start with the good news.'

'Emily and I are going to Dublin on the 8th of December to buy the ring.'

'Oh Trevor!' was all she could say before bursting into tears. Trevor knew they were tears of joy so he took her in his arms and said, 'I thought you would be happy about that.'

'Oh I am, we love Emily. Everybody will be so happy for both of you. Whatever the great news is it must be fantastic because that is great news.'

'Now, I know you always went to Dublin on the 8th of December and you are going this year. I know it will be different without Beatrice. So what I want you to do is bring Doris and Sofia with you and your mother. Having them with you will help to keep your mind busy. They would enjoy the day. We will go together on the early morning train. Emily and I will leave you when we get to Dublin. We will not be coming back on the train. We are meeting James Taylor after we buy the ring and have a nice meal. He is driving us home in Dad's new car.'

'Has his father bought a new car?'

'No, my Dad's new car.'

'What are you talking about? Your Dad hasn't got a car new or old.'

'That's the great news, he has one now. He doesn't know it yet. It is a surprise. Before Beatrice died she was saving all her money to help your parents buy a car for him.'

'My parents and Beatrice were buying George a car. Are you serious?'

251

'Yes!' he said.

'I knew nothing about this.'

'No, you were not supposed to know. I'm only telling you now because James is collecting it today and driving it down for him. He doesn't know anything about it. So what I want to know is do you want James to drive it to our house or do you want him to leave it in his Father's garage until Christmas and surprise him then?'

'No, bring it to our house today. He will be over the moon. Wait until we get home, before you bring it. I must be there for this.'

'OK,' Trevor said. 'I hoped you would like this news. It will give Dad a great lift, which he really needs.'

'Who was it that thought this one up?' she asked.

'Granddad and Grandma were talking to Beatrice one time about how excited George was when he was driving Mr. Taylor's car. Your mother said that if she had the money she would buy him a car. Beatrice asked what kind of money they were talking about? She decided if they put all the money she had saved to theirs in a few more months they would have enough. That is how it happened. When Beatrice got the bad news she gave your Dad every penny she had saved. There were lots of tears that night. Your Dad promised that George would have a car for Christmas. He wrote to James and told him the plan. He told him the amount of money they had and asked him to buy a car from the same guy his Dad had bought his car from, hoping the salesman would do him a deal on the price. James said he would do his best to get him a bargain. If he could, he certainly would. When he had one he would let him know.

If he trusted him to buy the car, and couldn't make the trip to get it, he would drive it down for him. Mr. Cramp was so grateful. He knew nothing about cars so if James was willing to do that for him, that would be great. It didn't take long when he heard from James. The garage had a beautiful car for sale. It was not brand new, it was the car the garage used to drive prospective buyers around in. It was in great condition, and he had agreed to a great price. It was a lovely red colour, James said he would love it for himself. The garage was willing to hold on to it until James heard from him by return post. They had lots of interest in it so he had to make up his mind quickly. Mr. Cramp wrote straight away and told him to buy it.'

After explaining all of the background, Trevor said, 'Isn't that great news?'

'It is fantastic news.' Ethel said. 'Such a lot to take in, I don't know where to start.'

Trevor said, 'Start by telling the girls you are taking them to Dublin. Don't mention the engagement. That's supposed to be a secret.

But you know me Mum, I could never keep anything quiet. I have such a big mouth. I don't see the sense in secrets, what's the big deal when you know, you know. Emily is as bad as me. She won't be able to keep it a secret. I bet by this time tomorrow all the village will know. She is dying to get the ring. I love the way she gets so excited about things. She doesn't know about the car, I nearly let it slip so many times, she thinks we are all coming home on the evening train. I have arranged to meet James at a certain place when we are finished shopping. He just appears as if by accident and offers us a lift home. I will accept and she will worry about you waiting for us at the station.'

'That's a bit mean," his Mother said.

"Then I'll tell her the truth after a while and let her enjoy the drive home. I'm so looking forward to it.'

Having told his Mother all this news made him feel a bit better himself. Life in this house has been so miserable for so long. Some cheerfulness would be nice for a change. When Doris was told about the trip to Dublin she would be looking forward to it. Her and Sofia could start making plans about what they would buy. He would give them a pound each to spend. George, the Grandparents and Mr. and Mrs. Solomons would give them spending money also. They would have plenty of money to spend. They could buy whatever they wanted to, for themselves or for friends. Sofia celebrated Christmas with the same joy as Doris. She bought presents for friends. She thought Christmas was lovely and saw no reason why she should not celebrate it. Her parents didn't mind that, she was only a child.

Chapter 40

The 8th of December came very quickly. There was so much fussing around, George thought they would never go. Mr. Solomons was taking them to the station. Doris was very excited, which was unusual. Trevor was very nervous, not at all like him. Ethel was so excited with her secret that George didn't know what to make of them all. When they left he was able to get on with what he had to do in peace and quiet. The train was packed as always on this date. The six of them could not get seats together, but Doris and Sofia got two seats together. They were thrilled. Ethel and her mother were near each other, but Trevor and Emily had to stand. They didn't mind, they were so excited. When they arrived in Dublin, the girls left Trevor and Emily and off they went. It was great for Ethel and her mother to have them. They would have to keep an eye on them. The streets were crowded, and the shops were bursting with people. They never once got a chance to miss Beatrice. The girls could not wander off on their own to buy presents, which they wanted to do. So Mrs. Cramp told Ethel to take them on their own, and do their shopping with them. At the same time she would do her shopping and meet back at Arnotts in two hours. The girls loved this arrangement, because they wanted to buy presents for Grandma and Grandpa. Ethel would be a great help to them as they never had so much money to spend. They wanted to get really nice things for everybody. Even if it meant they had to buy some things between them, and put from the two names on the cards. Ethel thought they were great, they didn't want anything for themselves. They wanted to spend all their money on presents. Ethel didn't stop them, she felt if that was what they wanted to do then let them enjoy doing it. The two hours flew by and it was time to meet up with Grandma. When they met she told Ethel to stay there and take a rest, she wanted to take the girls around Arnotts herself. She wanted to choose something nice for themselves as a gift from her. A gift for always being so good. They weren't expecting that, so they both chose the same thing. A jewellery box the same colour. Then she asked them if they would like a ring to go into the box? They both said no, the box was enough. They went back to Ethel and went for lunch. After lunch they went to Grafton Street, taking their time admiring the shop windows. They had all their big shopping done so if they saw a shop with not so many people in it they would go in, if not they were quite happy with what they had already got. They were lucky at the top of the street there was a lad selling cheap jewellery from a stall. The girls were so excited they bought lots of things from him, so many he gave them a tiny angel each, which he pinned on their coats for free. They couldn't believe it. That made their day. All their money was spent, except two pence each. They heard singing and there at the corner a crowd had just gathered to hear a group of boys and girls singing Christmas carols. They had time to listen for a while, and head to the station for the evening train home. They put their last two pence into the collection box for the carols. The adults were so proud of them. This would be a day to remember. It could not have gone better for all of them. When they got to the station nobody mentioned Trevor and Emily. When they arrived in Rathdrum station George was there waiting. He asked where Trevor and Emily were but Ethel didn't say a word.

Mrs Cramp nearly died. 'How could we have forgotten to meet them at the station?'

Ethel told George to take them home. There were no more people on the platform. Trevor must have decided to stay the night in Dublin. If they had gone to visit Aunt Phyllis, to show her the ring she would have made them stay.

George said, 'I hope you are right, let's get going then.'

Ethel was delighted, George believed her and didn't make a fuss. She knew exactly where they were, and was so excited she thought she would burst. They dropped Mrs. Cramp off first, then Sofia. In a couple of minutes they were home. Ethel and Doris went into the house, while George sorted out the horse for the night then he came into the house.

Ethel said she would love a cup of tea. George said he would have one made in no time and put the kettle on. Ethel said that they had got everything they wanted but she wouldn't open the bags until tomorrow. They were very tired. Then she heard the car coming up the drive.

She looked at Doris and whispered, 'Don't say anything.'

George was in the kitchen and didn't hear the sound of the car because of the kettle boiling in his ear. James could not have timed it better. Trevor knocked on the door and Ethel said, 'Who could that be at this time of the night?'

George opened the door and when he saw Trevor he asked him where he had come from.

'Dublin.' Trevor answered.

'I know that, but how did you get here?'

Trevor said, 'By car.'

'Whose car?' George asked.

'Ah now, that would be telling.' Trevor said.

While all this talk was going on in the hall, Ethel and Doris had gone around the back and told James to reverse the car and leave it at the hall door. Then they went back into the house. Trevor was now sitting at the table still talking to his father. George asked Ethel and Doris where they had been. They started to laugh.

'What's going on?' he said.

Then there was another knock on the door.

Trevor said, 'I'll get it.'

Then he shouted to George,

'It's for you, Dad.'

George got up annoyed and muttering to himself, 'Who wants me at this hour of the night?'

When he came to the door Trevor stood back and said, 'That's the car I came home in and it's yours.'

George said, 'Very funny,' and walked back into the house.

Ethel said, 'It's not a joke, the car is yours.'

James knocked on the door.

Trevor said, 'You answer that one Dad.'

When he opened the door James handed him the keys and said, 'The best of luck in your new car.'

For once George was stuck for words.

James said, 'It is a gift from your wife's parents and Beatrice. They want you to have it for Christmas. Come on, I'll drive you down there now and you can thank them.'

'Is it really mine? Are you serious?'

'Yes,' James said. 'Would I joke about something like this.'

'No, I suppose not.' George said. 'But I don't know where to start asking questions about this fantastic present.'

'Don't ask anyone you because will not be told.'

It was the first time James had seen George so flustered. He really was dumbfounded. He handed the keys back to James and said,

'Well, if you are telling the truth, you had better drive because I'm in such a state of disbelief I don't trust myself to drive.'

Trevor, Ethel, and Doris came round from the side of the house where they had been listening and peeping around at George to see how he was taking it all in. They came round and Ethel and Doris hugged and kissed him. He was overwhelmed, Ethel had never seen him in such a state. She told him not to go to the shop that could wait until tomorrow.

'Go with Trevor and take James home. Then Trevor can drive home if you don't feel like driving tonight.'

'Oh my God! There is no way I could drive tonight. I cannot believe this.'

'Now come in everybody and we will have a cup of tea before you lads leave. Then you can take your time coming home and enjoy the ride. We'll be in bed before you get back.'

Doris asked her Mother when they were gone if she knew about the car. Ethel said she did.

'You are great at keeping secrets!' Doris said.

'It was difficult but I got away with it. I never would have been able to keep it secret until Christmas. It was better to give it to him now. By Christmas he will be very good at driving, he will have had plenty of practice. He will love it I know, when he realises it belongs to him. Your Dad

259

deserves it. I am so happy for him.' Ethel said.

She and Doris went to bed. A lot had happened for one day. They were asleep as soon as they lay down. Trevor drove the car back, taking his time as he was not used to it. He parked in the garage that Ethel had cleared enough room to be able to put the car in, without it being obvious to George. When they came into the house Trevor handed him the keys and said, 'Safe driving Dad!' Then Trevor went to bed.

George sat for ages in disbelief at what had happened. He could never have imagined owning a motorcar at this time. He knew Beatrice had lots of money, and was very sensible. She was always generous, but he never expected her to do something like this. He walked back out to the garage and looked at the car. He was still in shock, at the same time he knew he would love it. But he thought Beatrice should have given the money to her father to buy a car for himself. Maybe she had suggested that to her Dad and he didn't want to start driving at his age. Maybe he thought it would be better to buy one for George. Whatever had been the plan he would not ask. He felt he had to accept it and be thankful for the lovely family he had married into. He went to bed, and was awake for ages. Eventually he fell asleep, when he woke he went out to the garage to make sure he wasn't dreaming. The car was there. He sat in the driver seat, it was so comfortable. He was over the moon with excitement. He couldn't wait to drive it. He would drive it to church, although it was a very short drive. Trevor, Doris and Ethel felt a bit foolish getting into a car for such a short drive, but they didn't want to disappoint him. He was going to drive to the shop after the service and thank his in-laws for such a wonderful gift. He would take Mr. and Mrs. Cramp for a drive in the afternoon. They would love that, they had great faith in his driving ability. George would take his time and let them enjoy it.

Chapter 41

Trevor was right when he said Emily would tell everybody she was engaged. He didn't mind, she was so excited, he wasn't going to take the good out of it. Her family were very fond of Trevor and were delighted she was going to marry such a nice lad. The ring was more often off her finger for the first few days. Every girl she met had to have a try on the ring and make a wish on it. She was really enjoying it. She couldn't wait to get the second one. She kept asking Trevor when they would make a definite date for the wedding.

'Not before June.' he said. He was not in a hurry. He wanted to get everything right. They were going to live over the shop, and he wanted it beautiful before they got married.

Emily would have moved in the way it was, but Trevor was sure of what he wanted. The whole lot had to be painted in nice bright colours. He was adamant about that. He didn't want to have painters in after they were married. It was all going to be done beforehand. Trevor did not want to hear anything about it until after Christmas. He was more interested in the car at the moment.

Emily found it hard not to talk about the wedding. June seemed so far away. She wanted a big wedding, and everything to be perfect. She wanted her Mother, Ethel and Mrs. Cramp to go to Dublin with her to buy the material for the wedding party. She included Mrs. Cramp in everything and valued her opinion on lots of things. Doris and Sofia were going to be bridesmaids. Emily's brother Paul and Trevor's brother Philip, were best men. Sofia was delighted, she liked Philip. Doris liked Paul, so they were really looking forward to coming down the aisle with them. That was all that was talked about so far. Everything else had to wait. Emily had everything planned but she just couldn't mention any of the plans. It was killing her having to wait, she was dying to talk to them. She had to be fair. The motorcar was the big thing at the moment. Trevor and George were like two kids talking about it, every chance they got. Ethel didn't mind; she was as happy as they were about it. Joseph and Philip were coming home for Christmas, and she knew she wouldn't be seeing much of them. George would be so excited taking them out in the car. Emily wouldn't see much of Trevor either. He would want to be part of the *car crew*. With all the men busy with the car, the girls could talk about the wedding. So then everybody would be happy. It was going to be a great Christmas. The best in a long time. Ethel had never seen George so happy, and he deserved to be. He never had a present like this before. He couldn't get used to the fact that he owned a car. They did the right thing by giving it to him before Christmas. He was getting very good at driving it. It was great to have it for all the trips that had to be made over Christmas. Joseph was coming from England by boat. He was driving to Wexford to pick him up and he brought Ethel and Doris with him for the long drive. It was a beautiful day for December. The car was very cosy, but it was cold outside. They didn't have to worry about that until they got to Wexford. They stayed in the car until the boat had docked and the people had disembarked. George went on his own to collect Joseph. When they got back to the car and Joseph saw Ethel and Doris he couldn't believe it.

He said, 'You are very brave to come all this way with Dad

and bring Doris with you.'

'Why wouldn't we come? Your Dad is a great driver,' she said.

'Only joking.' he said. 'Let's put my bag in the car then go for a nice meal before we make the long journey home.'

That's what they did. When they arrived at the house Joseph praised his Dad and said, 'Mum you are right! Dad is a great driver. I'm really looking forward to this Christmas. It will be great having a car to travel around in. It is a real luxury. Dad you deserve it, and I wish you the best of luck with it.'

George thanked him and said, 'I'll enjoy taking you all around, I love driving it. It is so comfortable, everybody should have one.'

They laughed and Joseph said, 'I suppose nobody else is allowed to drive it.'

'Well that depends on who it is and where they want to go.'

'That's generous!' Joseph said.

'Nobody has asked to borrow it yet. I don't know how your Mother might feel about lending it, but if it was you borrowing it I think she would be OK with it. Philip I'm not so sure about. I'm collecting him at the station tomorrow evening. You can come if you like for the drive. I'd like to have your company, it's nice to have you home. I miss you a lot being the eldest.'

Joseph spent the next day out in the motorcar with his Dad. They had a lot of things to do. He enjoyed every minute of it. He went with him to the station and when Philip got off the train, as a surprise, Aunt Phyllis was with him. George and Joseph were delighted she had come. She was invited every Christmas, but she never came. Their Mum would be so pleased to see her. Philip sat in the front seat and thought the car was great. He told his Dad he was a great driver.

'Why are you all so surprised I'm such a good driver? Do you think Mr. Taylor would have allowed me to drive his most expensive car, if he thought I could not drive.'

'No Dad, it's not that we think you can't drive, you do it like you have been driving all your life. You are just a natural, that's all.'

When Ethel saw Aunt Phyllis she was so pleased. Phyllis was great company. No trouble as a guest. Looked after herself and great fun to be with. George would bring her down tomorrow to see Mary and John. They would want her to stay with them. It was up to herself, Ethel didn't mind, they would still see her a lot over Christmas anyway.

As Ethel expected, Mary really wanted her to stay with them so she did. She was going to be here for a while now, if Mary got fed up with her she could come back to Ethel. There was no fear or that. They were sisters after all and had a lot to catch upon. Ethel was happy enough with her two sons home for Christmas. Doris was upset that she didn't have a present for Aunt Phyllis. Ethel told her she would give her the money to buy something for her and not to worry.

Like every other Christmas dinner was in the parent's house. This Christmas they had Aunt Phyllis and that was a real treat. The Solomons were invited as usual. This year they felt it was a bit much. The children were now all grown up and could be considered adults. That made no difference. They had better come this year because next year, please God, Trevor and Emily will be living here and they might have different ideas.

Trevor said, 'Gran, you are still the boss. Whatever you want to do is OK with us. Let's enjoy this Christmas before we start talking about next year.'

Trevor still had a lot to do and he wanted to get on with it. The time was flying and he wanted everything to be perfect. He was so happy on Christmas Eve when he closed the shop. He was delighted that tomorrow was Christmas Day.

There was a lovely atmosphere at the table. Pulling crackers, homemade of course, they made no bangs but were a lot of fun. Trevor had them all laughing at the stories he had to tell. Mr. Solomons had Aunt Phyllis laughing so much, she couldn't eat anything. She hadn't met Mr. Solomons before and she thought he was hilarious. Mrs. Solomons had to tell him to stop. They had all heard his stories before. Nobody minded hearing them again, they loved listening to his half Wicklow half Russian accent and his broken English.

The meal was fantastic. Not a scrap left on any plate. Mrs. Solomons had made a dessert that looked wonderful. It was a square chimney and a Santa's hat sticking out the top. It appeared he had just dropped down the chimney. It was a shame to eat it. There was a great variety of desserts. But everyone wanted the Russian one. Mrs Solomons dished it out so that everybody got a taste of the different layers. It was as lovely to eat as it had been to look at. There was plenty to go round but nothing left for seconds. Nobody wanted any more of anything, they were all so full. They sat at the table for ages, nobody wanted coffee at that moment so Mrs Cramp said, 'Now lads, you can do the washing up. We ladies are going to retire to the sitting room.'

The men didn't mind doing the washing up. The women had done all the cooking and that was fair. When the kitchen was spick and span, the men joined the ladies. Most of them were asleep in no time. That was OK. It had been a very busy time for all the adults and they were very tired. The younger ones went back to the dining room and played games quietly. When the adults woke up it was time to go to the Boles' house. The party began there soon after they all arrived. It went on for hours. By the time all the guests left everybody was so tired, they were nearly asleep on their feet. They went to bed and were asleep in seconds. Tomorrow would be a lazy day everybody could stay in bed all day if they wished. No cooking today. Plenty of leftover turkey, ham, and spiced beef which was George's favourite. Everybody could make their own sandwiches or have whatever they wanted.

George would go out for a drive on his own. He would want to just relax and drive without all the talk that he had to listen to since he got the car. Tomorrow, driving would be great. Nothing on the roads. Not a human being would be in sight. He would feel the whole village was owned by him. This Christmas has been magical. He would treasure the memories of it forever.

Chapter 42

When Christmas was over and Philip, Joseph and Aunt Phyllis had left, the house seemed so empty. January was always a miserable month in Ireland. This year will be no different. Emily was already talking about the wedding. She wanted to go to Dublin for the sales. She insisted on going on the first Saturday in January. So off they went. The shops were so busy it was like Christmas week. They had a great time and got plenty of bargains. She got beautiful material for the clothes for the wedding party. She knew exactly what she wanted, no messing about. Ethel was amazed at how good she was at choosing the best quality. She would check with Ethel if that material would be easy to work on. Ethel could not have done better herself. They shopped till they dropped and were laden down with parcels. It was a very successful day. Emily was such a lovely girl, she made everybody feel their opinion was very important to her. She got beautiful night wear for the honeymoon at a great price. She was so excited, she made the whole shopping party feel great. Mrs. Cramp loved the way she made her feel as important as her own mother. The two mothers got on very well, which was really terrific. Ethel hoped that, if and when Doris was getting married they would have as good a time as this shopping trip for the wedding. Ethel felt sad, only for a second, that she and her mother had been so left out of all the plans for Lydia's wedding. But this day had well made up for it. The months before the wedding were very enjoyable. There was always something happening. Every time Trevor came home from work, there was a message from Emily. What did she think about this or that? Did Trevor tell her about getting a present of the invitation cards and other things they got? She was always calling in to show something, or to ask about things. The months flew by.

The big day had arrived here and the excitement of the whole family was palpable. Trevor, the man of the moment, was the coolest of them all. Philip, Doris, Sofia and Ethel panicked about everything. George was ready to take them to the church. Then he had to collect the bridal party. As he is the minister, the bride would be on time. When Trevor saw Emily coming up the aisle, he fell apart. George thought he was going to faint. Philip held onto him, he pulled himself together. Emily was stunning. The dress was beautiful. The colours of the bridesmaids' dresses were exquisite against the white of the bride's dress. The whole thing was perfect. The reception was in the church hall. There was a sit down meal for one hundred people. After the meal, there were pictures taken. When the hall was ready the music started. The bride and groom led the first dance. Then everybody was up dancing. Now the wedding was in full swing. There is nowhere in the world a wedding is like an Irish one. It can go on for days. After a couple of hours the bride and groom left. They got a great send off. Then the rest of the village arrived. There were tables along one wall full of all kinds of food and drink. You could help yourself. Drinks of all kinds. Some made by Mrs. Solomons, the type that they drink at weddings in her country. You have to be careful of them. They are very strong. Only for adults. Maybe even too strong for adults!

The music played non-stop. When one band had a rest, another played. Ethel and George danced for hours.

They hadn't danced like this for years. They really enjoyed themselves. They left the hall at 2am and there was no sign of anybody else leaving. George had arranged with a few of the men from the village to let it go on, as long as there was food and drink there but at 7am close the hall and hold on to the keys. By 7am, Philip, Doris, Paul, Sofia and a few more young people were the only ones left. The musicians were leaving and the young people left with them. The men closed the hall, and were glad the day had gone well for both families.

The Boles deserved a bit of luck, after all they had gone through in the past year. It was a great wedding. The whole village had a marvellous time. It would be a long time before there would be a wedding as good as that in the village again. There might be a couple of affairs after this wedding. There were a lot of young people getting on very well together and who knows?

Going to a wedding is the makings of another is said in Ireland. It often does happen.

Chapter 43

Philip was home from college now for the whole summer. He would work in the shop and Doris would help as well. In the evening all the young people would gather in groups, and enjoy themselves. Ethel was feeling very lonely in the evenings. She missed Trevor so much, and she was losing interest in the business. Mrs. Solomons noticed she was not taking on much work and said nothing. She had big news herself and could never get the chance to tell Ethel. She thought she might say something to George, but that would not be right, she worked for Ethel.

So she said to Louie, 'I think we should ask Ethel and George to come down here to visit sometime soon. I cannot do it on my own, they will be so upset when we tell them.'

Louie said, 'Tell them yes, but what do you think will happen when we tell Sofia and Doris?'

'I know and I dread it,' Olga said. 'But it has to be done sooner rather than later.'

'I'm very worried about Ethel. I don't think she is well and it couldn't be worse having to tell her this news now.'"

'There is never going to be a good time. So let's tell them soon and get it over with.' Louie said.

The next day Mrs. Solomons asked Ethel if she and George would like to call down some evening to their house to have a chat. Ethel said, 'Yes, I would love that. Say on Friday next, would that suit you?'

'Yes, that would be great,' Mrs. Solomons said. 'Friday then, that's settled.'

When she told Louie he was pleased she had decided Friday. But he was sick to his stomach thinking what might happen.

Louie said, 'We'll make that nice Russian drink they both like and that cake they love. Then have a nice chat before we tell them. We'll make sure we have told them before the girls come in.'

'I don't know how we are going to face them.'

'It's not going to be easy, no matter what we try. So we'll come clean and tell them out straight.'

Louie said, 'What if we just tell them and not the girls? I don't want to ruin the summer for them. At the same time I want to tell the adults now.'

'We'll see what they say, I think they will agree that the girls don't need to know yet. The end of the summer will be plenty of time to tell them.'

When the Boles arrived on Friday night Louie offered both of them a drink and some cake. They both accepted. George and Ethel felt there was something different about this visit. Louie and Olga didn't pour a drink for themselves which was not like them.

Louie spoke first. 'My dear friends,' he said. 'We invited you here tonight for a reason.'

He hesitated, looked at Olga and said, 'I don't know where to start.' He couldn't do it.

Olga said, 'We are leaving the village in September. We are going to live in Dublin.'

There was complete silence. George and Ethel nearly dropped their drinks. Ethel started to cry, Olga went over to her, put her arms around her and she started to cry. The two men looked at each other and said nothing.

A few seconds later Louie said,

'Come on girls, Dublin is not so far away. We will always be best friends, and keep in touch.' Now that he started talking there was no stopping him. 'We can visit you and you can stay with us when you come to Dublin. Now that you have a motorcar, you can drive up in no time..

'Stop!' Olga said to him. 'We know what we can do. Give George a chance to say something.'

George didn't know what to say.

'I'm in shock.' George said. 'You know how sad we are to hear this news. We were not expecting to hear news like this tonight. I don't have to tell you how upset we are.'

'Does Sofia know?' Ethel asked.

'No, we are not going to tell her.'

'What do you mean you are not telling her?'

'We are not telling her, can you imagine how she is going to feel. We could not cope with her, she will be furious. We are asking you not to tell Doris either. We hope you will agree, it would be the best thing for all of us.'

Then Ethel asked, 'How are you going to do that?'

Louie said, 'It will be difficult, but not as hard as it was to get out of Russia. We will rent a furnished house in Dublin, in the next few weeks. I will go up a couple of times with the things we have to bring. Then we are going to tell them we are going on holiday to Dublin. When we get there let them enjoy a few days sightseeing and then tell them we are not going back to Wicklow.'

'Oh my God!' Ethel said. 'That's awful. Sofia will want to bring Doris on the holiday, what are we going to say to her?'

'That's the biggest of all our problems. We will have to put our four heads together and come up with something. They are young and will get over it. They are going to have to separate sometime. Make their own lives, they can still be best friends. We are going to be very strict with Sofia. She will suggest Doris coming and living with us, and we would have no problem with that. But that would not be fair to you. Likewise Doris will suggest Sofia staying here and living with you. That would not be fair on us. It's going to break their hearts. How are we going to live with them, while they come to terms with this trauma? It will be a trauma, there is no doubt about that.'

Ethel said, 'There is not going to be any easy way to tell them. I think what you have decided is one way of doing it. Maybe not such a bad idea. But for us, Doris will be here with us. She will go mad, I have no idea what to do.'

George said, 'We have plenty of time to come up with something. Getting Sofia to go to Dublin without her will be hard for you. Telling Doris she is not coming back will be awful for us. They all agreed they should never have allowed them to stay so close for so long.'

'Since the wedding, they have been going around with Philip and Paul. Not on their own with them only, but in the group, but still they seem to be together. It is a lovely friendship and it doesn't have to end. They can write to each and visit and have stay overs. Philip will be going back to Dublin. Sofia can meet up with him. Paul works here in the village and Doris can be friendly with him. So they both will have

274

somebody to console them, while they get used to being apart. We never thought it would come to this.'

George said, 'We thought you were staying here forever.'

'So did we, but things have changed. There are a lot of buildings going on in Dublin. The scrap business is booming. If we stay here I would have to go up and down and stay overnight. That would be no life for Olga and the family.'

'Oh you are right, you have to go where the work is.' George said.

Ethel said, 'We will miss you both so much. You have been so good to us in all our troubles. You have been wonderful to us, from the time we came, to this very day.'

Olga said, 'Our friendship is never going to end either.'

Louie said, 'We will never forget your kindness to us. You will never understand, leaving your homeland, coming to a strange country. Not able to speak the language. Everybody is a stranger. Wondering who you are. Why are you here? It cannot be explained. But we could not have come to a better place. The Irish people are so kind, generous and helpful. I could go on and on. You know how we feel about you and I mean every word.'

Then the tears started again, all four of them were crying. When they stopped crying Louie poured out drinks for himself and Olga, Ethel and George still had theirs, and he said,

'Let's drink to a different future for all of us.'

Ethel and George drank their drink and ate the cake. They wished the Solomons the very best of luck, and hoped everything would go well for them in Dublin. Then they went home broken-hearted. Ethel walked straight up to bed. By the time George had put the car in the garage and had come into the house Ethel was asleep. He was so thankful, he thought it was going to be another sleepless night. He would not have been able to do it. He really liked the Solomons and he was going to miss them as much as Ethel was. How they were going to deal with Doris was going to be a nightmare. He was not going to think about that now. He fell asleep, exhausted.

Chapter 44

The next day, being Saturday, there was nobody coming into the workroom. Ethel went out there and had a good look around. She decided when all the dresses were made and the wedding outfits she was working on were finished she was going to give it all up. She had already lost interest, but after last night's news there was no way she could carry on. She didn't feel a bit sad about giving it all up but she had had enough. It had been fantastic for years but now it was time to let it go. She could make a new life for herself. Visit her mother more often. Go for walks with her. Get George to drive them to nice places in his spare time. Take both her parents out for drives. Now with Trevor and some staff they had more time on their hands. It would be lovely. She smiled to herself. Locked up the workroom and thought, only a few more weeks and I'll never have to come out here again to work. She went back into the house when George was not there. She was glad.

Doris and Philip were still in bed. She had the house to herself, and pottered around. Doing nothing really, just thinking. She made herself a nice breakfast, ate slowly, and admired the beautiful flowers and trees that George had put so much work into planting and looking after. She counted her blessings. The life she had as a result of the Solomons coming here to live. She felt sad for a while thinking of Desmond, whom she loved dearly. The short life he had and all he suffered. That wasn't fair. Who was she to ask herself to question what was right and what wasn't?

Doris came into the kitchen, and was all chat about

the night before, and how good a time she was having. There seemed to be a lot of youths the same age this summer. The wedding had brought them all together. Ethel asked if there were any couples in the groups.

'Mum.' she said, 'Are you mad? We are all kids, just friends.'

That was the answer she was hoping for. Philip arrived then and the three of them talked for ages. She had a great relationship with them. She began to think Doris might not be so hard to handle when the summer ended, and Sofia had left. It remained to be seen. When George came home she got him to drive her to the shop. She just wanted to have a chat with her mother. Her Mother was delighted she had called, and had lots of news to tell her. They talked for ages, something Ethel very seldom did but today was the start of her new life. It felt so good not rushing around. Her Mother was surprised she stayed so long. She was waiting for her to tell her some bad news. But after about two hours she said she would walk home. It was such a lovely day and she was in no hurry. She left and walked as far as the church yard. She saw George there, putting flowers on the grave and asked him.

'How often do you do that?'

George said, 'Every week.'

She thought, 'That's good.'

She very seldom visited the grave, she left that to him.

George came up with what he thought was a great plan. He wrote to a minister friend of his in Cork. He asked if he, his wife, and twelve year old daughter could come down for a week's holiday. The last week in August. It was very important he would explain everything to him later. If he could write back quickly and let him know. He would really appreciate it. He told Ethel what he had done, and explained to her his plan. If the Rev. Mr. Smyth could take them for the last week in August, and they told Doris she had to go with them. When they came back Sofia would be gone. That would make things much easier.

'Doris won't go without Sofia.'

'I'll tell her Sofia cannot come. That it is part holiday and part work for me. You and Doris have to come as there are days of activities for the family.'

'But that's a lie. What activities could you be doing?'

'I don't know, when we got there Mr. Smyth could say they were cancelled or something. We have to have Doris out of Wicklow when the Solomons are leaving, or Sofia will not go.'

'That's for sure, but Cork? A minister holiday? Work? I don't think she will fall for that.'

'Have you any ideas?' he asked.

'I was thinking if any of your Minister friends could send you a letter and say there was a four day workshop training in London and you could bring your wife and daughter. All expenses paid. Do you think she would fall for that?'

She might if we tell Sofia's Dad to say under no circumstances is Sofia allowed to go.'

'That would make him look like he is the baddy. No we can't do that.'

'They are as anxious as we are to come up with something that will work. The whole thing is ridiculous. We should just be able to tell Doris, Sofia's parents are leaving Wicklow. Let her fret for a while then she will get over it.'

'Now, to be fair she has had to get over her brother leaving, and dying, her aunt and her real mother dying.'

'She is only twelve. Another person leaving her life could destroy her.'

'Well, I can't think any more about it.' George said.

'The only other thing is,' Ethel said, 'I was thinking we should get together, the six of us. Tell them out straight and see how they take it. Then they will never have anything to hold against either set of parents. If we do it any other way, somebody is going to have to lie.'

'You are right, that's exactly what we will do. I will call down to Louie this minute and see if he agrees.'

George was delighted with Ethel coming up with this idea.

'That will work. I know it will. I should have had more faith in you Ethel. You never let me down. You are fantastic.'

'I know." she said.'

They both smiled and felt this might work. George was out the door as quickly as he could. He was back in a flash. Louie did agree, that's exactly what they would do.

'After all this toing and froing, the solution was a simple one. The truth usually works at the end of the day.'

'We haven't reached the end of the day yet. Hopefully we will. Now it's a matter of when we decide to tell them.' Ethel said. 'I think the last week in August is time enough.'

They left it at that.

While all this was going on Ethel felt awful. She didn't say how she was feeling to anybody. She knew she would be fine once all this business with the girls was dealt with. The weeks were going quickly. The girls had a wonderful summer. The weather was beautiful. They were out all day every day and they all had great suntans, which made them look so healthy. On the Friday before the last week in August it rained.

'A gift from God.' Ethel thought.

Philip went to work in the shop. When Olga came to work she had Sofia with her. Ethel asked her if Louie was at home?

'Yes.' she answered.

Ethel got George to go and get him right away. When they came back Sofia was upstairs in the bedroom with Doris. Ethel went to the workroom and brought Olga into the house.

'Now,' she asked, 'Who is going to start this conversation?'

Louie said, 'I will, after all we are the cause of all this by leaving.'

So Ethel called the girls down. When they came into the room and Sofia saw her parents there she asked, 'What's wrong?'

Her Dad said, 'Sit down both of you. I have to tell you something, and I don't want either of you to get upset.'

He said, 'Sofia we are leaving Wicklow and going to live in Dublin.'

'What?' she said, 'Are you mad? I am not going anywhere. If you are leaving you, are going without me.'

Doris didn't know what to do. She sat there like a zombie. She could not believe what he had just said.

'Doris please do something,' she screamed at her. 'They

281

can't take me away. I was born here and I am not leaving.'

Doris said, 'What can I do? I don't want you to go, but if your Dad tells you they are going, you have to go with them.'

'Please! Please Doris! Don't let them take me!' she begged her.

Doris put her arms around her and started to cry. Sofia was distraught. There was no consoling her. Doris asked Ethel to do something. Ethel felt so sorry for her, she never heard a child cry like this in her life. She was afraid she would go into convolutions. She took Sofia and Doris out to the sitting room and with one of them on each arm she stayed like that with them until they could cry no more. Then she brought them up to her bed and told them to have a good sleep. They were very tired after the hectic weeks they had. They were up very early this morning. They would feel better after a good rest. She made them nice and snug and stayed in the room until they were asleep. Which didn't take long. She left the room broken-hearted. She was in dread of them waking up. George put the kettle on. Olga made tea. Louie felt they should have done this in their house. He said sorry so many times, George told him not to be sorry. It had to happen. It made no difference where they were. George knew when the girls woke up, and the Solomons were gone home they were going to have to face Doris. The girls slept for hours. Ethel kept checking on them, making sure they were alive.

When they woke they came down and behaved as if nothing had ever happened. Ethel asked if they wanted to eat. They said they were starving. She made them a nice meal and they ate every bit of it. They got ready to go out and asked George for a lift as it was still raining. He was more than happy to oblige them. In the car they were chatting away to each other as usual. He left them at their friend's house. They thanked him and told him to collect them at ten o'clock. He drove home in absolute shock. Young people, never understand them. The Solomons stayed and had a meal, more confused than ever.

'We will just wait and see what happens in the next few days.'

They were not going to talk about it again. When the Solomons had gone, George asked Ethel, 'What did you think of the way Doris reacted to the news?'

'I thought she was very good. I think she was so upset about Sofia that she never thought of herself. We won't mention it again and see how long it takes her to bring the subject up. They are leaving next Saturday. That gives us a few days to prepare for trouble. Doris won't react like Sofia, she is not leaving Wicklow. Her situation is very different. Yes, she will miss her best friend terribly. But we can point out to her how things are not always as bad as they appear. When school starts back in September she will be very busy. She will make new friends and Paul will still be here, and his friends. Doris is very sensible and much easier to handle than Sofia. We'll keep a close watch on her and if she is having a bad day we'll make a fuss of her. Let her know we understand how she is feeling. The sad part is that we are feeling very upset also. We will miss the whole family. It had been such a wonderful friendship for all of us. But we have lovely memories of all the very exciting times we had together. The nice food, drinks, and other things they brought into our lives. Some of the Russian customs, the few words we can speak in Russian. The Russian dances that everybody in the village can do, at least one of them. Mr. Solomons playing the balalaika and singing. We had never seen a balalaika before they came. We should be thankful for all they shared with us, and made us better people. They have been so grateful for all they have learned from us. It would be nice to give them a big party when they are leaving. There is no way that can happen. Nobody wants to go to a party. That would be a disaster. We will adhere to their wishes and let them leave quietly. Anybody who wants to make a card of good wishes, or saying goodbye may do so.'

Ethel said, 'We as a family will give them presents. The rest of the village can do whatever they like. I'm not getting involved with collections or anything like that. They would hate that. They are only going a few miles up the road and we will be keeping in touch with them all the time.'

'Mrs. Solomons is very upset about leaving.'

'I will miss her so much.' Ethel said. 'She really loved living here.'

'The children will get on great in Dublin. They will make their own lives. Meet good Jewish partners, have families of their own. There was nobody for them to make a life with here in Wicklow. So we have to appreciate, the move was really for the family. Only for those reasons they never would have gone. It is very important for Jewish people to marry into their own religion, that's very understandable. Some mixed marriages are very successful, but in a small place like this it would be a lot more difficult. We would never have minded if Philip and Sofia had got together as a couple and did marry. Her parents might not have liked it, and that would have been awful, for all of us. We know they liked each other but only as friends, that was great. Philip might keep in touch with her when he goes back to college.

That would help her to settle in Dublin.'

'When Sofia starts college and gets into her studies she will love Dublin. I'm sure of it.' Ethel said.

Chapter 45

When the village woke up on Saturday morning, like the way they came, The Solomons were gone. Nobody heard or saw anything. How they went, or who they went with was a mystery. It was just as well, Ethel was no good at goodbyes. She was so upset herself she was not in the mood of having to console Doris.

When Doris woke up and had her breakfast George asked her if she would like to go to Courtown with him and Ethel. He was surprised when she said yes. Get your swimming gear and whatever else you want to bring and we'll be off. She sat in the front seat and talked all the way. Not one mention of The Solomons. They stayed on the beach for hours. They got in for a swim, and had fun in the water. Then they went for a nice meal, and left for home. She sat in the back this time. She fell asleep for most of the journey. It was one of the best days the three of them had had in ages. They loved each other so much. There was no way Doris was going to be selfish and spoil this day for them. She felt so sorry for her parents. It was a big loss for them also.

She had noticed Ethel did not look well for a while now. She hoped it was nothing more serious than the news of The Solomons leaving. She would wait until the Solomons were gone a while, and see how Ethel was before asking her how she was feeling, and suggest a visit to the doctor.

A week later Doris had a letter from Sofia. She hated everything about Dublin. The other two, referring to her brother and sister, seemed to be delighted with themselves.

She hated them. Her Mother was upset, but she was nice to her. Her Father was interested in buying a house on the South Circular Road, and never stopped talking about it. He was going around like a headless chicken. She hated him. The house where they were living now, she hated that. She hated the whole world and was going to kill herself. She used the hate word so much, and never once asked Doris how she was feeling. Doris was annoyed with her. She threw the letter on the table and told Ethel to read it.

'That's just the way she was feeling when she wrote it.' Ethel said. 'You know Sofia doesn't hate the world. Write back a nice letter to her to help cheer her up. Tell her how much you miss her. The next letter from her will be completely different. I know that for sure. Tell her we wish her Dad the best of luck buying the house. Remember Doris, Sofia had to leave the only place she had ever lived in where she knew everybody. She had to leave you, her best friend since the day she was born, and me, I brought her into the world. How do you think I feel? So don't be hard on her. Her whole world was shattered. She will recover in time, sooner rather than later we hope. Once they get a home of their own, she will feel different. When she is settled down and you can go and stay with her, she can stay here. Then it will be as if she never left. A friendship like you two had is forever. It will not end no matter where you are in the world.'

Doris said, 'I know you are right.'

She went back upstairs. She answered the letter right away and gave it to George to post. She felt better after that and got on with her plans for the day.

Doris received a letter from Sofia every Saturday. She answered right away and Sofia got her letter every Tuesday. Three months later on a Saturday morning when Doris

287

opened the letter, there on the right hand side of the page, in big print, was the new address.

80, South Circular Road,

Dolphin's Barn

Dublin.

The first words to Doris after Sofia said hello were, 'We got the house. See our new address. You have to come and stay. It's a lovely house. Huge after our little cottage. Lots of rooms, when you come you can have a room of your own if you like. But I think we would like to sleep in the same room, I know I would. The house is just a couple of doors down from the Jewish Synagogue and right across from the Protestant church. So you won't have far to go to your place of worship. We think Dad bought the house so near the Synagogue, to make up for lost time when we lived in Wicklow. He goes there no matter what's on. Every Saturday we think, in fact we know he is first in the door. We think he has gone a bit *religion mad*. He is doing things he never did in Wicklow. He is carrying on as if he has just discovered he is a Jew. He is very strict about what we eat. He has Mum walking down to a street called Clanbrassil Street, full of Jewish shops and buying all the things we could never get in Wicklow. Some of it is good and Mum still cooks nice things, but we miss all the lovely things your Mother gave us to eat. He is going over the top about all Jewish festivals. But he always did that. Making sure we would never forget who we are, and where we come from. He is driving us all mad. Apart from that I am very happy with the house. I can't wait for you to come up and stay for a whole weekend. Say you will come soon. I know you will love it. Tell your Mum and Dad there is plenty of room for them also and they are very welcome.'

Doris read no further, she told her Mum the great news. 'I have to go next week Mum and see Sofia! I have to go!'

'Yes, you are going next week. We promised you could go when they got a house and we always keep a promise. You are going on the early train. I'm sure Sofia will be there at the station with her Dad to pick you up. This is only a day visit. We have to give them time to settle in before you stay over. The next holidays you have you can stay as long as they allow. I think it would be nice for you to stay for half of your time there and if Sofia spent the other half down here with us. That would be fair. I'm sure Sofia would love that.' Ethel said.

Doris agreed and was so excited. Ethel was delighted to see that big smile back on her face again. Then Ethel realised how quiet she had been and distant, but still as nice a child as she had always been. But that smile was always missing. What a treat to see her so happy again. She was never in what you would say bad humour. But she had never been her old self since Sofia left. She must have really missed Sofia a lot more than she pretended.

'Thank God we can all get back to being a bit more normal again now.' Ethel thought.

Since Trevor got married and moved in over the shop his Grandparents seemed to be in great health. Not working agreed with them so much. Ethel thought her mother would miss the shop more, not a bit of it. They were having a great time, for which she was pleased for them. They had worked so hard, they deserved a good retirement. It was great they had each other. She never thought when her Dad was sick, he would get better and live as long as this. On nice fine days, George and Ethel would take them for a drive. Her

Dad loved this, her Mother might bring a picnic. If not, they would eat in a hotel. Once they brought them to Dublin to visit The Solomons. All four of them really enjoyed that day so much.

Things went very well for all the family for the next six months. Ethel's health deteriorated very quickly and Doris left school to look after her. George didn't agree with this. Ethel did not want to go into hospital, and Doris made up her mind she was staying at home. As long as she could manage to keep her comfortable. She was such a good Mother to her, she was going to do her very best for her. The Grandparents helped out. George was very good. Some neighbours were brilliant. But Doris was on call twenty-four seven. She never complained. When Ethel could sit up and felt a bit better they had a good laugh. Some days were very depressing, looking at her so sick. She had to be put on strong drugs and the doctor really wanted her in the hospital. He agreed Doris was doing a great job. But she needed professional care. She was a lot more poorly than Doris realised. He explained to Doris that by keeping her at home was being cruel to her. She needed round the clock medication by intravenous tubes and that could not happen in the house. Doris had to give in and let her go. The ambulance would be there in the morning to take her to Dublin. Doris sat with her all night and never stopped crying. George begged her to take a break, and if she slept she could go with her in the morning. She went up to her room. She didn't sleep. She prayed that Ethel would die before the ambulance came in the morning. George peeped in at her and she pretended to be asleep. Two hours later she came down, and George was asleep with his head on the bed. She woke him and told him to go to bed, she would

290

take over now. He went to bed and Doris had her all to herself. She told her how much she loved her, and said she had suffered enough. And was giving her permission to die. She lay on the bed beside her and kept telling her all the things she loved about her. A little sound came from Ethel. Doris sat up and there was a smile on her face. She hugged her until the life left her body.

She got her wish, she would not be going to hospital now. Doris was amazed at herself. She didn't cry, she didn't scream or shout, she didn't wake George. She treasured this time alone with her. She felt it was a beautiful way to die.

After two hours she woke George. Then she cried. Both of them cried so much.   George went for the doctor. There was no need for an ambulance now. The two sisters in the village who looked after the dead would be sent for and they would do all that was necessary to have Ethel looking her best. Doris could do no more for her. George made her go to bed. She had had so little sleep for so long she would never be able for the next couple of days. She went to bed and slept right through for twenty-four hours. A lot had happened while Doris was asleep and George was pleased that she missed all of it.

The only thing she asked about were the funeral arrangements. George told her a friend of his was coming from Arklow. He was having a service in their church in the afternoon then Ethel would be laid to rest in the cemetery. After which they were going to Trevor's place. He had made all the plans. The Grandparents didn't go to the church, they were so devastated. Ethel was their third child to lose, and a grandson. This they would never get over. It just was not fair. They felt so old now and wanted to die. The three

291

boys, The Taylor family, Emily's family, the Minister, and The Solomons were all that were there. After the meal, George and Doris left quietly without saying goodbye to anybody. Philip and Joseph stayed a little longer. Eventually the Grandparents left, Trevor and Emily were on their own. Life would never be the same again.

The boys stayed home for the rest of the week. Doris loved having them. When they went back, she missed them so much. Only her and George now. She decided she was not going to school anymore. She was going to mind George. Which she did. Everybody was against that including George, but there was no talking to her. When Doris made up her mind nobody on this earth would change it. She was so like her birth Mother Lydia in some ways.

Chapter 46

When Ethel was six months dead, Sofia came down with the intention of bringing her back with her to Dublin for a break. She would go with her on condition that she could leave anytime. That was arranged and she went. Mrs. Solomons was delighted she came, because a friend of hers was going to offer her a job. Doris was sixteen now, she should be in school or working. Looking after George was not good for either of them. She deserved to have a life, and this job was ideal for her. Doris settled in very quickly, and was quite cheerful. Mrs Solomons had to wait for a chance to mention her staying in Dublin and going to work. So, she told her a friend of hers down from them had a new baby and was not doing very well. The sad part was she worked for her husband. He was a money lender and she did all the paperwork. He was really stuck for somebody to do the books. It was going to be very hard to get somebody, because they would have to live there, be very honest, and become one of the family. They were Jewish and that was another problem. Mrs Solomons was helping out as much as she could, but he really needed a proper bookkeeper. Sofia asked Doris if she would like to see the baby tomorrow, when her mother was going in to help. She said she would. The next day Sofia and Doris went with Sofia's Mum to see the baby. He was tiny. Doris asked if she could hold him, when Doris held him she felt overwhelmed. The tears rolled down her face and right onto the baby's head. Mrs Solomons nearly died; she did not know what to do. She went to take the baby from her and she wouldn't let it go. 'Oh Doris! I'm so sorry I didn't mean to upset you.'

293

'Oh, it's OK.' she said. 'I never held a real baby in my arms before. He is so small he reminded me of when Sofia and I carried our dolls around before we got our prams.'

Doris felt a warm glow holding the baby and she thought, 'I love this baby.'

Mrs. Marcus thought she was a lovely girl and hoped she would take the job. Doris didn't know that was the real reason she was here. Mr. Marcus came into the room and Doris nearly burst out laughing. She thought if you rolled him the snow, he would be the perfect snowman. He introduced himself. He had a nice, warm handshake and Doris liked him right away. He was very small and very fat. He was roundy, with a huge moustache covered his whole mouth. But there was something likeable about him. They had had a drink. The girls left and Mrs. Solomons asked, 'What did you think of her?'

They both said, 'She has to come and work for us. She is exactly made for the job. She loved the baby, we will employ her as a nurse, if she is not interested in bookkeeping. We'll have to see how long she is staying with you this time, and see if she mentioned coming to see the baby again. How are we going to ask her to leave Wicklow, and come and live here?'

After a week Doris had not mentioned going home. They called in a few times to see the baby. Mr. Marcus told Mrs. Solomons the next time they called in he was going to ask her if she would like to live with them and mind the baby.

'There is no other way we can do it. She can go home and think about it. We will wait for her to make up her mind. If she decides to come, and gets homesick she can leave straight away.'

'Well, the best of luck with that!' Mrs. Solomons told him. 'You had better say you just thought of that now and you can take the blame for the consequences. She can only say yes or no. Do not mention my name. She would never forgive me if she thought I had anything to do with this.'

'No, I will not. I'll ask her if she likes Dublin, and have a bit of small talk before I mention it, until I feel it's safe to do so.'

Sofia and Doris called to see the baby the next day. He still seemed no bigger than a doll. They stayed a while, then Mr. Marcus asked Doris if she would like to take him home with her.

'What do you mean to take him home with me?'

'Only joking.' he said. 'But you do like him, don't you? So how would you like to come and live with us, and mind the baby and get paid for it? You could mind the baby every day, as paid work. You would see Sofia every day and take the baby for walks. Would you think about doing that?'

Doris looked at Sofia.

'Is he serious?' she asked her.

Sofia said, 'Ask him, don't ask me.'

Doris said, 'Are you really offering me a job?'

'Yes, we are.' he said. 'Just think about it and don't take long. We need someone now.'

Doris was in shock but she never suspected this was why she was here. She said, 'You know, I never thought of leaving Wicklow. This week has been wonderful. Now you

295

are offering me work a couple of doors from my best friend. I don't have to think about it. I will take the job.'

'Are you sure?'

'Yes!' she said.

Sofia said, 'How are you going to tell George?'

'He will be happy for me. He hates me looking after him. If I was gone he would make a life for himself. If he knows I am happy and safe in Dublin then that's all he wants for me. I'll go home the day after tomorrow and tell him. That fact that I would be part of a family, and living so close to Sofia's family will appeal to him.'

When they came back to Sofia's house Mrs. Solomons was chopping vegetables at the table. She kept her head down, to give the impression that she was not that interested.

Doris said, 'You will never guess what has just happened?'

'How could I guess? Tell me.'

Doris was so excited.

'Mr. Marcus has offered me a job minding the baby. I am going to live with them and I am getting paid for it. Right here beside you, my friends. How lucky is that?'

'When did this happen?' she asked.

'Just now when we called to see the baby. He asked me if I would like to take him home. I didn't know what he was talking about, he was only joking. Then he asked me if I would like to come and live with them, mind the baby and get paid.

'What did you say?' Mrs. Solomons asked.

'I said I would.'

'You what?'

'I said I would.'

'Just like that.'

'Yes, just like that.'

'How are you going to tell George?'

'I will tell him very nicely. I know he won't mind. He knows I will never go back to school so he will be glad I'm going to work, doing something for myself.'

'I hope you are right, don't give him a big shock and break it to him as if you are asking for permission, not telling him you are going. He can stop you if he wants to. You are under age and you need his permission. Don't leave with bad feelings that would be awful. Ask him how he feels about you going.' Mrs. Solomons said.

'I know it will break his heart, but if it is what I want I know he will never stop me.'

Doris knew very well how to get around George, and she was right. She told him the minute she got home. Before he had a chance to ask her if she had enjoyed herself. He just acted as she had expected.

'If that's what you want to do you go with my blessing.'

She hugged him and thanked him, but when he put his arms around her he couldn't let her go. They both started to cry. It was much harder than she thought it was going to be. She had always acted very grown up about things, but she suddenly realised she was only sixteen, going up to Dublin was a big step. She told him they were very nice people. They knew she was a Protestant and the church was right across the road from their house. They would never talk about her beliefs.

'That's good.' he said. 'I'm happy about that. Never forget your place of worship.' he told her.

'As if I would. Sure I love getting dressed up for church. I wish I had further to walk so I could show off my Sunday best clothes.'

That made him smile. Doris was a real show off, as well she could be, with the beautiful outfits her Mum made for her. Nobody in the village had anything to wear like the style Ethel kept Doris in. She asked him if he would do her a favour and not tell anybody she was going until she was gone.

'If that's what you want then you have my word.'

'Thanks Dad.' she said. 'You are a real star.'

He loved it when she called him a star, it felt like she was still his little girl again. She had always called him a star when she got what she asked for. To be fair to her, she never asked for much. So when she did ask he could never refuse her. She always called him a star when he drove her anywhere or picked her up with her friends. She was a great child and never had to be slapped. She just did what she was told. A very happy little girl and so kind. She had brought such happiness into their home. He was distraught, and had to pretend he didn't mind her leaving. He didn't ask when she was going, he just couldn't. He went out for a walk, to try and come to terms with what had just happened. He felt he was going to collapse in the street, so he went back home. He told her he would drive her to Dublin. He wanted to meet these people who his little girl was going to work for.

She said, 'No, we will both go to Dublin on the train someday.'

'I want you to meet them, but not the day I'm leaving. I could never let you go back to Wicklow without me. That would be hard on both of us. We'll tell Trevor we are going to Dublin for the day in about two weeks before I'm going to stay. He can drop us to the station and collect us.'

'That's a good idea.' he said and was happy he was going to have her for a couple of weeks more.

The Solomons were delighted she was coming. Although it was none of their business, they felt she would have a better life in Dublin. She was doing nothing in Wicklow, only looking after George. She kept the house spotlessly clean, and was a great cook. She loved what she was doing and never complained. But every time Sofia went home after staying with her, she felt Doris needed to do something for herself. So when the Marcus family were looking for somebody to bookkeep Sofia remembered how good Doris was at maths in school. She thought it would be great for Doris and she would have her best friend back living beside her.

Sofia had settled down well and was going to secondary school. She had nice friends that she was going to introduce Doris to and they would have a good social life. The next day Sofia had a letter from Doris telling her she was coming to Dublin on the following Thursday with her Dad. She told her how things had gone and he was very good about her leaving. She wanted him to meet the family before she came to live with them. She was writing to them now to check if Thursday suited them. They were coming by train and would her Dad collect them at the station? Sofia was so happy she hadn't changed her mind. She wrote back at once. Just a postcard with the code they used when they wanted to say something without writing a letter. Doris had arranged with George to take her to a town a few miles away to post the letters. She did not want them going to her Grandparents post office. It depended who was working there and how much nose disease they had. They were used to her writing to Sofia every week. But her posting two letters would be noticed. She didn't want that. She had told Sofia when she got her letter to ask Mr. Marcus if he had got his. She told him not to answer, just tell Sofia if the answer Thursday was OK, she would let her know. On Saturday, Sofia's letter arrived as usual. Thursday was perfect and Mr. Marcus was collecting them, in his motorcar with his chauffeur driving. Sofia said lots more nice things about her coming. She gave the letter to George, while he was reading it he got upset.

'What's wrong?' she asked.

'Nothing wrong,' he said, 'I'm just thinking how lucky these people are to have you coming to live with them. My loss is their gain, but they seem like good people. I know they will be good to you. Any problems and you come home. Always remember you have a home here, no matter how long you are away. Homesickness is a funny thing. It may happen soon after you leave, it might take a long time before it happens, and sometimes it never happens at all. If it does happen to you, you will know it. It's not like any other illness, not a nice feeling at all. You will only be a few miles up the road and I can be there in a couple of hours, and bring you home. So you have no need to worry. I often think of all the young people who left here to go to America, and they had no hope of ever getting back. They must have longed to see their parents. Thinking of all the family events they missed. I get consolation from the fact that I can come and see you anytime. I'm sorry for getting upset, I didn't mean it. I'm fine now. OK, let's look forward to Thursday and see how we get on.'

Things couldn't have gone better. The Marcus family was so welcoming. They had a beautiful table set, and a huge fire blazing in the room. It was lovely and warm. George got on great with them. The baby was asleep so Doris didn't disturb him, but she never took her eyes off him. They talked for ages and then a nice lady asked if they were ready to eat yet. Mr. Marcus asked his guests if they were OK with eating now? They said yes and she started to serve food they loved, Mrs Solomons had told them the things they loved, and they went to all that trouble to get them. Doris couldn't believe it. That was one thing she had never thought would happen, living with a Jewish family, eating Jewish food which she loved. George loved it also, and they ate everything put in front of them.

Mr. Marcus was so pleased to see them enjoy the food so much. He offered some to them to take home. Doris told them she would start working on the first of March. That was great for them. They told her they were going to make sure she had everything she wanted. They wanted her more than she wanted them and they hoped she would like working for them. They told her they had put an extra single bed in her room. Whenever she wanted Sofia to stay over, that bed was for her. Doris thought this was really very kind.

They thanked them for everything. Told them they were going to see their friends and were leaving on the evening train. Mr. Marcus told them his driver would take them back to the station. George was happy enough that

Doris would be well looked after. Doris was happy that her Dad liked the family she was going to live with and work for.

When they got on the train they were very tired. It was dark and they both fell asleep. Doris woke first, she didn't know where they were. She hoped when it stopped next time she would find out where they were. They were OK, two more stations and the next was their stop. She woke George about ten minutes before they had to get off. He couldn't believe he slept like that for so long. Trevor was there to meet them.

'Where's all the shopping he asked?'

They nearly died. They had nothing with them.

George said, 'we left it with Sofia. Doris is going back in a couple of weeks and she didn't need what she bought. It was all for Easter, and she is going to be in Dublin then.'

'Let's get going then,' Doris said. 'She wasn't sure if Trevor believed what George had said and she didn't care.

They had nothing to eat. They went straight to bed. It was a good day. She was glad it went so well, and it was over. The next two weeks were going to be hard. She would have to visit her Grandparents before she left and that was awful. She was leaving without saying goodbye. They were so old now, she would have loved to hug and kiss them but she couldn't. Trevor would be happy for her to go. But it wasn't fair to ask him to keep it secret and not tell them. He had enough on his plate and he worked so hard. She was going to try and get home at least once a month. The month would fly and she would hardly be missed. George always did the shopping anyway so they didn't see her that often. When she came home she would spend plenty of time with them, she told herself.

302

Chapter 47

At the end of February George brought her to the station. She hugged and kissed him without a tear in her eyes. He left the platform before the train pulled out. He never did that before, but it was just as well. Nobody sat beside her and she felt very lonely.

'Oh, my God!' she thought to herself. 'Am I homesick already?'

She didn't feel a bit happy. What was she thinking of leaving home at sixteen? Would she get off the train at Bray and go back? She started to cry. No, she told herself, she would go all the way and if she felt it wasn't right she would come home tomorrow.

At Bray a lovely young girl sat beside her and talked all the way to Harcourt Street. That was a great help. When she saw the chauffeur waiting for her she felt a bit better. He talked to her and told her he hoped she would be happy in Dublin. It was a nice city and easy to get around. He asked her if she had any relations living in Dublin. She told him she had a brother living on the north side, and a married brother and his wife on the south side and an uncle by marriage on the south side and her Mother's aunt Phyllis. He told her if she ever wanted to go and see them Mr. Marcus would allow him to drive her there. 'Are you sure?'

'Yes,' he said.

'That's very kind of him.'

'Oh,' he said. They are very nice people to work for, if they like you, they will be very good to you.'

She believed that. George said he felt that when he met them and who could not like Doris? They knew how lucky they were to get her. The last girl they had was a lot of trouble, and they couldn't get her to leave.

When they reached the house they welcomed her the same as before. There was a nice meal ready for her. When she said she would go to bed Mrs. Marcus brought her up to her room. There was an oil stove in it and it felt nice and warm. There was a hot water bottle in her bed. She just took a night dress out of her case and left the unpacking until the morning. The bedroom was huge. She felt like a sparrow in it. She would have to get Sofia in here as soon as she could. She knew it was going to take some time to get used to this big change in her life. She was going to give it her best shot. If it didn't work out at least she had tried. As her Dad would say; *He who never made a mistake, never made anything.* She opened the book she had brought to bed, and she fell asleep after a couple of pages. Mrs. Marcus saw the light on and was going to tell her to sleep well. When she saw the book she took it from her without disturbing her. She marked the page and left it on the bedside table.

In the morning she asked Doris if she had slept well? Doris said, 'I must have. I don't remember turning out the light.'

Mrs. Marcus laughed and said, 'Or closing your book.'

'Oh,' Doris said, 'I must be more careful in future, I'm sorry'.

'No harm done, you are lucky we have electric light. Somebody would always check if a light is on long after midnight. No need to worry. Do you always read in bed?' Mrs. Marcus asked.

'Well, most of the time.'

'But I never fall asleep with the book in my hand.'

When breakfast was over Mrs. Marcus brought Doris to the nursery. She showed her where everything was. There was a place for everything and everything was in its place. 'You don't have to know or remember all this, but if I need something in a hurry I just want you to know where it is and get it for me. I don't have very good health at the moment and looking after the baby is hard for me. I love doing everything with him, but bathing him is difficult. I think you could bathe him if I show you?'

'If I am going to be the baby's nurse, then that's part of the job. I will bathe him. I am very nervous, I have never done it. If you sit beside me and guide me then I will learn. I will do my best and my best is always good enough.' Mrs. Marcus was delighted with her answer. She was not being smart but her answer was full of confidence and that was what she wanted. If she was going to give over the minding of the most precious thing in the world to this young girl she was going to have to be able to take on the responsibility of him. It was a big ask, but if she could do this she could do anything. They did everything together and she was so confident, Mrs. Marcus felt she had a real treasure here. She carried out all instructions perfectly. When they had everything ready she told Doris to sit down. She spread a big towel across her and said, Ready?'

'Yes,' Doris said.

She put the baby on her lap and showed her how to undress him. Now place him in the water and she did everything exactly as she was told. Took him out, dressed him and placed him down for his nap. She was delighted with her achievement.

'Well done that was perfect, the one thing you will have to be very careful with is when the baby gets a bit bigger he will move in the bath.'

'That's OK'

'When you go to take him out make sure you have a good grip on him. He will be slippy so get the towel around him as quickly as you can. Don't worry that won't happen for a while yet. As he gets bigger you will take him out and lay him on the bed. That will be much easier for you. Now, how do you feel?' Mrs. Marcus asked her.

'Great, I really enjoyed it, but I would like you to stay with me for a few more mornings before I do it on my own.'

Of course I will, once you are enjoying it, you will be good at it.'

While the baby slept she told her to tidy up the nursery and then take a rest. Doris lay on her bed for a while after tidying. Then she got up unpacked and put all her things away. She felt good and wondered what she should do next. She came down to the kitchen. There was nobody there. She would like to do something, but what? She waited for a while then Mr. Marcus appeared and asked her how she got on, she told him and asked what she should do now.

'That's the Mrs.' Department, she will be down soon. Rest yourself until she comes.'

She sat down, picked up a paper and glanced over it. Then Mrs Marcus arrived. She told her again how pleased she was with her.

'Your work is all about the baby. When he is asleep you can rest, read, look after your own clothes. We have a person who comes in to do the washing, but she does the big wash.

Look after your smalls yourself. If you have anything big she will do it. We don't like to give her things that we can rinse out ourselves, you know what I mean?'

'Yes, of course I'm well used to looking after my smalls' and they started to laugh.

The morning went quickly and then it was lunch time. The lunch was huge and lovely. If she ate like this every day she would be as round as the boss himself. She would have to watch what she ate. This was her first day and she was not going to leave anything. But she couldn't do this every day. She was dying to get the baby in his pram and take him for a walk. She asked Mrs. Marcus when she could take the baby for a walk.

'Oh, any time you want to. I thought today you might like to wait for Sofia to come home from school, and you both can take him out.'

'Oh, that's a great idea I'd love that. Do you want me to do anything while I am waiting for her?'

'Well, he is fed and changed, just get the pram ready, he will need to be wrapped up well. It's a beautiful day but still a bit cold. You can go and meet Sofia if you like and walk home with her. You know where her school is don't you.'

'Yes, that would be a nice surprise for her. Can I do this every day?' she asked.

'Do it today and see how you get on. Then we can think about every other day. Once the baby is not put out of his routine, you are free to do whatever you want. I know you will act responsibly and I trust you not to do anything foolish. Prove me wrong and you will be out of a job.'

They laughed again. Doris felt life here was good.

When she walked out with that beautiful pram. She felt fantastic. She was walking down towards Sofia's School and she was a bit nervous. She had walked these roads with Sofia many times, but the responsibility of the baby was a lot to bear. She was afraid of crossing the road. There was a lot more traffic than there was in the village. This was a real baby and she didn't own it. It was not a doll. When she saw Sofia coming she was so glad. Sofia was glad to see her. She told her how nervous she was and wanted to get back as soon as possible. Sofia told her not to be silly. The baby was fast asleep and they could walk slowly and she would get used to the pram. She relaxed a bit more and started to enjoy it. They talked all the way home. They couldn't believe they were here in the capital city together, after being so long apart. It was just fantastic. Doris wasn't going home in a few days, she was here to stay.

When they got to Sofia's house. She threw in her school bag and told her mother she was going for a little walk with Doris and the baby.

'Don't go far,' her Mum said. 'You have to do your homework.'

'I know,' she shouted back and was out the door.

While the two of them were together Doris got more confidence, but she would not give Sofia a go of the pram. Sofia got annoyed but not for long. She understood Doris was taking her job seriously and she was right.

Doris told her, 'I'll ask if I can give you a go. If Mrs. Marcus allows it, then we will have chances, I will push him out and you can push him back. The next time we will do it the other way, that's fair right?'

Sofia agreed as usual.

Chapter 48

Doris went home for Easter and Sofia went with her. George thought Doris looked very healthy. He was delighted to have her back. She settled in as if she never left. The first thing she did was visit her Grandparents.

Doris couldn't get over how old and fragile both of them had become in such a short time. That made her very sad. Trevor and Emily were doing great in the shop, as well as taking care of the Grandparents. George helped out a lot, by taking them out for drives to give Trevor and Emily a break. They loved going out with George, and it gave him something to do. It took him out of the house, and made him feel useful. What he was doing was really appreciated by Trevor and Emily and it was good for George also.

Doris told him not to stop what he was doing for the Grandparents because they were there. Herself and Sofia were well able to walk, if they wanted to go anywhere which they didn't. He did take them for drives which they enjoyed. The couple of days they were there flew by. Suddenly he was driving back to the station.

No tears this time, Doris told him if he cried she would never come home again. He didn't even hug her. He left them on the platform, said cheers and was gone. That nearly killed Doris; she knew he was upset. If he had cried she knew she would never have gotten on that train. It was great to have Sofia with her.

When the train arrived it was packed, but they were lucky they got the last two seats together. They talked all the way and without realising it they were in Dublin. Mr.

Marcus was there waiting for them. Doris was happy to see him, she was dying to see the baby. She had missed him but never mentioned him all the time they were away. She knew Sofia wouldn't let her talk about work and she didn't.

When they were home Mrs. Marcus gave her a big hug and said, 'We missed you, welcome back.'

When she went to her room the same welcome as before. She got into bed and slept like a baby.

She woke at ten o'clock. That was late but nobody called her. She rushed down and said, 'Sorry I'm so late you should have woken me.'

Mrs. Marcus told her, 'There is no hurry if you sleep late, but I will make you work longer in the evening.'

She laughed. 'I'm only joking, you don't work from nine to five here. All you have to do is mind the baby during the day and when he goes to bed you are free to do whatever you want.'

Doris was happy with that and asked, 'Where do I start now?'

'Where would you like to start?'

'The bath'

'Right answer, let's go and get the baby. I had everything ready and I waited for you. So, we'll get that done now, then I have a few more things to discuss with you before you take him out.'

Doris was surprised she felt so confident. She remembered everything she had been told to do. It all went very well and she actually enjoyed it. When he was all dressed up she cuddled him for ages before putting him in his pram. This time she was much better at getting the pram across roads and up and down steps. She discovered if she walked on the other side of the road she would have a lot less crossings. She didn't realise the soldier's barracks was on that side. When she passed one of them shouted after her, 'Hello Nurse! How is baby?'

She got such a fright she never walked on that side again.

Doris loved working for the Marcus family. The baby was getting bigger and more interesting. Every hour he was awake she played with him. When Sofia was on her school holidays they both had a great time with him.

Then one day Mrs Marcus told Doris they were going to Bray for the month of June for holidays and she would have to come with them. She asked if Sofia could come and Mrs Marcus said, 'Yes of course! How could we not take her, she is like your other half.'

Doris was so thankful because a month away from Sofia wouldn't be a holiday for her.

Sofia was glad to be invited and then they started making plans. All they talked about was the holiday. A month at the beach sounded fantastic for two country girls who didn't live near the sea. They couldn't wait.

June came and it was exciting as they hoped. One day Doris and Sofia were walking along with the baby in the pram. A train passed into the tunnel at Bray head. Doris stopped walking and started to cry. Sofia got an awful fright. 'What's wrong?' she asked. Doris was sobbing by now and Sofia couldn't control her. She still didn't know what was wrong with her. Sofia took the pram and told her to walk on the inside until they got back to the house. When Mrs. Marcus opened the door and she saw them, she nearly had a stroke.

'What happened?' she asked.

Sofia said, 'We were just walking along and Doris started to cry. I don't know why.'

Doris was still sobbing, and then said, 'I want to go home.'

'Home, where to Dublin?' Mrs. Marcus asked. 'No,' she said, 'to Wicklow.'

'What brought this on?

'I saw the Wicklow train going towards Bray Head and I suddenly wanted to be on it.'

'Oh, that's Ok! We can get you on the train tomorrow if that's what you want. That's what they call being homesick. That's no problem. Don't cry anymore. Mr. Marcus will have the car brought out and drive you home if you cannot wait until the morning.'

'No,' Doris said. 'I will wait and Sofia will have to come with me.'

'That's fine.'

Mrs. Marcus knew she would have to let her go home. But hoped she would come back. They would wait for her for as long as they could. She really was part of the family.

The next day off the two of them went. George had got the message from Trevor to pick them up at the station. He thought they had come on holiday. When he saw Doris he recognised homesickness. She looked untidy and distraught. She put her arms around him and wouldn't let go. Eventually he got her into the car. He felt sorry for Sofia if Doris decided she was never going back to Dublin, Sofia would have to go through going back on her own again. He would cross that bridge when came to it. He tried to get some kind of conversation going, to find out what had happened. He then decided to wait and see what they were going to do.

Doris was quiet for a couple of days. She didn't want to go anywhere. She and Sofia stayed in her room most days until the afternoon. The weather was beautiful and George thought it was such a pity to waste all that sunshine, but said nothing.

Then Doris announced she was going back. He was delighted, and so was Sofia. He brought them to the station before she changed her mind. They got off the train in Bray. When Mrs. Marcus opened the door and saw them, she hugged Doris so tight. She was sure this would never happen again. And it never did. The rest of the holiday was great.

Chapter 49

They went to Bray every year for the month of June, and Doris loved it. She stayed working for the Marcus Family for the next seven years.

She never had a boyfriend. She was tall, slim, with long black hair and violet eyes. Plenty of young men were interested in her, but she was not bothered.

One day Mr Marcus introduced her to a handsome, wealthy Catholic man. It was love at first sight. So much so, she began taking instructions in the Catholic faith and changed her religion to marry him. They were married in July 1925. They were married for fifty-four years and had ten children. All did well for themselves. He died in July 1979 six years before her. She was lost without him, and did not want to live anymore. She died in September 1985. 'Happy,' as he said herself, 'to be going home to God.'

All her family is sure that is where she is now.

Sofia had worked for her Dad who had a lot of business in the city. She had no interest in men. Until one month after Doris met her husband, Sofia fell in love with, and married a rich Jewish man in August 1926.

They were married for fifty-four years and had six children. All did well for themselves. Sofia's husband died six years before her in 1979. She died in February 1985.

They had been friends from the day they were born until they died. Sofia visited Doris every Saturday and Doris visited her every Wednesday. Their children played together and were great friends. There would have been at least two marriages between those families. The only barrier was the difference of religion. Sofia and Doris would never have minded if any of the children had married. They never discussed it with their husbands, so we will never know what might have been. All of the children got married to people of their own religions. All of them were very happy with the people they married. Only one husband died when he was fifty years old. His wife never married again. Another husband died when he was sixty-six and his wife never remarried.

Those children still kept in touch for all those years. Some of the Jewish family went to live in Israel. Most of them are still alive, the eldest being ninety-five. The youngest being seventy nine.

Of the ten children, Doris had there are now only four alive living in Dublin. One of Her sons went to New Zealand. That had a terrible effect on her, him being so far away. She cried for weeks when he left home. She missed him a lot. She could not understand why he chose that country. When there was very little chance of any of the family going there for a holiday or him making the journey home. But he did manage to get home on holiday and all of the family including his parents did make it to New Zealand to see him at different times and got to know his five children. But in her heart she always felt he missed a lot of family celebrations. The day he got married she cried all day. There was no consoling her. She kept saying, there he is now getting married and not one of his own to celebrate with him. That put the rest of her family off ever leaving home.

They all did very well staying in Ireland and she loved that. Doris was so proud of her family. Her thirty one grandchildren and sixteen great grandchildren. They all loved her so much.

If any of her grandchildren had to be corrected, Doris would say to the parents, 'Leave them alone, the world will beat them time enough.'

The children knew they would get away with anything if Grannie was around, and they made the most of it. All of her children that are alive are still married, one couple for sixty years, another couple for fifty-eight years, the next couple for fifty-five and the youngest for fifty-one years.

All of Sofia's family are still alive. The friendships are going on to the third and fourth generations. This should be in the Guinness Book of Records. Three religions with the greatest respect for each other. Everybody was able to attend each other's celebration. The Catholics celebrate all the Jewish ones; the food and drink, mostly homemade, were delicious. They all love the matzah the Jews ate at Passover. They always gave a couple of boxes as a present to Doris and her Catholic family. A box to send to Wicklow to Trevor and Emily's Protestant family. Sofia's Jewish family celebrates Christmas with the Protestants and Catholics. Santa always came to them when they were small. That might have been confusing to them, as Santa never came to their other Jewish friends. They often laughed about that to this day. All three groups are so happy that their parents were such good friends. They feel that friendship gives them a wonderful outlook on life. They are all able to hold a conversation wherever they go in the world on all three religions, with great confidence and no fear of contradictions. This had added a great richness to

316

all their lives. Today we are so lucky to have Educate Together Schools in Ireland. Already they are making a great difference in all our lives. If these schools had been around when the three families this book is about they would have suited them very well.

That was the thing that upset them most when they were children and moved to Dublin. They had to go to different schools. No time to be together during the week, only seeing each other at weekends. But they were great weekends with fantastic memories. How rich all our lives would be if we could have friendships like these. What a wonderful world we could have if everybody was a bit more patient and kind to each other regardless of religious beliefs. After all, nobody has come back from the dead to tell us if there is a God or a Heaven.

Mrs. Solomons always said, 'The people that were there when Lazarus was brought back from the dead should have asked him. But nobody thought of asking him.'

Her saying this always made everybody laugh. Lots of comments like these were thrown out there but nobody ever took offence. The older ones of the families often had great laughs discussing what they would ask God if they did get to heaven. Some of the things they said were hilarious.

One day Mr Solomons said he was going to ask God, 'Why did Eve eat the apple and not just leave it at that? No, she had to give it to Adam so he would also be in trouble. Like my vife she always makes me eat what I do not vant. So you see, men were in trouble from the beginning of time. I hope someday somebody will make something that can fly right up there and have a good look around and get into heaven without dying.'

When he said things like this he used to have them all

laughing a lot. He was very funny and loved the attention he got. These conversations went on for ages, one trying to outdo the other, being more adventurous.

In those days it was their way of having fun. No television, mobile phones, video games etc. Life was a lot less completed then. A slower pace of life. Although mothers had a lot of work to do in the home. Hand washing, no washing machines, dishwashers, vacuum cleaners or any of the other machines we have now. They always had time to enjoy life and make the most of what they had, doing simple things.

Friends

A Poem By Anne Deally

Hearts reaching out to each other
Minds in harmony
Respect and kindness always outweighing a difference of
opinion
We have shared the best of times
Loved Laughed and Cried together
Our gift to each was friendship
Unbroken through the decades
Holding us up when all we
wanted to do was fall
Heads held high we continue through life together
The bond we had between us unbroken
Because of our friendships loneliness has never touched
our hearts
Thank you my beloved friends.

The years following the tragic
accident where James lost Lydia and
the impact on all the families will be
further explored and elaborated on
in book two.
